# GOOD JOY,
# BAD JOY

ALSO BY MIKKI BRAMMER

*The Collected Regrets of Clover*

# GOOD JOY, BAD JOY

A Novel

## MIKKI BRAMMER

PENGUIN BOOKS

PENGUIN BOOKS

UK | USA | Canada | Ireland | Australia
India | New Zealand | South Africa

Penguin Books is part of the Penguin Random House group of companies
whose addresses can be found at global.penguinrandomhouse.com

Penguin Random House UK,
One Embassy Gardens, 8 Viaduct Gardens, London SW11 7BW

penguin.co.uk

First published in the United States of America by
St. Martin's Press, an imprint of St. Martin's Publishing Group 2026
First published in Great Britain by Penguin Books 2026
001



Typeset by Six Red Marbles UK, Thetford, Norfolk
Printed and bound in Great Britain by Clays Ltd, Elcograf S.p.A.

The authorized representative in the EEA is Penguin Random House Ireland,
Morrison Chambers, 32 Nassau Street, Dublin D02 YH68

A CIP catalogue record for this book is available from the British Library

ISBN: 978-1-405-97634-3

For Hilda Edwards, who lived a wonderful life
and always felt like home

Let us greedily enjoy our friends, because we
do not know how long this privilege will be ours.

—*Seneca the Younger*

# GOOD JOY,
# BAD JOY

**1**

It starts with the gentle tittering of birds outside my window. The warm, filtered sunlight nudging my cheeks. Then a smile spreads across my face.

I am awake. I am alive.

For most people, these are not mind-blowing revelations. But when you're eighty-nine years old, each morning your eyes flutter open again is a pleasant surprise.

I don't say that to be flippant. It's just that, in the past twenty years, I've endured the loss of my husband and most people I've known from my generation. I sometimes think of those intrepid adventurers ascending Mount Everest who have to persevere in spite of their fallen companions. If they are still alive, they're expected to keep climbing. It's the same for me. I am alive and so it's my duty to continue living.

My cell phone dings merrily on my nightstand. More a relief than a surprise—it means that Hazel, my one remaining contemporary and my best friend since childhood, is still climbing too.

I fumble for my glasses wedged between the pages of a book. Hazel's message is to the point, as it is every morning.

**Still kicking.**

Grinning, I peck my response with my pointer finger.

**That makes two of us!**

Most days, that's the extent of our morning check-in. **But today my phone dings again.**

**Hallelujah.** (Intended in the secular sense—Hazel's **not a fan of** religion.) **Looking forward to seeing you on Sunday.**

I send back a flurry of hearts and flowers.

**Me too!**

When it's clear no further response is coming, I lie **back down and** stretch my limbs one at a time in my daily assessment, **checking for** anything of concern. Knees: not as flexible as they used **to be, but not** painful. Lower back: a small twinge, but that's to be **expected when** you spend most of your days gardening, isn't it? Heartbeat: **strong,** steady, and reassuringly rhythmic.

Compared to most aging bodies, mine is in great shape. **I can walk** several miles unaided, minus the supportive inserts in **my orthopedic** sneakers. I do my stretches every day, along with a **few sun saluta**tions. I can easily lift a bag of soil and carry my own groceries. **I drive** wherever I please (except for highways, but I've always **avoided those)** and live by myself in the house I've called home for **more than sixty** years. Every annual checkup, I brace myself for that **inevitable bad** news almost everyone else my age has received—cancer **or, worse,** dementia—and yet it still hasn't come. High cholesterol **and blood** sugar are my only health blemishes.

In the grand scheme of things, I know I'm not that old. **I read about** a woman in the Amazon who is 107 and still walks miles **through the** forest each day. And another who took up running in **her hundredth** year and set world records. But for whatever reason, my **particular** generational cohort was dealt shorter life straws. I never **imagined** I'd grow accustomed to losing people, but when you've **mourned the** majority of humans you've known in your life, well, it becomes inexplicably bearable. Or perhaps you just become resigned to the inevitable.

So I do my best to focus on the bright side.

As the tittering of birds grows louder, I roll out of bed, **open the** curtains, and revel in the sunshine, summoning deep gratitude for the fact that I am here another day. Not many of us get to live this long, so I try to squeeze everything out of every extra moment I'm given—it would be disrespectful if I didn't, now wouldn't it? In honor of those who can't, I make sure to savor the small pleasures of being alive, capturing them like a sensory photograph to tuck away in my memory for safekeeping.

*The refreshing coolness of the kitchen tiles beneath my bare feet.*

Just as I have every morning for the past sixty years, I gaze out the window as I wait for the coffee maker to warm up. I'll admit it took me a while to get used to making one cup instead of two. For a long time, I kept Thom's khaki-green mug lined up on the counter next to my sunflower cup, even though I only ever filled one of them. Now I just keep it at the back of the cupboard in tribute.

*The sparkle of sunlight through the crystal vase on the windowsill.*

As is my habit, I check the wall calendar for significant dates, in case I need to send someone a card. It used to be filled with birthdays and wedding anniversaries, but those have slowly been replaced with sadder reminders, the people I send them to increasingly younger. Sometimes I wonder if they feel I'm rubbing it in somehow, as if to say, "I'm still here when your parents aren't." But hopefully they just feel comforted that someone is thinking of them on an especially painful day. I hope someone will do that for my daughter, Elizabeth, when the time comes.

I make a note to send a card to Audrey Michaels—her mother, Esme, was a lovely, generous woman who made a spectacular blueberry cobbler. I miss her.

My first triumph of the day: managing to carry my coffee out to the porch without spilling a drop.

I settle in the rattan armchair that has miraculously endured decades—it creaks more than it used to, but then so do I. Goodness, how much time have I spent in this chair? Those increments of minutes, hours, must add up to a significant portion by now—months, years?

*The bees buzzing happily over the hydrangeas.*

When you're old—and I've been old for a while—you have plenty of time to watch the world go by. You have nowhere to be, no need to rush. So I adjust the cushion and relax into the chair to watch the neighborhood I've known for more than half a century slowly come to life, just as I do every morning.

The routine is comforting. Patty Cole hurrying out barefoot in her dressing gown to grab the newspaper so she can read it in bed with her husband. Sally Anderson's snooty poodle strutting down the sidewalk with such majesty that all the other dogs seem shabby in her presence. (I have a soft spot for those shabby ones—much more character.) The Lopez kids walking together to school, little Flora's hand clasping tightly onto her big brother Manu's. My, he's getting tall. I've watched so many kids grow up over the course of these mornings—and sometimes I've even watched their own kids grow up.

There's only one aberration in our street's familiar fabric today: a car I don't recognize parked outside the bungalow a few doors down. Until recently, the house belonged to the Jacobsons, who decided life in Florida was more their rhythm after becoming empty nesters. I was sad when they left. It was just one more reminder that the world moves on, whether you want it to or not. Sometimes it's hard not to feel left behind.

I sip my coffee, trying to bring myself back to gratitude. But I'll be honest—lately, I've been finding this ritual more of a challenge. You see, there's been a question niggling at me that I just can't find an answer to.

Why am I the one who's still here?

# 2

carefully count the twenty-dollar bills onto my kitchen table, smoothing out the creases, the dog-eared corners, until I have my allotted amount.

Thom's investments, along with Social Security, made sure I'd be cared for financially after he died. But I'm not sure any of us expected me to live this long. Things have gotten tighter recently, and since I don't know how many more years I'll be around, I try not to live beyond my means, especially since prices keep rising.

I'm quite adept at saving money. I allocate myself a budget, going to the bank once a week to withdraw enough to last me until the next visit. It helps that my garden is dependably bountiful and I bottle and preserve the surplus fruit and veggies to last me through the fallow months. And as long as I limit my meals to my homegrown fare along with canned beans, pasta, and rice, my grocery bill stays reasonable. Admittedly, my passion for baking inflates it sometimes—whenever I see the cost of eggs in the grocery store, I wonder if I should start keeping chickens.

I also try to keep only one light on in the house at a time and mend all my clothes, bedding, and other household items that have worn thin or fallen prey to ravenous moths. It's been years since I bought anything new that wasn't a direly needed replacement, like my electric kettle. It'd be a travesty not to offer guests a cup of tea, and I'd feel uncouth boiling the water in a saucepan, so I deemed that a necessary expense.

My sixteen-year-old grandson, Finn, likes to joke that my house is a time capsule because most of the objects are from eras long before he was born. But what's the point of accumulating more stuff when someone's going to have to sort through it when I'm gone? I've gradually been giving items away so there'll be less to get rid of. Finn says I should sell them through the consignment shop in town, but that would feel like taking advantage of people. If they're looking for things secondhand, it probably means they're tight on money like I am. And if I'm not using that thing anymore, why shouldn't they have it?

Plus, I love setting something out on the sidewalk and peeking through my window to watch folks browse through the boxes, delighting when they discover something they need or love. It tickles me when young people remark how "cool" and "vintage" the things are, like my old leather-bound transistor radio or Thom's collection of vinyl records. Those are just normal household items to me.

I slide my allotted spending money into my purse and fetch my grocery caddy.

I look forward to Sundays for several reasons. When nothing much happens in your life, things that used to feel like a chore—grocery shopping, for example—become a treat. And today I have added purpose for my shopping: Elizabeth, Finn, and Hazel are all coming for dinner.

It's rare that I'm able to coax Hazel up from Brooklyn to my small town of Beacon; she's a city slicker to the bone. I avoid metropolises if I can help it, so it's a miracle our friendship has lasted this long. But just as Hazel occasionally tolerates small-town life on my behalf, I return the courtesy by venturing down to endure New York City once in a while. And during the months in between, on top of our morning check-ins, we speak on the phone every Sunday evening (when she's still in the country—disparate time zones make it difficult sometimes).

I was flabbergasted when Hazel suggested, without a nudge, that she come up for dinner tonight in lieu of our call. She's even agreed to spend the night instead of taking a late train back to the city like she usually does. In celebration of this rarity, I saved some of my grocery money from last week so I could splurge today. I'm hoping to entice Hazel to come more frequently by making her favorite foods. She loves my cooking—her diet consists entirely of takeout, unless she happens to be dining at a restaurant—and a home-cooked meal is one of the few things Hazel covets that I can actually offer.

Ordinarily, I walk as much as possible or take the bus, but it's hard to manage so many groceries on my own, so today I'm driving. Sundays in Beacon are especially busy with visitors up here on day trips from New York City. It's more challenging to find a parking spot, but I welcome the energy the city folks bring, and I understand why they're here. Our beautiful town is nestled in the foothills of Mount Beacon overlooking the Hudson River, with one of the most charming main streets you'll ever see—there's even a waterfall at the end of it. And you should see the way the sun sets the red brick architecture aglow in the afternoons. It's simply heavenly.

I try to buy what I can from the independent stores on Main Street—the baker, the greengrocer, the butcher—but even that's a challenge now. It's been so sad watching those small businesses struggle just because everyone values convenience. Finn told me that people order their groceries over the internet these days, but why would you want to miss the chance to interact with others? So impersonal. I love chatting with cashiers while they scan my items, though it frequently elicits impatient grunts from the customers behind me.

Heavens, there really are no parking spots today. I've been circling the block in my yellow Suzuki Swift for ten minutes and there's not a single one to be seen.

Wait, is that one up ahead? I hunch over the steering wheel and hastily don the glasses hanging around my neck (technically I'm not supposed to drive without them, but occasionally I forget). Ooh, lucky me—a red Toyota Corolla is pulling out of a plum spot.

I slow down to give the Corolla enough space to exit and sit patiently with my blinker on. But as it drives away, another car that's come from the other direction is waiting with its blinker on. I suspect I might have gotten here a second or two sooner, but can't say for sure.

We sit for a few seconds in a standoff. I'm already later than I planned, so I'd really like this spot. But the person in the other car might be in an even greater hurry—perhaps they're late for a doctor's appointment—and who am I to say my needs are more important? I don't want to be presumptuous, so I roll down my window and wave them in to signal it's theirs. I'm surprised they don't wave back in thanks, but that's life. I drive off to find another spot.

It takes me another fifteen minutes before I do, and it's farther than I'd have liked, but the walk will be good for me. I wheel my grocery caddy the few blocks to the butcher, where I'm planning to spend my extra budget on a leg of lamb. I don't eat much meat anymore because it feels like an indulgence for just little old me, so this will be a nice treat for all of us. I'll even get us a bottle of Rioja—Hazel's favorite.

The wheels of my grocery caddy rattle against the sidewalk as I hurry towards the butcher, making sure to say hello to everyone I pass. Once upon a time, there'd have been many familiar faces among them—friends and acquaintances I'd known for decades who'd be happy to stop for a chat—but now it's mostly become a blur of blank stares. It's disconcerting to feel like a stranger in the town you've lived in for the majority of your life.

My friendly greeting to each passerby yields mixed results. One yoga-mat-toting woman smiles tightly and slides on her sunglasses to avoid eye contact. Another fashionable couple return the greeting but quicken their steps, probably fearing I'll monopolize their time with a long conversation. Only one woman who appears reasonably close to my age—long gray hair and skin so pale that the two almost blend—offers me a warm smile and an equally enthusiastic "Hello."

It's enough to keep me from feeling completely deflated. Even on a Sunday, everyone is rushing. The world moves faster than it used to, and I wonder how people have any time to admire the smaller joys of life.

*The soothing symmetry of a picket fence.*

*Ivy sneaking its way up a trellis.*

*Paw prints forever etched into cement.*

What a sad existence that must be—so focused on the next thing you're doing, the next place you're going, that you forget to appreciate the very moment you're in.

My grocery shopping takes me about an hour. Unfortunately, very few cashiers are in the mood for conversation. Even Ramona, the bubbly woman whose family has owned the greengrocer for several generations, is more curt than usual as she weighs my bundle of carrots.

"I hope your mother has recovered from her hip surgery," I say, referencing the tidbit she had shared last time. "How is she doing?"

Ramona glances at the queue of people behind me. "She's fine, thanks for asking."

"And what about that little girl of yours? Did she enjoy her first year of school?"

Grimacing, Ramona replaces the carrots with potatoes on the scale. "She did, thank you."

Sensing she's in no mood to elaborate, I open my wallet, ready to pay so I don't take up more of her time. It must be stressful having many customers waiting. And while I'm loath to generalize, I've observed that a lot of these visitors who come up from the big city tend to be rather impatient.

At least there's something to look forward to—the true highlight of my weekly grocery shopping ritual. I reward my efforts with a cappuccino and a slice of lemon cake that's divinely sweet and just moist enough that it melts on your tongue.

All sorts of fancy coffee shops have sprouted along Main Street lately, catering to the discerning city crowd, but those are too intimidating for me. I'm a creature of comfort, so I continue to frequent the quieter one at the end that's been there the longest. Unfortunately, even that's full of tourists today, and I'm a tad crestfallen when I see that there are no available tables. I like to sit and savor my treats—I daydream about them all week—but today I suppose I'll have to get them to go. Perhaps I can sit by the waterfall and do some people watching.

I take my place in line, my tongue tingling in anticipation of that sweet, tangy lemon cake. There's one slice left in the glass cabinet, and I'm relieved when the person in front of me doesn't order it.

I search for a recognizable face among the staff, but everyone seems new. Before, I didn't even need to say my order, they knew me so well. I'd feel like a bit of a celebrity when they'd say, "The usual, Mrs. Bridport?" as soon as they saw me. But today the blond woman taking orders just looks at me expectantly, without so much as a "How may I help you" or even a "Hello."

"Oh, I'm sorry," I say, flustered. "I'll have a small cappuccino and that slice of lemon cake, please."

An annoyed sigh erupts from behind me.

I turn to its owner, a short woman with blunt bangs, wearing sweatpants. Did I do something to bother her? I didn't realize I was taking that long. Perhaps I inadvertently bumped her with my grocery caddy.

"I'm sorry, dear," I say. "Is everything okay?"

"Yes, it's fine," she says. "It's just that I've had a shitty day and I really wanted that piece of lemon cake. God, my life sucks."

I notice the dark circles under her eyes and the over-chewed state of her fingernails. My empathy swells; I can live without a slice of lemon cake this week.

"Why don't you go ahead and have it then?" I wave at the blond, who's about to seize the slice with her tongs. "Hello there—please save that piece for this woman here. I'll have . . . a doughnut instead."

The cream-filled kind gives me indigestion, but it'll do. I'll just take an antacid when I get home.

Nodding, the blond wordlessly fulfills my request.

The sweatpants woman offers a half-hearted smile. "Thanks."

"You're welcome."

Honestly, I'd expected a little more gratitude. But maybe her day has been so terrible that it's hard to muster any kind of cheerfulness. And it's not truly a good deed if you expect a reward.

I'm on my way out of the café when I finally hear a familiar voice. "Joy! Have you heard?"

I don't need to turn around to confirm who it belongs to. Rita has lived on my street for forty years and often begins her conversations with that very sentence. If our town were to have a queen of gossip, she'd be crowned unopposed. That's why we've never been more than acquaintances—I purposefully keep her at arm's length. It's a shame, really, since she's one of the few people I've known who are close to my age and have managed to stay alive.

"Oh, hello, Rita," I say, turning to face her. "Aren't we lucky with all this sunshine we've been having?"

I try my best not to gossip, and with Rita it's easiest just to deflect to a different topic. It's hard for something to catch fire if you don't give it any fuel.

Rita shuffles closer and looks around for anyone else she can reel in as her audience. I'm sure she's disappointed it's just me.

"Someone's moved into the Jacobsons' old bungalow," Rita says, eyes furtive. Her glasses are perched on top of her head, as usual—I'm not sure I've ever actually seen her wear them.

"How lovely!" Maybe her gossip isn't so nefarious this time. "I did see a car I didn't recognize parked in the driveway. Have you met them yet?"

Rita shakes her head. "Not yet, but I've heard *all* about him." Here we go. "Nancy's grandson works at the police precinct, as you know, and apparently this new guy has a criminal record." Rita pauses to make sure she has my captive attention.

I smile politely, worrying I'm encouraging bad behavior.

"He's spent time at *Sing Sing*," she says, gleefully emphasizing the name of the maximum-security prison just down the Hudson River from Beacon.

My stomach lurches, and I'm annoyed at myself for letting Rita's gossip influence me. Everyone deserves the benefit of the doubt and I've already made a judgment on this man without knowing anything about him.

"Is that so? Perhaps there's more to the story than Nancy conveyed," I say, mostly to convince myself.

Rita rolls her eyes at me. "What more do you need to know except there's a criminal now living next door to us? This town is going downhill fast."

"Well, actually, it's a lot safer than it used to be. You were here in the eighties—remember how it was back then?" Thom wouldn't even let me come to Main Street unaccompanied.

"I suppose I do," Rita huffs. "But do you really want to return to those days?"

The knot of concern tightens against my will.

"I'm sure one person's presence wouldn't do that," I say. "And we don't know anything about him. We've all made mistakes, and so we all deserve grace."

Rita crosses her arms. "A criminal is a criminal, no matter how you paint it."

There's no use trying to reason with her when she's in one of these moods. But I worry how many people she's already swayed with her gossip. I feel sorry for the poor fellow, having his new neighbors all form a perception of him before he's even had the chance to introduce himself.

So I make a show of looking at my watch.

"Goodness, time has flown. I'm so sorry, Rita, I'd really love to stay and chat but I'm cooking dinner for Elizabeth, Finn, and a friend tonight, so I've got to get home to heat up the oven."

Rita arches an eyebrow. "Elizabeth is coming over? Haven't seen her around in a while. How's she doing after that messy divorce?"

I bristle for several reasons. Rita doesn't know any details of my daughter's divorce—I hardly know them myself—but I also don't want my family's personal business becoming part of her gossip repartee.

"She and Finn are both doing really well—thanks very much for asking."

I'm hoping my response conveys more confidence than I feel. It's been so hard to get my daughter to share anything with me lately—I have no idea how she's doing. She just seems exhausted.

I position my body towards the exit. "I'd better be going, Rita. Have a lovely afternoon!"

She's still talking as the café door drifts closed behind me. A bit rude on my part, but she'll find someone else to gossip to before long.

Irritatingly, she's already planted the seed in my head.

Do we really want a convicted criminal living in our midst?

# 3

I'm slicing carrots into medallions—Elizabeth's preference—when there's the thud of a car door outside. The wall clock assures me I still have two hours before anyone is due to arrive; the creak of the garden gate and the rhythm of footsteps on my porch beg to differ.

I've barely set down the knife and wiped my hands on my apron when Hazel appears in the kitchen, one arm stretched up the doorframe and the other on her hip, as if posing for a photo. Her turquoise kaftan, embroidered with cheerful tropical birds, contrasts with her bright red hair.

"Still the same old Joy," she says with a sly smile. "So trusting you don't even lock your front door."

The sight of her is like sliding on my favorite pair of slippers—instant comfort, settling into a groove slowly formed over time.

"Well, that's just one of the many perks of living in a small town," I say, resuming our playful tug-of-war over our dwellings of choice.

The rainbow of resin bangles on Hazel's wrist clatters as she takes hold of my shoulders and kisses my cheeks, left then right. Those European greetings always confuse me. Which side first? Do I kiss the cheek or the air? Hazel has eleven inches on my five feet, making it all the more logistically awkward. A flamingo greeting a duckling.

I'd much prefer a plain old hug, but I'll take any affection from my friend, awkward or not.

I gesture at the clock. "I was planning to pick you up from the five o'clock train you said you were taking." Surprising people at the station is one of my favorite things; the way their eyes light up at the sight of you on the platform, the realization that someone cares enough about them to make the effort on their behalf.

Hazel reaches over me to pluck a carrot medallion from the chopping board.

"I know I said that. But I was ready with time to spare, so I thought I'd hop on the earlier one."

It's rare for Hazel to be early; she shows up when she shows up. Even though I call her at the same time every Sunday, she's always in the middle of something—an art project, a crossword, a salsa lesson—but I know not to take it personally. Hazel's life is one of constant motion. Unlike me, she needs to be constantly doing, seeing, making, and enjoying.

"Well, I hope the taxi wasn't too expensive."

She can easily afford to take cabs, yet deems them a waste of money in New York City. But the public transit system in Beacon isn't as robust.

"Oh, I didn't bother with a taxi," she scoffs. "I just got a ride with some man who was on the same train as me."

She tosses the carrot in her mouth like popcorn, smirking as she awaits my response. I should've learned by now not to react to Hazel's attempts to shock me, but I can't help it.

"You got in the car with a stranger? You should have called me to come and get you!"

"And miss out on the thrill of potentially being kidnapped?" Hazel crunches the carrot with satisfaction. "I thought you said safety was a small-town perk?"

Outwitted, I elbow playfully past her to the coffee machine.

"Well, since dinner is hours away, how about a cup of coffee?" I extract her mug—vivid yellow hand-painted giraffes, a gift she brought me years ago from Tanzania—from the cupboard.

"Actually, I'll have peppermint tea if you've got it," she says, easing herself into a chair at the kitchen table.

Tea for Hazel? That's a new one.

I rummage through the clutter of boxes on the tea shelf, many of which I suspect have been there a decade.

"I don't think I do," I say, chagrined to disappoint Hazel. "But the mint in my garden is flourishing, so I'll just pop out and pick a few leaves."

"You're a doll, Joy, thank you."

She brushes away a lock of hair—always that same deep shade of red—and wearily closes her eyes.

I know better than to ask if she's okay. "That train journey takes more energy than it used to, doesn't it?" I say, locating my herb scissors in a drawer. "The guest room's ready if you want to take a nap before dinner. I'll bring the tea in for you."

Hazel's eyes blink open. "Nonsense—I'm here to spend time with my best friend."

I wait for her punch line. The one implying that her "best friend" is in fact someone else—another long-running bit between us—but it never comes. It's rare that Hazel's compliments come without the veil of humor or a hint of sarcasm.

I'm unexpectedly touched.

The thud of two car doors signals Elizabeth and Finn's arrival later that evening.

Just as Hazel and I are heading through the screen door to greet them, I turn to my friend.

"I should warn you that Elizabeth hasn't been herself lately," I whisper. "A little distant and surly—I think it might be the divorce. She and Jack aren't on good terms."

It's such a shame things didn't work out between Elizabeth and Jack. I always liked having him as a son-in-law—he was charming and funny and brought a lightness to Elizabeth's intensity. But then a couple of years ago they announced they were separating, and Jack moved to the other side of the country. From what I understand, his new job at some dental technology company has him flying all around the world. At least, that's the excuse he gives for not seeing Finn more often.

Since Jack left, I've felt a distance growing between my daughter and me. Not because of a particular argument or falling out, more of a gradual drifting, the way you might be swimming at a beach and suddenly realize that the current has pulled you much farther down the shore. It feels like I've been fighting against the tide ever since, trying to get back to where we were, back when she was a small girl.

As if to emphasize that distance, Elizabeth immediately contradicts the warning I've given Hazel. Her face and body animate with delight when she catches sight of my friend.

"Hazel!"

Elizabeth leaps up the steps as if I wasn't even there.

They exchange air kisses with an ease I've never managed.

"Hello, lovely Elizabeth," Hazel says, equally delighted. "It's been too long, hasn't it?"

Thank god Finn is here so I'm not left standing there like a third wheel.

"Hey, Nanna!" He greets me with arms wide, pulling me into the kind of tight hug that his father was so good at. It's only been a few days since I last saw Finn and I swear he's taller. My head barely reaches his clavicle now; it feels like yesterday that he used to snuggle into mine while falling asleep on my chest.

After he releases me, I open my arms hopefully towards my daughter. "Hello, my darling."

Elizabeth accepts my hug. "Hi, Mom."

Any other day, nothing would feel amiss in this interaction. But the delight I witnessed in her moments earlier with Hazel is noticeably absent. I suppose Elizabeth does see me much more frequently, even if her erratic shift work schedule as an intensive care nurse makes it challenging.

Hazel takes Finn by the shoulders. "I think you've finally outgrown me," she says dryly. "If only by a hair."

Finn grins proudly, then sniffs at the scent of roast lamb and rosemary mingling with the sweetness of the evening jasmine. "Smells great, Nanna—what's for dinner?"

"Hazel's favorite," I respond, pleased. "Lamb roast."

I catch Elizabeth's shoulders tensing out of the corner of my eye. Funny how you become attuned to every subtle movement of your child's body, desperate for a tell, a clue to the emotions simmering beneath.

"I'm not eating much red meat these days," Elizabeth says, stepping onto the porch.

I mask my disappointment with another smile—an action so practiced, it's innate. "Well, that's no problem at all. I've got some chicken breasts I can rustle up for you."

Finn puts his arm around Hazel. "Don't worry, we'll eat her share of the lamb."

I hang back on the porch, watching them walk inside chatting, grateful to have gathered my favorite people for one rare evening together.

But during dinner, as I observe Elizabeth's interactions with Hazel, little jolts of envy needle at me. They've always had a special bond, cemented from when Elizabeth was a kid and Hazel would send her postcards from remote parts of the globe and return with gifts and stories that would have my daughter transfixed. I loved that Hazel opened up Elizabeth's eyes to the world in a way I never could, but at the same time, her adventurous spirit seemed to shine a light on my inadequacies. What wisdom did I have to offer my daughter, having been raised in one small town before living the rest of my life in another?

I see that transfixed look now, in both Elizabeth's and Finn's eyes, as Hazel regales them with a story. It's one I've heard before, about the time she locked herself out of her apartment in Australia and persuaded some nearby construction workers to put her in the front of their Bobcat and lift her up high enough that she could climb onto the balcony and through the sliding door she'd left ajar. It's not just the stories that make Hazel so compelling, it's the charisma with which she tells them; she could make a trip to her accountant sound like a wild, captivating escapade. I've heard all her travel tales hundreds of times, but that's why our friendship works—Hazel loves telling stories and I love listening to them. I used to think she shared those often-sordid details about her life to shock me, but then I began to understand she wanted me to live vicariously.

It's a concerted effort, but I manage to push my envy aside—for tonight, at least.

Hazel and I stand on the porch, watching Elizabeth's car disappear down the hill.

I reach for the screen door. "How about a round of gin rummy before bed?"

Hazel is a night owl, so I want to make an effort to stay up later, if only to bask in her presence a while longer.

She puts her hand on the door, stopping its momentum.

"Could we just sit out here for a little while? It'd be such a shame to miss the stars coming out." An impish twinkle. "The one small-town perk I'll concede to."

"Of course." I'm delighted to have some company for the evening ritual that's felt intensely lonely of late. "Shall I make us some tea?"

Hazel keeps her hand on the door. "Let's just sit."

She moves Thom's old rattan chair closer to mine and lowers herself into it.

The evening air is thick with the spice of humidity as the cicadas announce their presence with gusto. I'm overcome with contentment;

in this small moment, everything feels exactly as it should be. It's like balancing a soap bubble on your fingertip; all the more beautiful because it's so ephemeral.

With a satisfied sigh, I turn to Hazel to see if she's enjoying it as much as I am. But she isn't gazing at the stars; she's looking at me.

I wait for the sassy comment I'm sure is headed my way. But she remains silent, her focus steady.

My hand shoots self-consciously to my cheek.

"Do I have raspberry coulis on my face?" I'd drizzled some over the chocolate cake for dessert, and it does tend to get everywhere.

Again, the absence of a quip is glaring. Hazel just shakes her head, a soft, indecipherable smile on her face. It gives me pause—I thought I knew all her facial expressions by heart. Something isn't right. I'm not sure I like this new, subdued version of my friend.

"Tell me what you've been getting up to in New York City," I say, hoping the prompt will inject some life into her.

Hazel has lived in the same loft apartment in Brooklyn since the seventies, her "home base" when she wasn't flitting about the globe for her business importing artisanal rugs and textiles. Back then, her neighborhood wasn't the polished enclave it is today, but Hazel loved its rawness, its unpredictability—and the electric creativity that came with those things. Even at the age of eighty-nine, my friend adores anything audacious and unconventional. Probably because that's exactly what she is.

"Well," Hazel says with an odd laugh. "I'll tell you, but I don't think you're going to like it."

My rattan chair crackles as I shift to face her. "What happened?"

A silence.

"I suppose I should just come out with it." A hint of exasperation. "But before I do, you have to promise you won't make a big deal out of it. I'm only telling you because we don't keep secrets from each other."

My hands grip the chair. What could Hazel have done? Is she in some kind of legal trouble?

"Of course I promise," I say, mind racing with the possible crimes she might have committed. As feisty as she can be, I'm positive she's not capable of killing someone. Well, not intentionally.

"I have cancer," Hazel says matter-of-factly.

My mind had ventured so far in a different direction that it takes me a few moments to reel it back to what she's just said. When the gravity of it finally hits me, it's like a fist closing around my heart.

I can barely manage a whisper. "Cancer?"

What a terrible friend I am, that this feeble response is all I can muster.

"Yes, my dear, cancer." Hazel's signature wryness has returned. "The bastard finally got me. With all the things I've done to my body over the years—as enjoyable as they were—I'm surprised it didn't come for me sooner."

I try to focus, to come up with something supportive for my friend. Unfortunately, I fail.

"But . . . what kind of cancer?"

It's disorienting to hear Hazel's laugh when she's just delivered such devastating news. And yet it's also befitting of her—cavalier, even in the worst of times.

"Does it matter?" she says. "The long and the short of it is that my death warrant is signed. I've been lucky to live a wonderfully fulfilling life and now it's coming to an end."

"But what about treatment?" It's impossible to temper the panic in my voice. "They're getting so much better at curing cancers these days. Surely there's something that can be done?"

"And spend my last months being poked and prodded, injecting my body with all sorts of chemicals? No, thank you." Months? "Joy, I've made my peace with this and I need you to as well. Remember, you promised not to make a big deal of it."

"But . . ." I say, struggling to articulate a belief I've long held but never acknowledged. "It's just, well, I assumed I'd be the one to go first."

Hazel laughs again. "Haven't I always been the one who tries things out before you to show you how fun it is?"

"This isn't the same as getting your driver's license, Hazel."

"But it's an adventure nonetheless," she says. "Now, I'm tired of this doom and gloom. Let's talk about something else."

As Hazel launches into a story about her downstairs neighbor, I'm barely listening. I sit in my chair stunned, as I realize my greatest fear is about to come true.

Soon, I'll be the last one still climbing the mountain.

# 4



Is this what cows feel like when they're uprooted from the field they were raised in as calves and plonked in an unfamiliar one?

Mama told me to be brave on my first day at my new school. That if I was polite, followed all the rules, and observed closely how everyone else did everything, I'd get along just fine with my second-grade classmates. She hasn't been feeling well these past few days and I don't want to give her a reason to feel worse.

But as I stand in the doorway of this little schoolhouse, twenty pairs of eyes boring into me, panic rises in my throat.

I already miss my classmates in Madison. Mama explained that school would be different in our new town, a small farming community close to the Minnesota border. That, instead of many classes of kids, each in their own room, the twenty pairs of eyes currently inspecting every aspect of my appearance comprised the whole student body. And this musty one-room building, with a single outhouse tucked several yards behind it, was the entirety of our schoolhouse.

I'd tried to put on a brave face when Daddy sat me down and told me he was leaving the city medical practice he'd worked at my entire life, to become the sole doctor for this place that's a mere speck on the map.

"Remember that this is a small town, Joy," he said this morning as he walked me to the schoolhouse door. "You are representing our family, just as I am. So I expect you to be on your best behavior at all times. I know you'll be a good girl."

I dread seeing the pool of disappointment in his eyes whenever I fall short of his expectations, like the time I got the giggles during church, disrupting the service. I couldn't help it—the more I knew I shouldn't be laughing, the more my body wanted to. I can't even remember what I found so funny in the first place. Afterwards, he didn't yell at me, or even admonish me, he just shook his head and remained silent until dinner.

So I'll do my best to live up to his idea of a "good girl" at this new school. The problem is, none of these kids look like they want to be friends with me.

My panic subsides briefly when the lone adult in the room—Mrs. Farnsworth, the school's only teacher—guides me to a desk in the front row. I whimper my thanks and take my place, snickers erupting around me as the wooden chair groans like an embarrassing bodily function. Feeling the eyes now burning into the back of my head, I sink lower to make myself as small as possible, willing the hands of the clock to magically gain pace and whisk me away from this painful experience.

We're halfway through our morning lesson—memorizing the names of the forty-eight states—when the door to the schoolhouse flies open. A girl around my age saunters in confidently, her dark blond hair a mass of unkempt curls. The energy in the room shifts and everyone's attention draws to her, like sunflowers turning their faces towards the warm glow of the sun.

Even Mrs. Farnsworth greets her with an amused smile. "And what, dear Hazel, is the excuse for your tardiness today?"

Hazel nudges the door closed with her hip. She pauses, noticing me in the front row, and cocks her head with curiosity.

"Dad's tractor broke down, so I had to walk," Hazel says, nonchalantly weaving her way through the rows of desks to the empty one in the back corner.

I wait for everyone else to laugh, but no one appears surprised. Did everyone ride farm machinery to school? Our teacher's skepticism seems less about her mode of transport and more that it's a well-worn excuse.

"Broken down, again? What terrible luck your father's been having," Mrs. Farnsworth says with good-natured sarcasm.

As our geography lesson continues, I'm relieved the class's attention has turned away from me. I already know all the forty-eight states by heart, but I hold my tongue, since Mama says no one likes a know-it-all and I suspect my best means of survival in this tiny new community is to blend in. So I resolve to stay quiet, keep my head down, and try not to be noticed.

My strategy works until lunchtime.

We're lined up with our bowls, awaiting our allocated spoonful of beans that Mrs. Farnsworth is doling out from a large can on the pot-bellied stove at the back of the room. The shaggy-haired boy in front of me, likely a few years older than I am, points at my shoes—black leather lace-up boots that reach just above my ankles—and laughs.

"High-tops," he sneers. "So old-fashioned. I thought you used to live in the city?"

Snickering fills the room again.

Panicked, I compare my footwear to everyone else's. They're all wearing the same style of patent-leather shoes, none of which rise above their ankles. I've never given any thought to my shoes—I just diligently wear what Mama sets out for me every morning.

"Maybe she just doesn't want to follow the crowd, Billy," a voice pipes up from the other side of the room. Hazel is sitting on top of her desk, legs crossed at the knee. "I like that. Not everyone is a sheep."

Billy's shoulders droop as he stammers a response. "Oh, yeah, I guess they're okay."

The others murmur in agreement. Though Hazel is among the

younger kids in the room, it's clear she holds court. I've never encoun-tered a girl who is so confident, so assured of her place in the world. She certainly isn't a sheep.

Hazel flashes me a grin. All I can offer in return is a bewildered but grateful look.

She shimmies off the desk and takes her place in line behind me.

"So you just moved here?" Hazel says, fingernails tapping a cheer-ful rhythm on her enamel bowl.

"Yes," I say shyly, feeling the watchful expressions of the others. "My family came here from Madison."

Hazel grins again, revealing a cluster of wayward bottom teeth. "A city slicker, huh? Half your luck. I'm dying to get out of this thumbtack of a town."

The line shuffles forward and Billy holds out his bowl for the scoop of beans.

"It seems like a nice place to live." My nerves won't let me think of something more creative.

"Only if you like a life where nothing ever happens," Hazel says, standing next to me as we both receive our portions.

I'm about to head back to my desk up front, when Hazel puts her hand on my shoulder.

"Hey, Billy," she calls out to my tormentor, who's already shoveling his beans into his mouth at the desk next to Hazel's. "You won't mind switching desks with Joy, will you? I'm going to show her the ropes around here, so it makes sense for us to sit together."

The older boy manages to swallow before he pouts. "But this has always been my desk."

Hazel shrugs. "And it's good to change things around sometimes—right, Mrs. Farnsworth?"

She looks at our teacher like an equal rather than a superior, sure of her support.

Mrs. Farnsworth pauses doling out legumes. "Yes, that's a lovely idea to help Joy settle in." She turns to Billy. "Won't you be a nice boy and let Joy have your desk for now?" She holds up a finger to silence his imminent retort. "We can revisit the arrangement in the fall."

Billy slumps glumly into his seat, pushing his spoon around his near-empty bowl. "Fine," he mumbles. "I'll do it after I finish my lunch."

Hazel winks at me and my heart lifts.

Life is suddenly looking much more exciting.

**5**

Talk about an awkward morning after. What do you say to someone when they shuffle into the kitchen for breakfast, the morning after telling you they only have a few months left to live?

"Good morning!" My chirpy tone borders on manic. "I'm making crepes!"

Hazel squints like she has a hangover, despite barely touching the wine last night.

"I'll just start with some tea," she says.

"Of course." I hurry to fill the kettle. "Is there anything else you need? Aspirin? A warm compress?"

Suggesting those things for someone with terminal cancer is like fighting flames with an eyedropper, I know, but I need to do something.

Hazel, now seated at the table, eyes me sternly. "Don't fuss over me, Joy. You know that's not what I want."

She smooths her hair with her palm. Hazel's not a natural redhead, but she's been dedicated to the same vibrant shade for most of our lives, so it feels like she is.

I dip my head in contrition. "I know."

"Let's do some shopping today before I head back to the city," she says, rubbing her palms together. "I've found so many treasures at that little vintage clothing boutique on Main Street. All the places in Brooklyn have been mercilessly picked over by those 'hipsters.'"

I dare not question the point of acquiring more things when you're not going to be around for much longer.

"That's a wonderful idea," I say, pouring the water over the crushed mint leaves, the calming aroma a welcome balm. "I'll get dressed as soon as we have breakfast."

Contrary to my dressing gown and slippers, Hazel is already fully attired—an oversized purple blouse with a dramatic ruffled collar and matching wide-legged pants, topped with a menagerie of accessories. She always looks put together—I've seen photos of her hiking through muddy rainforests while still exuding glamour—but she usually arrives at my breakfast table in her dressing gown, an elegant silk number with a bright calla lily print I adore. She must be eager to get started with the day.

While tending to the crepe mixture, I surreptitiously study her for any signs of illness. When someone is eighty-nine years old, it's hard to discern what is normal deterioration and what might be something of concern; we're both covered in wrinkles and age spots. She's wearing a full face of makeup, so the flushed rouge of her cheeks is misleading. From what I can tell, her five-foot-eleven frame stands as tall as it always has, but then most people look tall to me.

What I can gather, at least, is that Hazel is tired. So I suggest we drive instead of walking into town as we have in the past—my guise being to bring her overnight bag in the car so we don't have to rush home before the train.

"Maybe we can even squeeze in lunch!" I say, to firm up my reasoning.

As we walk down Beacon's retail artery a couple of hours later, I'm reminded how differently people view me when I'm with Hazel. When I'm alone, I generally escape notice altogether; when I'm with Hazel, people greet us with looks of delight. We must make quite the pair: Hazel, tall and unique in every way; me, short and unremarkable in every other. It's fruitless for me to try to match her style—and that wouldn't be me, anyway—so I'm in my usual elastic-waist slacks, button-down shirt, and comfy orthopedic sneakers.

"Love your outfit," says a young woman with more piercings than I can count. There's no need to clarify whom she's referring to.

"Thank you, darling!" Hazel says with a regal gesture of the hand.

It's not that she tries to attract attention, it's more of an innate knowing that she deserves it. That same confidence I sensed instantly when we first met in that classroom in Wisconsin.

After we've browsed the racks at the vintage clothing shop—Hazel bought several silk scarves—she stops in front of a secondhand store, just as I knew she would. It's not a visit to Beacon if we don't go through this ritual.

She holds open the door, determination in her eye. "Shall we?"

I walk through it obediently, preparing myself for the battle of wills that's coming.

Seth, the owner of the shop, looks up from the newspaper spread out next to the cash register.

"Hazel Scottsdale," he says, eyebrow raised. "Haven't seen you in a while."

He looks at me blankly. I always accompany Hazel on her visits to his shop, but he never seems to recognize me. I've even encountered him a few times in line at the bank over the years and received that same blank look.

That's probably why I take quiet pleasure in the ink that's spread all over his forearms from leaning on the newspaper. I wouldn't even feel bad if it smudged onto his white shirt.

"Hello, Seth." Hazel pokes nonchalantly through a large salad bowl of costume jewelry. "Still chasing hearses to swoop in on those estate sales, so you can overcharge rich city folk for junk?"

She picks up an old music box and twists the key until it plays "Clair de Lune."

Seth forces a laugh.

"Don't pretend you haven't done the odd unscrupulous thing in your time, Hazel." The piece of hair ineffectually masking his bald patch floats in the breeze of the desk fan. "I knew you in the seventies, remember?"

Hazel waves a dismissive hand. "Once a rumormonger, always a rumormonger."

And yet she winks at me.

"I'm just going to the back corner to browse the books," I tell her, knowing I'm not required for this encounter.

This store is a minimalist's nightmare, shelves arranged in narrow, mazelike passages, each piled high with a miscellany of used objects. I imagine there are some real treasures buried among it all, but you'd have to be angelically patient to sift until you find them. Still, I'm hoping today is the day I'll finally find something compelling in the dusty collection of used books. As much as I love browsing our local bookstore, it's beyond my budget to buy anything new. And the wait for most books I put on hold at the library is months long, which also requires angelic patience.

Even though I'm tucked away out of sight behind the shelves, I'm still privy to Hazel and Seth's conversation.

"Something tells me today's the day you're ready to finally sell me that."

I don't need to look to know that Hazel is pointing at a ceramic hand-painted vase that's sitting on the counter next to Seth. I can picture its sleek form with swaths of turquoise, purple, and white. Too abstract for my taste, but Hazel has asked about it every time we've come in here since Seth opened the store about fifteen years ago. Once she even offered him $5,000 for it; I tell you, I almost choked on my lemon cough drop when I heard that. Even more so when Seth declined the amount.

But I know why she wants it so badly. The first time we stumbled across it here, I could tell instantly that it wasn't just any old vase. Hazel's reliably unfazed demeanor faltered, if only momentarily, and only in a way that someone who'd known her for decades would catch.

I asked her about it while we were at lunch later that day.

She placed her fork down and clasped her hands, elbows on the table; a sign she was about to tell me a story.

"Do you remember, back in the seventies, I had an artist friend named Eric?"

"Of course." I only met him a few times, but I remember the deep melancholy behind his eyes. "He did quite well, didn't he?"

"In certain circles," Hazel said. "He was quite a celebrated ceramicist, though he clung too tightly to the starving artist fallacy to ever fulfill his potential. Anyway, we both knew Seth back when he ran a gallery in Manhattan—he was a young upstart on the scene. He repeatedly offered to represent Eric, but Eric always declined. Said he just didn't like Seth's 'energy.'" Hazel sipped from her water glass, leaving a scarlet imprint on its rim. "And it was true that Seth didn't really appreciate his art, nor even really understand it. He was more into the social prestige of the art scene, just wanted the notch in his professional belt of representing the artist *du jour*."

I abandoned my quiche to focus on the unfolding plot.

"As you may also recall," Hazel continues, "Eric died young, the way many artists did—and still do—by chasing one too many highs."

"I do remember that," I said solemnly. Among the throngs of Hazel's friends and acquaintances I'd met over the years, Eric also stuck out because of how deeply his death seemed to affect her. She was uncharacteristically withdrawn in the aftermath, her sparkle absent for months.

"Well, that vase was the last thing he made," Hazel said, contemplative. "And I wanted to make sure it would be treasured by whoever ended up with it. But when it went to auction, Seth outbid me at the last moment—I was still building my business at that time—and though I offered to buy it from him for much more as soon as I had the means, he refused. I've tried many times since, but he's a stubborn cow. I'm not giving up, though; I owe it to Eric to get that vase back. It deserves to be with a person who really appreciates it, not one who's keeping it out of spite."

And perhaps today is her last-ditch effort.

I peek through the shelves to see Seth's reaction to Hazel's proposition.

He puts his hands up as if it's beyond his control. "Like I tell you every time, Hazel, that's the one thing in this store that's not for sale."

Hazel's myriad accessories jingle as she crosses her arms, painted fingernails tapping on her forearm. "Not even if I let you name your price?"

"Not even then." Smug is the only description for Seth's expression.

I do my best to muzzle a sneeze from the dust floating in the tungsten-lit glow. I should've thought to take a Zyrtec before coming into this store.

"What a shame," Hazel says. "I could have made you a rich man—rich enough that you could give up swindling hipsters."

I know Hazel did well for herself running her textile-importing business, but surely she must be bluffing about how much she's willing to pay. Then again, when your time on earth is quickly dwindling like hers is, what's the point of saving your money?

Seth's forehead twitches, a hint that he might finally be tempted. Then his smirk returns.

"A shame, indeed."

Unable to contain my sneezes any longer, I unleash them in a barrage, providing a dramatic end to their conversation.

I wait until we're seated at an outdoor table for lunch before I broach the subject of the vase with Hazel.

"Have you ever considered that maybe Seth really did love the vase and wanted to enjoy it?" I shake salt into my hand then sprinkle it over my pasta.

"You only assume the good in people, Joy." Hazel has been stirring her bowl of soup in a figure-eight since it arrived, yet she's barely eaten any. "No, I'm fairly certain he's just vindictive. He always suspected Eric turned down his representation because I told him to, which wasn't true—Eric did what he wanted. But the fact that I want the vase makes Seth want to keep it from me. I do wish he'd just give in at this point, as much as I enjoy sparring with him."

One of the many ways we are chalk and cheese—Hazel relishes an argument or any kind of confrontation, whereas I avoid them at all costs. All our lives, she's the one who complained to the server when our meals were subpar, the one who challenged men when they catcalled us on the street or made a dirty joke at our expense, the one who stood up to any kind of bully, really.

I've gotten so used to Hazel playing that role in my life, letting her handle conflict so that I didn't have to.

What will I do when she's gone?

**6**

Yoo-hoo! I'm not dead yet.

Hazel's morning message arrives on schedule. But it brings no relief, her gallows humor stirs no mirth. It feels like the beginning of an ominous countdown, the end of which could be anywhere from months to weeks away.

I hardly slept, waking in fits and starts to check my phone for her text, the way you do when you've got an early flight to catch and don't want to miss your alarm. The sunlight caressing my cheek this morning is just cruel confirmation that the events of the past few days weren't a dream. I don't feel like doing my sun salutations and stretches. I want to stay in bed and wallow, to pretend for one last hour that Hazel's diagnosis isn't true.

But I can't, because I have a piano lesson to give.

I've only ever had one job in my life—working as a receptionist in my father's medical practice in Wisconsin in the years following high school. When I moved to Beacon and married Thom in my mid-twenties, I floated the idea of getting a job, but he almost took it as an insult.

"Don't you have everything you need?" he said, exasperated.

He had a point—as a lawyer, he earned more than enough for the two of us. He preferred I dedicate my time to taking care of the house, playing hostess, and, when the time finally came, being a mother. Elizabeth's arrival in my late thirties was somewhat of a miracle, since we'd all but given up hope of having children. Given that blessing, it seemed only right that I devote myself to being present for her whenever she needed me.

But before she was born—as a way to ease the yearning of not being able to have children—I began offering free piano lessons to the kids in the neighborhood. Back then, many of the families in Beacon couldn't afford music lessons for their children; such things were labeled unnecessary luxuries. And since I didn't need the money, and had been playing piano since I was four, it seemed like a small way to contribute to the world. More than sixty years later, I've lost count of how many young little fingers have caressed the keys of my old piano.

Unfortunately, piano lessons are an even bigger luxury for many families now. So I'll keep offering them for free for as long as I'm physically able. It's an absolute treat to open a child's mind to the treasure of music. To watch their eyes light up in that moment when it clicks, when it moves from the drudgery of memorizing notes and keys to something magical that stirs their little souls. I'll never grow tired of that.

As I hurry to make my coffee, spilling a few drops in the process, a timid knock on the screen door announces the arrival of today's student. Sunny is a precious little seven-year-old whose mom, Perlah, brings her on the bus and then waits patiently outside for the duration of the thirty-minute lesson. Without fail, I invite Perlah to sit in the living room and listen, but she says she wants Sunny to have her time all to herself. As the youngest of three sisters, it's something she rarely gets.

After Perlah and her daughters moved here last year from the Philippines, the organist at my church told me how Sunny would hang around after Sunday service asking all kinds of questions about the instrument. When I had a word with Perlah about giving her weekly lessons for free, it was as if all of the little girl's dreams had come true.

Our lessons are at seven thirty in the morning so Perlah can drop her at school before going to work as a home attendant.

"Mrs. Bridport!" Sunny says, sitting stick-straight on the piano stool, legs dangling, not yet long enough to reach the pedals. "I memorized three scales—watch!"

Sunny's delicate fingers tap expertly through the notes, hesitating only once on the F-sharp in the G major scale. Since most kids loathe scales, I rarely enforce them, but Sunny begged me to teach her some.

"Very impressive, Sunny," I say. "Especially since I only taught them to you last week. How did you practice?"

It's not just her memorization that's impressive—she doesn't have a piano at home. Few of my students do, since families who can't afford lessons definitely can't afford a piano. I used to have an open-door policy for neighborhood kids who wanted to practice on mine. Well, technically I still have it, but parenting has changed and kids don't roam freely as much as they used to. So I've developed a relationship with the local music shop to keep an eye out for any secondhand electric piano keyboards that might come their way. They do me a deal, and then I tell a parent that I've heard about someone giving away a keyboard and ask if they'd like it. Technically a fib, I know, but that way they just feel like luck is smiling on them for once, instead of being given what they might see as a handout—most of them are too proud for that. And I'm happy to forgo a few extra groceries for the month if it can provide that happiness. I see how hard these parents work to give their kids a good shot at life. It makes me wonder if Thom and I made it too easy for Elizabeth by giving her everything she could ever want.

Sunny beams up at me. "I made a keyboard at home with a marker and some cardboard—well, Mommy helped me a little—and then I practiced the scales fifty times each day."

I clasp my hands. "What a clever idea!"

Sunny pulls back her tiny shoulders, bursting with pride. "I bet you I can even do it with my eyes closed."

"That would be a neat trick, wouldn't it?"

I pull my chair closer to show her I'm a captive audience.

But even as Sunny makes good on her prediction and then plays me another song she learned by heart, I struggle to give her my full attention.

All I can think about is Hazel.

I'm mad at myself for not being more supportive when she told me her news two nights ago, but it was such a shock. And the way she was so matter-of-fact about it was disorienting. She calls me a softie because I tear up easily when something moves me or if I see someone in distress. But how am I supposed to contain those emotions and "not make a big deal out of it," as she said, when the one person who knows me better than anyone—better than even my husband—announces that she won't be around for much longer?

"Mrs. Bridport?"

Sunny's gentle tugging on my sleeve severs my daydream. How rude of me. These lessons are supposed to make the kids feel special— I'm especially ashamed when I see our time is almost up. Desperate to atone, I send her on her way with two chocolate chip cookies instead of the usual one (I like to give the kids a freshly baked treat as a reward for their hard work).

Sunny's eyes light up like it's Christmas.

"Whoa, thank you, Mrs. Bridport! Now Mommy and I can each have one instead of sharing."

Now I feel even worse for never having thought to give her an extra baked treat for Perlah, waiting so patiently outside.

I stand on the porch watching the two of them walk hand in hand to the bus stop, touched by the way Sunny keeps looking up at her mother with such admiration.

Still feeling out of sorts, I close my eyes and scrutinize the weight in my chest, trying to pinpoint the emotion it holds. Sadness, of course. Helplessness, understandably. But tucked away under all of that is something surprising.

Betrayal.

It's selfish, but Hazel has been my rock, my protector, the one I've always been able to turn to when life got hard. Though there was always a 50 percent chance of her being the first one to go, I'd never stopped to consider what it would be like if she actually did. And I'm a little resentful that she's leaving me behind.

It's ridiculous, and yet it's the truth. What a terrible friend I am.

Through the open screen door, I hear the chime of the antique wall clock Thom's sister gave us as a wedding present.

It's only eight fifteen in the morning—I can't waste the entire day feeling sorry for myself.

I have my weekly board games group at the church this afternoon, so maybe I'll bake some peach muffins for the snack table. That will provide a welcome distraction. Meditation isn't something I've ever mastered, but baking is the closest I come to it—measuring, sifting, stirring my mind into a state of calm.

Once the muffins are in the oven, I check the little digital pedometer I keep clipped to my waistband. I'd better get my steps in for the day if I'm going to be sitting and playing board games all afternoon. And it'll do me some good to move my body—I could use those endorphins.

Only a few wispy clouds interrupt the blue expanse when I step outside. It's a glorious day for a stroll around the neighborhood, especially because everyone's gardens are in full bloom this time of year. I hope it's not too boastful to say that my garden is one of the most spectacular, if only because I've been cultivating it for the longest. I remember the day Thom drove me here a few months after we were married, when we'd been living in his tiny studio apartment above a hardware store on Main Street. He insisted I keep my eyes closed for the drive, not letting me open them until we were standing at the front gate.

I tell you, my heart almost burst when I saw our new home with its charming pitched roof, dormer windows with forest-green shutters, and cozy front porch.

Thom stood behind me, arms around my waist.

"I can't wait to create millions of memories with you here," he whispered, pressing his cheek against mine as we gazed up at the house, with nothing but the potential of our lives ahead of us.

The only hint of a garden back then was a sad-looking rosebush that needed to be put out of its misery. But little by little, I brought that unloved swath of dirt to life—every single thing that grows there now started as a seedling. I may not have achieved much of note in my life-time, but I sure am proud of that. And this house does hold those millions of memories Thom promised. They weren't all happy ones, but I suppose that's what life is. Show me the person who has only happy memories. The important thing is not to succumb to the unhappy ones.

The neighborhood is quieter than usual, since most people are at work. A shame, since a nice conversation might help me out of this funk. In the distance I see Daphne, our bubbly mailwoman. I was sad when the man who'd long delivered our mail retired last year, but Daphne has such a positive and zesty presence that it feels like she's always been part of our neighborhood. I walk in her direction, hoping she's not in too much of a rush. Perhaps I can even entice her for a quick glass of lemonade on the porch. I often try to give her some of whatever I've baked that day, but she rarely accepts or only nibbles at it if she does. These girls have so much pressure on their bodies; I'd hoped things would've changed by now, but sometimes I wonder if it's only gotten worse.

I'm so focused on catching Daphne's attention that I don't realize I'm right outside the Jacobsons' old bungalow. And that its newest resident—a man who looks to be in his forties or fifties, though I find it harder to tell these days—is out front washing his car. (I couldn't tell you what kind it is except that it's silver, very shiny, and much fancier than any vehicle I've ever had.) Tattoos stretch down his arm as he polishes his windshield. It's at least seventy-five degrees out, so he must be sweating, standing in the sun in those black jeans, T-shirt, and boots, not to mention his thick beard, which must keep his face very toasty. And is that an earring I see glinting?

He pauses his polishing and glances up at me, perhaps sensing I've been standing on the sidewalk staring at him.

"Hello there, ma'am," he says, straightening. "Beautiful morning, isn't it?"

His smile is unexpectedly kind. No, that's rude of me. Why would I expect that it would be anything but kind? Goodness, I'm being so judgmental about this man, all because of Rita's gossip. All he's done so far is wash his car on his own property and offer me a polite and friendly greeting.

"Oh, hello . . . sir," I stammer. "Yes, it's such a lovely day."

A blur of brown darts out from beneath the car, startling me. I'm relieved when it materializes as a rotund wirehaired terrier with a hint of dachshund, sniffing excitedly at my feet.

"Hettie!" the man calls sternly, tossing his cloth on the car's hood and striding over. "I'm sorry," he says, scooping her up just as she's about to put her front paws on my shins. "She's a little too friendly sometimes."

Watching the dog nestle into her owner's thick, tattooed arms, I tell myself that this man can't be that bad since dogs are very good judges of character. I'd love to have a pup, but Elizabeth is allergic, like her dad was, and I wouldn't want to give her an excuse not to visit me. But it would be nice to have some four-legged company, especially when the evenings stretch into loneliness.

"That's okay." I scratch behind Hettie's ears. "People often accuse me of being that way too." The scruffy hound lifts her chin, and I let her lick my hand. "It's not our fault we like people, is it, Hettie?"

"It does help to have her as the welcoming committee in a new neighborhood." He gestures to his tattoos. "Softens my image a bit."

I glance at my feet to mask my guilt.

"Well, those tattoos are very . . . artistic," I say. "Someone obviously worked very hard on them and I'm sure they're very meaningful to you."

He looks surprised. "They are, thank you." He sticks out the hand that isn't bridling Hettie. "I'm Rowan—are we neighbors?"

"It's a pleasure to meet you, Rowan." I accept his handshake, noting his neatly trimmed nails. "Yes, I'm Joy—I live a few doors down, in the house with the green shutters."

It occurs to me that I probably shouldn't reveal my address to a former criminal.

"The one with the impressive garden?" Rowan winks at me. "Someone obviously worked very hard on that."

My cheeks light up pink.

"I did, thank you—even if it's taken me more than half a century to get it to this point."

"Good things come to those who are patient," he says. "Hettie and I were admiring it this morning on her walk. Was that piano playing I heard coming through the window?"

"It was! But it wasn't me—I give lessons to some of the little ones in the town."

"That must be very rewarding," Rowan says. "And a nice coincidence. I'm a piano tuner myself."

"How lovely! How long have you been doing that?"

I hope he doesn't think I'm fishing for details of his felonious past.

Rowan doesn't appear bothered. He squints, calculating in his head. "More than twenty years now. Most of my clients are in Manhattan, but I'm looking to branch out here if you know of anyone. I don't want to encroach on anyone else's territory, of course."

How respectful of him. So many men his age are cutthroat with their business ethics.

"I'll admit that I'm very loyal to the lady who's been tuning my piano for the past decade—her dad did it before that—but I'll be sure to keep an ear out for anyone else who might be looking."

"I appreciate it," he says. "Thank you."

He's so polite and friendly—it's hard to imagine this man being put in prison. Perhaps it was for something more benign like tax fraud. That said, in movies the best criminals are also the most charming and that's how they get away with things. It's probably safer for me to keep my distance.

"I'd better be going," I say, my guard back up. "But welcome to the neighborhood."

"Thank you, Joy," Rowan says. "I'm very happy to be here. Hettie and I look forward to seeing you around."

As I continue to the end of the block, I'm conflicted. I thought I'd be okay with having a new neighbor with a criminal record. But now that it's reality, I can't help feeling uneasy, especially without knowing the details.

When I get home, I'll make sure to lock the door behind me, just in case.

**7**

The fire alarm is squealing at the smoke billowing from the oven when I walk inside my kitchen.

I'd been so distracted when I left for my walk that I forgot I'd left the peach muffins baking. In between coughs, I frantically shove open the windows and wave the tea towel to coax the smoke away from the alarm. Then I balance precariously on a stool, trying to reach the button with the end of a broomstick to silence it before it alerts the fire department.

Once the crisis is averted, I check in with my body—my throat aches from the smoke, but otherwise I feel okay. I sit on the porch in my rattan chair until the kitchen airs properly, pondering the dire course this mishap could've easily taken. Adrenaline surges through my veins. What if I'd talked to Rowan a while longer or walked farther than just around the block? I could've burned the whole house down. Or, worse, died of smoke inhalation while trying to put the fire out. Of all the ways I've imagined I might fall off the perch, a fire wasn't one of them. Would I have been ready to go? Even for someone who contemplates their eventual demise daily, today feels a touch premature to be my last day. And it'd be a shame for it to happen just because of a silly little absent-minded mistake of overcooking some peach muffins.

*   *   *

My board games group is held at a church on the edge of town that's not on the bus route, so I drive. I've had my trusty Suzuki Swift for about eighteen years and she's still running reliably. I rarely drive outside of Beacon, but it keeps me feeling self-sufficient—even if I do have the occasional fender bender, like the lamppost I accidentally backed into a few months ago. I'm not proud that I fibbed to Elizabeth when she asked about the dent in my bumper, telling her it must have happened while I was parked at the grocery store. Thank goodness for my spotless driving record. I hate to lie—especially to my daughter—but this one was necessary. I don't want to give her a reason to take away my independence.

A few streets before the church, I nudge my foot on the brake, anticipating the car in front of me slowing down for the upcoming stop sign. My body tenses when the driver only slows briefly before zooming across the intersection. Sure, there are no other cars or pedestrians around, but the rule is that you come to a complete stop at the sign before proceeding.

As if atoning for that person's flagrant disregard for traffic law, I make sure to stop for a few seconds longer than usual, diligently checking both directions several times before proceeding.

I can hear Hazel's voice in my head, teasing me. Back in high school, she started calling me "Good Joy" because I'd never do any of the naughty things she'd get up to, like skipping classes, gossiping with the other girls, or smoking out in the parking lot. I didn't mind the nickname—I was proud of it. Without rules, the world would be chaos. They're there to keep us safe; they give us lines to color within, to show us how to behave. It unnerves me how often people blithely ignore the rules—my best friend being one of them.

I'm still a tad agitated as I park my car outside the church. But as soon as I walk inside, the scent of aged wood and warm candle wax greets me like an old friend. I've been attending this church ever since I moved to Beacon in the late fifties to be with Thom, though he was much more religious than me. My relationship with God has been complicated since he failed to save my ailing mother, despite my diligent prayers. But I still occasionally attend services, even with Thom gone, mostly for the company. I often think about the sheer amount of faith that must have been absorbed into the walls in the church's decades of existence. The opening of hearts in unison, the letting down of emotional walls to send your deepest hopes skyward. You don't need to be religious to be touched by that.

The back room of the church is already full of people. Since the peach muffins were burnt to a crisp, I've brought the brownies I made a few days ago—to soothe myself after Hazel left—to contribute to the snack table. I position them between a bowl of mini candy bars and a plate of sad-looking cookies labeled GLUTEN-FREE, SUGAR-FREE, and VEGAN.

Then I hover nervously, clutching my handbag for comfort.

I've been a regular at this board games meet-up since it began about twelve years ago. But as the years have passed, the familiar weathered faces have been replaced by new, youthful ones much closer to Finn's age than mine. A few of them glance up from the games they've already started setting up, huddled in their various groups. Their smiles are polite, but I catch a few pointed looks conveying a hope that the old woman doesn't ask to join their table.

Sometimes I question why I keep coming, when what was once a fun weekly gathering of my contemporaries has shifted to something that's just as likely to cause me anxiety. A place that emphasizes how the world no longer has room for me.

I scan the clusters of people. My favorite game used to be Trivial Pursuit, but the version they use here is newer and I struggle with the pop culture questions—they're just a series of names and phrases that remind me how out of touch I am. Monopoly I can handle, but that group has already started playing, so I can't join.

With few options, I timidly approach the UNO table.

"Hello there," I say to the three twentysomethings positioned around it. "Would you mind if I joined your game?"

The one holding the stack of cards pauses their shuffling. From their hair and what they're wearing, I would say they're a man, but Finn tells me that you can't just assume these things anymore, and I want to be respectful. It's taken me a bit to get used to, and I often forget, but it's so lovely that younger people have more freedom to express themselves. I try to keep up with the language changes, but it feels like I'm unlearning a lifetime. Luckily I have Finn to keep me in line, otherwise I'd be offending people all over the place.

"Of course," they say, though their tone feels forced. The other two nod politely, moving their phones from the space in front of the empty chair.

"Thank you, that's very kind." I take my place as quickly as I can. "My name's Joy."

"I'm Ty," the shuffler says. "And this is Raven and Benny."

"It's a pleasure to meet you all." I gather my cards as Ty tosses them in front of us.

As we begin to play, I sit back and listen to their banter. I thoroughly enjoy being around young people. They're so expressive of their thoughts and feelings, even the negative ones. My generation—women, especially—were taught to button up and pin on a smile, no matter what.

I nod along to their conversation, laughing at jokes and references I don't understand. While they do their best to include me, I can't help feeling a little invisible—something I've become well acquainted with as I've grown older.

There isn't a precise moment when it happens. It's a gradual fading away, like a bright painting in a sunny living room that becomes more muted over time. There are hints when invisibility descends, of course. On the bus, when, instead of meeting your eye, people seem to look through you. On the sidewalk, when they bustle past, not stopping to apologize when they bump you firmly enough to test your balance. At the doctor's office, when they talk at you, rather than to you, dismissing your concerns and questions.

Eventually, you come to a disheartening realization. In society's eyes you are superfluous and no longer have value to add.

Because you are an elderly woman.

Turns out, it's even worse when you're a widow. Until Thom died, I remained somewhat visible, but only in his company, and only by proxy. We were a package deal. Without his commanding presence next to me, I've entirely faded into the background.

Today, I see it in the belittling head tilt of my opponents each time I make a move in this UNO game. The kind of tilt you'd give to a chubby-faced toddler or a clumsy puppy—the one that says, "Oh, look how cute you are" to someone whose antics are charming but not to be taken seriously. If only they knew some of the things I've been through—I'd tell them, but I don't want to ruin their afternoons.

Even when I play the dreaded Draw Four card to Ty, they don't groan in displeasure or threaten payback like they would with the other two players. I'd love it if they did—I enjoy some competitive banter. Instead, they just accept it graciously and ponder their next move.

Most days, I do my best to take it all in stride. I tell myself I'm being too sensitive. After all, how can I know for sure what folks are really thinking? Perhaps it's just my own insecurities creating a story in my head. Nonetheless, it's a blow to the ego, especially when you enjoy being around people. It's hard to engage with others when they don't take you seriously, when your mere appearance renders your ideas and opinions invalid. How can you squeeze everything out of life when nobody seems to notice you anymore?

Raven is the first to call UNO. After Ty plays a Reverse card, I have the chance to play a Draw Four card against Raven, but I don't. What's the point? Since no one has played a single penalizing card against me this whole game, I suspect they've all been going easy on me. They don't see me as a worthy adversary but someone to be pitied. I'm sure it's well-intentioned, but it stings all the same.

When Raven wins on the next round, Ty gathers up the cards to shuffle again, asking if I want to play another.

"Oh, thank you," I say as brightly as I can. "But I'd better get going."

Benny looks at me, perplexed. "You came here just to play one game of UNO?"

Fair point. Most people—me included—stay for the whole three hours. But this hasn't been the spirit-lifter I'd hoped it would be.

"Busy day, unfortunately." It's the best I can come up with. "But it was a pleasure playing with you all. Have a lovely afternoon!"

I hastily reach for my handbag, but it's caught on the leg of my chair. Flustered, I tug at it, causing all the contents to fall out.

Ty and Raven slide out of their chairs to help me, but I wave them away, squatting to gather everything. "It's fine, it's fine—thank you!"

The people at the next table turn around, alerted by the unhinged pitch of my voice.

I put my hand on the chair to hoist myself back up to standing, but before I have the chance to try, Ty and Raven rush to help me, each taking one of my arms to support. Now the whole room is watching and I'm humiliated.

Raven hands me my bag with a sympathetic smile. I know they were both just being kind and thoughtful, but I could've easily stood up by myself.

I'm so embarrassed that I can't even look them in the eye.

"Thank you," I say quietly and hurry towards the door, feeling everyone's eyes still on me. I don't turn around until I'm safely outside the building.

That didn't make me feel better at all.

On the drive home, I fight back tears, my nerves already frayed from this morning's brush with mortality. It was just a silly kitchen fire, but if I had, in fact, died today, what kind of legacy would I have left behind?

Hazel said she's accepted her diagnosis, in part because she's lived a long, fulfilling life. Could I say the same? If I'd have asked myself in my twenties what a fulfilled life would be, I'd have said having a husband and child. But looking back, as my final sunset draws nearer, I'm not sure that's all there is to it.

Hazel has squeezed every possible drop out of her existence. Her textile-importing business was wildly successful and she got to experience so many parts of the world. Thom and I rarely traveled outside of the United States, except for our honeymoon to Venice. That's never bothered me, since I'm a homebody and it was enough to live vicariously through Hazel's travel stories. But sometimes I do think about how interesting it would've been to meet all those people from foreign lands. To expand my worldview beyond this small town on the Hudson River.

When I look at other women my age in 2023—the ones who've made it as far up the summit of life as I have—my achievements pale in comparison. Nancy Pelosi is still wielding her political power (in stilettos, no less), Jane Goodall is still out saving the world's animals, Isabel Allende continues to write wonderful novels, Gloria Steinem hasn't given up fighting for women's rights, and Jane Fonda is getting arrested in the name of preventing climate change. Martha Stewart even did a stint in prison and is still running a business and being generally fabulous.

What have I done? Raised a child, taught piano, grown a garden.

Once in a while, Finn prints out stories he's found on the internet about women my age doing impressive things. The nonagenarians swimming long distances, or becoming ballerinas, or going back to university to become doctors. I know he means well, that he's trying to inspire me, but really it just makes me realize how inconsequential my life has been. All of those women have lived big, compelling lives, whereas I've just been living the same quiet existence on the same quiet street. Of course, I've loved teaching piano to all those kids over the years and I'm very proud of my garden, but I do wonder what might have happened if I had thrown caution to the wind.

Instead of resisting Hazel's influence, staying comfortable in my role as her opposite, what if I'd tried living more like her?

# 8

WISCONSIN, 1946

I check the window one last time to confirm Daddy's car is absent from the driveway. I wasn't expecting this opportunity.

He doesn't usually work on weekends, but when you're the only doctor for a small town, you have to go out when called. From what I could glean from his phone conversation, a baby delivery was imminent. I'm glad it's a happy occasion this time—last month he was called out on a Sunday just after we arrived home from church because someone had been kicked by a horse. If it were a similarly grim emergency today, I'd feel even guiltier about what I'm about to do.

First, I make sure I've pressed Daddy's shirts and prepared everything I need to have dinner ready when he returns. The more the house is in order, the less chance he'll realize what I've been up to.

Hazel says he's too strict with all his rules about how to behave, but I appreciate them. I like knowing what to do to make him happy—or at least, not make him unhappy. He's already so stressed, and I don't want to do anything to make him snap.

And yet there's one rule I've been willing to break repeatedly. I just can't help myself.

I creep up the stairs of our farmhouse and down the hallway. I'm relieved that my mother's bedroom door is slightly ajar; it feels like less of a misdemeanor if I don't have to turn the handle and push it open. I wedge my foot in the gap and peek through to the bed, where the sage-green quilt hugs my mother's delicate form. At first glance it looks like she's sleeping, but she's really just gazing up at the ceiling.

I lean on the door, flinching when it creaks.

Mama shifts her head ever so slightly and smiles in my direction. When she lifts a weary hand, beckoning me, I banish all feelings of remorse and scurry to the chair at her bedside.

It's rare that it's just the two of us. On weekdays a nurse is here while Daddy is at work and I'm at school. And though I'm allowed to spend time with Mama in the early evening—always with him sitting in the corner, reading over patient charts—it's only ever for fifteen minutes and I'm not supposed to ask her questions. I dare not mention anything about Hazel since Daddy disapproves of me spending too much time with my friend.

"Those parents of hers were almost kids when they had her," he's said on more than one occasion. "They let her run wild."

So I usually just tell Mama what I learned at school that day. Daddy says that speaking with her for any longer than fifteen minutes will drain too much of her energy. But I know from these clandestine meetings that she's capable of much more. I always remind her to tell me if she's getting too tired, but she just squeezes my hand and offers the same response.

"I treasure every extra minute I get to spend with you, my love."

I've never worried about Mama telling him about these visits. I know implicitly without her having to say that it's our little secret. It's not that I mind Daddy being there during my evening time with her. But his proximity puts me on edge, and I end up stumbling over my words, never saying what I mean to Mama.

The first time I snuck into her room, I just planned to sit quietly and soak in her presence without disturbing her. The next few times, I started reading to her from the book on her bedside—the way she gazed at me so intently, so lovingly, while I was reading made me feel like I was floating on a cloud. Each time I stopped to check if she'd had enough for the day, she would ask for more.

A few weeks ago, when Daddy was out helping a toddler who got his leg stuck in a fence, Mama looked at me in a way I hadn't seen before. With a sense of urgency.

"Joy, I hope I'll be around for a very long time," she said softly. "But it never hurts to prepare for the unexpected."

She studied my face, questioning whether I'd caught her notion. Though my conscious mind couldn't quite reckon with what she was implying, somewhere deep in my bones, I understood.

I nodded cautiously and waited for her to continue.

"How about I start teaching you all the things my mother taught me?" She looked around in that exaggerated, furtive way of stage actors, ending with a grin. "And we'll keep it just between the two of us, how about that?"

This time I grasped her meaning clearly: Don't tell Daddy.

I always wondered why she didn't tell him she has more energy than he thinks she has, that I'm not tiring her out. But I wouldn't dare say anything to her about it. I was just grateful for these sporadic interludes we got to have together.

And so our lessons commenced.

She began by teaching me the correct etiquette when dining with others, how to be a good hostess, how to respond to invitations and write a thank-you note. I started bringing a notebook to my visits to make sure I captured her words precisely.

*Never wear perfume in a confined space—and even outdoors, the scent should be a suggestion rather than a pronouncement.*

*When sitting, place your palms in your lap, one wrist draped over the other, ankles crossed and neatly tucked to one side.*

*Keep your voice to an agreeable tone at all times; try not to raise it, even in anger.*

*Being punctual is a way of saying you respect the person you're meeting, so always be on time, if not a little early. The exception is dinner parties, when you should arrive fifteen minutes late so the host has some breathing room to finish their last-minute preparations.*

*Never arrive at anyone's home empty-handed.*

Every evening before going to sleep, I'd read the words over, committing them to memory as the light of my candle danced on the wall. I'd seen the way everyone in our community lit up when they saw Mama, how her warmth and kindness towards everyone, no matter their social circumstance, never wavered. Who wouldn't want to follow that example?

Today, I sit, notebook at the ready, eager to capture more of her wisdom. The stark paleness of her skin this afternoon tightens my grip around the pencil.

"I want to be frank with you about matters of the heart, Joy," she says, wincing as she shifts on the mattress to face me. "I know you adore those fairy tales of great love, but romantic feelings can lead you astray. It's better to choose a man who is dependable—one who will give you and your children a steady, comfortable life. We're lucky in that way to have your father. Love can blossom in time, but it shouldn't be the priority."

Again, I search for the subtext to her words. I'd always imagined my own parents as having had a great love story.

Mama struggles to reach the water glass on the nightstand. I hurry to assist her, holding it gently to her lips the way I recall her doing for me when I was younger. Seeing the effort this takes, I hear my father's voice in my head, rebuking me for sapping her energy.

I return the glass to the nightstand and close my notebook. "You need to rest, Mama," I say contritely. "I'll get out of your hair."

She stops me, weakly placing her hand on mine. "Wait, darling." A deep, slow breath. "There's one more thing my mother taught me that I want to share with you."

There's no way I'd refuse the chance to bottle one more aspect of her presence. I reopen the notebook.

"Try to never be an imposition," she says. "Our family is blessed with many things—a sturdy roof over our heads, plenty of food to eat, people who care about us. Others aren't as fortunate as we are, so it's best not to burden anyone with your emotions and your troubles. Chances are they're struggling more than you, so try to always button up and smile, if you can. You're such a good girl, Joy. I know you can be a bright light for others."

I know enough from overhearing Daddy's phone conversations with my Uncle Jim that the world is suffering right now—first the Great Depression and then the war. I do have a lot to be grateful for. And I like the idea of helping others, being strong for them, being a comfort.

Especially to her.

I sit up tall and give her my brightest smile. "I'll do my best, Mama."

She relaxes back into the pillow, closing her eyes contentedly.

I take that as my cue to sneak quietly out of the room.

I wait until I'm safely down the hallway to unleash my sobs.

**9**

I squeeze the frosting onto the red velvet cupcakes in high swirls, just the way Finn likes them.

Elizabeth admonishes me for giving him sweet treats, but what are grandmothers for? That organic health food she feeds him all the time must be so boring. And I know for a fact she doesn't eat that way herself—I've seen a package of gummy bears sticking out of her purse more than once.

Finn was born a few years before Thom died, and it felt like divine timing. Something wonderful to fill a seemingly unfillable void. The afternoons I spent watching him were a salve for my disoriented soul. The school bus would drop him near my place every day and we would "hang," as he calls it now. It was a bittersweet day when Elizabeth informed me Finn didn't need babysitting anymore. Of course I was happy for his independence, but it meant I'd go days without another presence in my home.

Thankfully, Finn still drops by my place a few afternoons a week on his way home from school, and it's a gift I treasure—not everyone's sixteen-year-old grandson willingly spends time with them. I'm especially pleased for his company today; it's been just over a week since Hazel told me her news and I've been a bit blue. His cheerful bear hugs are as soothing as a warm bowl of soup on a bone-chilling day.

When Finn walks through the door today, however, he's lacking his usual sunniness.

"Hey, Nanna," he says, his hug looser than usual. He drops his backpack in the hallway and follows me into the kitchen, slumping into a chair at the table.

My heart twinges in that way only parents know—when you sense your child is hurting but you're not sure you can do anything to fix it. I assumed it would stop once Elizabeth became an adult, only to realize it's a perpetual feeling; they're a child to you no matter how old they become. It's the same with grandchildren.

Thank goodness I baked his favorite today. I haven't made them in a while because I've been challenging myself to try new recipes to bring some variety to my otherwise predictable life.

I stand behind Finn with my hands over his eyes. "Guess what I made today?"

I feel his cheeks rise into a grin. We've been playing this game since he was in elementary school.

Finn sniffs the warm, sweet aroma lingering in the kitchen, searching for clues.

"Pain au chocolat?"

"Nope."

"Portuguese tarts?"

"Try again," I trill.

"Lamingtons?"

"I still haven't quite gotten the hang of those, so no."

"Okay, I give up," he says.

I slide the plate with the warm cupcake in front of him.

"Yeessss, Nanna." He grabs it enthusiastically, hugging me with one arm. "Thank you."

I watch with pleasure as he carefully takes the top off the cupcake and flips it over to make a sandwich, like he's always done. His dad must have taught him that; Elizabeth prefers to lick all the frosting off first.

I wait until he's finished eating to try to find the source of his dolefulness. When he sits back in his chair and brushes the crumbs from his T-shirt, I try my luck.

"What's something interesting you learned today?" That question tends to work better than the generic "How was your day." Finn's very curious and loves sharing peculiar facts with me.

Today, however, he just shrugs, slumping deeper into his chair.

"I dunno." He fiddles with the cupcake paper on his plate. "School kind of sucks at the moment."

"How so?" I've never met a teenager who unabashedly loves school, but Finn generally enjoys his classes.

He folds the paper in half, then in quarters. I let the silence float until he's ready.

"A few of the other guys have been giving me a hard time because they saw me in the car with Mom the other day when we were singing to one of those stupid eighties songs she loves, and I was doing dance moves to try to make her laugh." He pushes the plate away. "I don't care that they saw us, but they made a video of it with a caption saying the reason I'm not on the football team is because I'm too busy dancing with my mom. But I could totally be on the team if I wanted—I'm way faster than most of those guys. I just don't give a shit about sports." His head snaps up. "Sorry, Nanna."

I pat his hand. "That's okay, dear—believe it or not, I've heard that word a time or two in my life."

It unearths a hint of a smile.

"I'm sorry you're going through that," I say, keeping my hand on his. "It's hard when you're not interested in the same things as your classmates."

Finn runs his finger over a blemish in the oak tabletop. "They've also been saying that it's probably the reason my dad left, because I'm such a mommy's boy."

I do my best not to overreact, but I ache for him.

"I know that whatever happened between your parents wasn't

about you," I say gently, even though I have no evidence of that. "Your dad loves you so much." Nor that one.

Finn frowns. "Then why does he never want to see me anymore? I was supposed to go stay with him in San Francisco for a few weeks this summer and all of a sudden he canceled, with some vague reason that it didn't fit with his work schedule. He didn't even suggest an alternative week."

"Oh honey, I'm sorry. I know you were looking forward to that."

Goodness, I'm disappointed in Jack. I thought he was better than that.

Finn shrugs again. "It's fine. I guess I can go to that STEM camp I was going to miss instead."

"That's a silver lining," I say, a little too eagerly. "And I'm sure you'll have plenty to teach me when you get back."

Finn's shoulders soften, and when he eventually looks me in the eyes, I catch a glimmer of the cheekiness I love.

"Have you finished that pile of romance novels you got from the library yet?" Now his grin is unmistakable.

"They weren't all romance novels." My cheeks burn. "There were some mysteries in there too. But yes, I have finished all my library books."

"Great," Finn says. "Want to go get some more this afternoon? I'm done with all of mine and Mom's too busy to take me. I really need to get my driver's license."

The library has always been our thing, even if our tastes in books diverge more than they used to and he no longer sits on my lap and lets me read to him.

"I'd love to."

As we're about to walk into the library, I stop to check for my keys in my handbag—I've accidentally locked them in the car on a few occasions.

"Hello there!"

My stomach sinks as I look up at an all-too-recognizable face.

Celeste Hobart has lived across the back fence from me for almost fifty years, though she's about ten years my junior. That said, the tennis outfit she's attired in is still quite daring for her age and she's wearing far more jewelry than is practical for playing any kind of sport.

I plaster on a smile to mirror hers.

She immediately focuses on Finn. "My, my, Finn. Look at you! It seems like just yesterday you were toddling around in the backyard."

"Hi, Mrs. Hobart," Finn says, politely enduring her fawning.

Finally, Celeste turns to me.

"Hello, Joy," she says in her grating, saccharine tone. "Your garden is looking lovely, but when doesn't it? I'm lucky to have such a pretty view from my back window."

I stiffen. "Thank you, Celeste."

She fingers the pearls adorning her collarbones. "I'm having my spring neighborhood potluck next Saturday," she says tentatively. "I know you haven't been able to make it the past few years, but I'd love to see you there if you can manage it."

To be precise, it's been the past twelve years I haven't been able to make it. Ever since Thom died, in fact.

I manufacture a look of disappointment.

"Darn, I already have plans on Saturday," I say. "What a shame that I'll have to miss it again this year."

"Of course," Celeste says quickly, as if anticipating my answer. "Maybe we'll have better luck next year."

I doubt it.

"Maybe we will," I say sweetly. "But I'm sure you've invited our newest neighbor?"

Celeste inclines her head. "A new neighbor?"

"Yes—a lovely man named Rowan moved into the Jacobsons' bungalow a few weeks ago."

Celeste's expression falls. "Oh. Yes, Rita told me about him."

Of course she has.

"An invite to your party would make him feel very welcome," I say, mostly daring her to invite a known criminal into her home. "And I know how hospitable you are."

Finn gives me a perplexed look.

"Yes, of course, that's a great idea," Celeste says, to my surprise. She adjusts the cluster of gold rings on her fingers. "I'll reach out to him tomorrow."

The three of us stand awkwardly until Celeste looks at her phone.

"Gosh, I'm late for my pickleball game," she says. "I just thought I'd return my library book on the way. See you both later!"

She brushes past before either of us can return her farewell.

As we step through the doors, Finn turns to me.

"Nanna, why do you never like talking to Mrs. Hobart? Haven't you been neighbors for like half a century?"

"I don't know what you're talking about," I say, knowing exactly what he's talking about. "I spoke to her just then."

"Yeah, but you're way friendlier with everyone else."

"There wasn't much chance to speak to her because she was in such a hurry."

Finn lets it go, though I know he's not convinced. But you don't have to like everyone you meet—even if you happen to be someone who's known for liking nearly everyone they meet.

He and I agree to find each other at the checkout desk in thirty minutes.

When I first started going to this library many decades ago, there was only one small shelf of romance novels to choose from. Back then, they were rather taboo and I couldn't help blushing when I checked them out, trying to disguise my tastes by also borrowing gardening books and mysteries. The first few times the librarian gave me a wink when my selection was somewhat saucy, I almost died from the embarrassment, until I gathered she was a fellow romance fan. It was like we were part of a secret society. Slowly but surely—after a few awkward run-ins with women I knew hovering by that single shelf—I realized just how many of us were members of that clandestine community.

These days, thankfully, it's not just a single shelf of romance novels—it's an entire section. It's so delightful to see the variety of women, and even men, I encounter while browsing. I have a penchant for the swashbuckling historical romances, but I've been trying to broaden my horizons with some of the more modern ones, which are quite a bit raunchier than I'm used to—I tend to get a little hot under the collar. Goodness me, they are certainly eye opening. It even makes me wonder if Thom and I could have been more adventurous, amorously speaking.

In the spirit of shaking things up, I decide to try something new today. I mostly avoid the "paranormal romance" shelf, but it couldn't hurt to dip my toe in. Running my finger along the colorful spines, I pick one at random. When I finally bring my haul of books to the counter, Max—one of the newer, younger librarians—holds up my selection approvingly.

"I love this one," he says. Then he leans forward for the sake of discretion. "A bit spicy, just FYI—it doesn't just fade to black, if you know what I mean."

Cheeks blazing, I glance around to make sure my grandson isn't within earshot. Not because I don't want to embarrass him, but because I'd never hear the end of his teasing.

"Thank you, Max." I swiftly put the book in my bag. "I wonder if you might kindly check on the book I have on hold to see how many weeks away it might be."

It was recommended by one of those lovely ladies who hosts a morning TV show I quite like. I've been on the holds list for a month now and I'm so eager to read it.

Max consults his computer screen, the bright light emphasizing the pink of his sunburned nose.

"Unfortunately, it looks like you've still got a bit of a wait ahead of you, Mrs. Bridport." The computer mouse grinds as he scrolls. "There are eight people ahead of you, so I'd say you've got at least ten more weeks before it's your turn."

"That's okay," I say. "I'll have something to look forward to then, won't I?"

Max grins at me. "Exactly. I love how you always look on the bright side."

I wish that were true, but these days it's getting harder. I'm taking the train to the city tomorrow to visit Hazel, and I'm a little nervous. I want to be strong and hopeful for her sake, but I'm afraid I'll crumble—exactly the thing she told me not to do.

Finn is still busy browsing, even though it's after our agreed meeting time, but I leave him be—he looks much happier than he did earlier this afternoon. I'll just wait for him by the entrance so I'm not in anyone's way.

As Max tends to the next customer, something catches my eye. Sitting on the top shelf of the holds stand, bright pink cover calling out to me, is the book I've been waiting for. Maybe I could just read the first few pages while I wait for Finn.

I slide it out from the shelf and crack open the cover, careful not to lose the paper slip with the name of its intended borrower. I only manage to get through the first page when Finn appears at the self-checkout computers. Disappointed, I go to return the book to where I found it.

Then an idea starts to form. An impulse that feels foreign.

What if I took the book now?

I know it's not my turn yet, but no one has claimed it. And technically I'd only be borrowing it for a short while before I returned it, so it isn't stealing. But I've never cut in front of someone in line in my life—that's against the rules. Do I have the guts to do it?

Finn is on his way over and my pulse quickens. Before I can overthink it, I stuff the book in my bag and hightail it to the exit.

"Sorry I took so long," Finn says, holding up his stack. "I couldn't decide."

"Oh, no problem at all," I say, playing it cool. Finn knows me so well that I'm sure he's going to guess something's going on.

He stands aside to let me walk out the door first. The security gate immediately starts beeping.

I freeze, heart now pulsing in my throat. Max hurries towards us and I prepare for my reckoning.

But instead of demanding to search my bag, he waves at me apologetically.

"I'm so sorry, Mrs. Bridport, I must have forgotten to demagnetize one of your books." He glances back at the line of people waiting for him at the counter. "Don't worry about the alarm—just go ahead. I trust you!"

I cringe, knowing I'm not living up to his generous assessment of me. Waving meekly, I step through the security gate again, wincing as it beeps loudly.

I walk briskly until I can't hear the sound anymore, incredulous that I'm capable of such an act. It's like someone else took over my body for an instant—someone more like Hazel.

"Nanna, wait!" Finn jogs behind me, trying to catch up.

Did he see me take the book? What a terrible example I'm setting for him after emphasizing the importance of being a good, kind person his entire life. I stop walking and turn to face him, ready to admit my guilt.

But he's just pointing down the street.

"Want to get some ice cream before we go?"

The tension in my body evaporates. "That would be lovely!"

As we amble down the block, it occurs to me that there might actually be an upside to being invisible.

<h1 style="text-align:center">10</h1>

When the train chugs into the station, it takes me by surprise. I was so engrossed reading on the platform that I hadn't even noticed it approaching.

Any repentance I was feeling about my little library book heist yesterday has been stifled by the fact that the book is as good as I hoped it would be. I've hardly been able to put it down since I started it last night.

It's peak hour for people commuting to Manhattan and the train is thick with body heat, competing colognes wafting from the collars of the slick-looking businessmen. I pull my bag—packed with meals in Tupperware for Hazel—onto my lap to free up the seat next to me.

A whisper of a moment before we're about to depart, I see a man running along the platform and jumping onto the train, breathless. When he appears in our carriage, I recognize him. It's my new neighbor, Rowan—with little Hettie sticking her head out of the canvas tote bag under his arm. He looks around the crowded carriage and I wave without thinking, alerting him to the empty space beside me.

Rowan smiles, relieved, and strides down the aisle. The train is already moving by the time he sits.

"Thanks for saving us a spot, Joy." His chest still heaves from running for the train. "I'm sorry, would you prefer Mrs. . . . ?"

"Bridport," I finish for him. "And Joy is just fine. Who needs formality between neighbors?"

"Definitely not me." He grins, leaning back into his seat. I catch the scent of laundry detergent—orange blossom, I think.

A wet nose nuzzles at my arm as Hettie's scruffy head sticks out of her bag. Delighted, I scratch her ears.

"Hello there, little one." She snuffles at my open palm.

"Hettie has great taste in people," Rowan says, stroking her wiry coat, which is almost the same color as my morning coffee—just a dash of milk.

At the sound of his voice, Hettie turns her big brown eyes up to him with that adoring gaze dogs save for their favorite human. Her tail wags a cheerful beat at the other end of the tote.

"I think she can just smell the food in my bag," I say. "But I sure do hope we can be friends."

We settle into silence as the train finds a steady rhythm. While Rowan stares passively ahead, I subtly examine the tattoos on his forearms poking out from his rolled-up shirtsleeves. They're quite mesmerizing.

I startle when he suddenly turns to me. "Are you on your way to Grand Central with all that food?"

I pivot in my seat to better face him. Another of Mama's life instructions: always look someone in the eye when talking to them.

"Yes, it's for my friend Hazel," I say. "She's not well at the moment." It comes out more somber than intended.

"I'm very sorry to hear that," Rowan says. "She's lucky to have a friend like you who cares so much about her."

"Oh, I don't know about that," I say. "I haven't dealt with her diagnosis as graciously as I could have. She's always been the strong one for me and I dearly want to do the same for her, but it was a bit of a shock to hear." My voice cracks ever so slightly. "We've been best friends since we were eight years old."

What am I doing pouring my heart out to this man I barely know?

I don't want to scare him off by bursting into tears, so I glance out the window and take a few slow, controlled breaths to keep them at bay.

Hettie sneaks farther out of her bag to rest her little chin on my arm, her brown eyes now shining up at me. How do dogs know exactly when to do that right when you're at your lowest? They really are magical beings.

"It's a rare treasure to have a long-lasting friendship like that," Rowan says, undeterred by my emotional revelation. "I can see why it's such a shock."

He follows my gaze out the window, and we watch the morning sun sparkle on the Hudson River, the breeze serrating it into ripples.

"I lost my mom a year ago," he says. "When she first told me about her cancer, it was hard for me to accept. She'd always lived such a full and robust life and I'd basically thought of her as invincible. It seemed so unfair that she'd be struck down like that."

"I'm sorry you lost her," I say, feeling selfish for wallowing in my own impending loss when he's recently experienced one. But I'm also glad that we're now equals in emotional revelation—perhaps it's true what they say about comfort in strangers. I don't think I've ever disclosed so much to someone I've just met.

"Thank you." Rowan squeezes Hettie tight. "I've lost a lot of people in my life—probably more than most people in their fifties—but some losses ache more than others, don't they?"

I meet his eyes. "They do."

I hadn't really considered that fact, but he's right. I've lost both my parents, my husband, and most of my friends. But there's something about losing Hazel that feels unbearable. And I don't think it's just because it means I'll be the last one left.

The resigned sadness in Rowan's eyes feels like a mirror to my own, a kindred spirit. What an unexpected blessing to have ended up next to this man and his lovely little dog this morning.

But just as I'm appreciating his presence, an awkward reminder looms on the riverbank next to the train tracks: Sing Sing, the maximum-security prison where Rita said Rowan had done time.

I'd always puzzled over the prison's rather whimsical name; it felt incongruous to the darkness I imagined it housed within its enormous walls. But Finn explained to me once that it comes from Sint Sinck, the name of the Native American tribe from which the land was purchased. I doubt they'd appreciate that legacy.

As the prison sails past the window, I surreptitiously monitor Rowan's body language for a sign the building might have been significant in his past. But he's just staring passively ahead again, almost oblivious.

Could Rita have been spreading false gossip? It wouldn't be the first time, but in this case, it'd be especially unfair to poison everyone in the neighborhood against him. I'm ashamed that I've been so militant about locking my doors these past few days because of her.

Determined to show him he's just as accepted as any new neighbor, I shift the conversation.

"And what brings you and Hettie to the city today? If that's where you're headed, of course."

Rowan's passive expression animates to a smile.

"My partner, Philippe—Hettie's other dad—lives there. We've been a couple for about twenty years but never lived together," he says. "He's a city boy through and through but I prefer a slower-paced life. That's why I finally made the move to Beacon."

That sounds like a very modern arrangement. Imagine being with someone that long and never living together—it must take a lot of trust in each other. I used to get anxious when Thom was just away overnight, as he often was when he went to his law firm's Manhattan office.

"It must be working if you're still together," I say. "How did the two of you meet?"

"We were in the same art history class in college, though we didn't interact too much back then," Rowan says. "Then we ran into each other years later and just clicked." A dreamy smile. "Sometimes it's as simple as that."

"You studied art history? How impressive," I say. "I didn't have the chance to go to college myself, but that sounds like a fascinating thing to study."

Rowan bows his head. "I didn't end up finishing my degree because of, well, life stuff," he says. "But Philippe did—even got his master's. He's the smarter one of the two of us."

"And what does he do now?"

"He's a very talented antiques restorer." The pride on Rowan's face is heartening.

"A piano tuner and an antiques restorer," I say. "What a splendid pairing."

He nods. "I like to think so. We have a lot of things in common and a lot of differences, but that's what makes it work. The great thing about living apart is that I always look forward to seeing him. You need the chance to miss someone, in my opinion—helps you savor them more."

I like that idea—savoring the ones we love.

By the time the train pulls into Manhattan, it seems like we only just left Beacon. I'm feeling much better about seeing Hazel—I'll be strong for her, even if it means tamping down my emotions. After all, I have many years of practice.

Rowan and I are walking through Grand Central when we hear a shrill whistle mimicking a bird call.

Rowan's face lights up as soon as he hears it.

"Philippe's here." He glances around to see which direction his partner is coming from, then waves at a short, dark-haired man walking towards us. He's more heavyset than Rowan, but dare I say a little more dapper, wearing a tailored suit with no tie and loafers with no socks. No sign of a tattoo.

"How did you know that whistle belonged to him?"

Rowan combs his hair with his fingers. "It's our secret call," he says. "It's more of a practical thing, usually, to find each other in a crowd." He dips his head, bashful. "But occasionally we use it when we're in different rooms of the house and we just want to let the other person know we're thinking of them."

Rowan leans down to kiss Philippe's forehead, and they share an adoring gaze. How nice to see two people who are truly in love.

"Philippe, this is my new neighbor from Beacon, Joy," Rowan says. "I think she might be Hettie's new best friend."

Philippe pretends to look aggrieved. "Well, Joy, you'll have to fight me for the honor." His accent sounds European—Hazel would be able to pinpoint it. "It's a pleasure to meet you."

We bid each other farewell in the middle of Grand Central, the wonderful celestial ceiling mural watching over us as if our encounter were written in the stars.

"I hope we run into each other again soon," Rowan says.

"I do too." Our conversation this morning on the train was one of the most meaningful and enjoyable I've had in a while.

I make my way through the station to the escalators. Usually Hazel comes to meet me at Grand Central because I'm skittish about riding the subway. Thom wouldn't let me ride it, insisting I take a cab to wherever I was meeting Hazel. But after he was gone, she convinced me that the subway isn't the terrifying experience it was in the seventies and that I should save my money. I felt safe because she was there with me. There's no way I could ask her to do that now, of course. When I called her last night to confirm what time I'd be at her place, I insisted I'd be fine taking it alone—even if I didn't quite believe it myself.

Now I stand in front of the turnstiles, sneaking in a few more calming breaths as people bustle by me, a lone rock in a rushing river.

I can do this.

I'm going to have to get used to doing things without Hazel.

# 11

The glare of daylight is welcome when I emerge from the subway in Brooklyn.

It's a relief to see a streetscape I recognize, even though Boerum Hill has changed immensely since Hazel moved here in the seventies, back when the rows of brownstones sat mostly in disrepair—so much so that there was discussion of demolishing them all to make room for an expressway. Hazel fell in love with the area's diverse, bohemian spirit, even if everyone (my husband included) told her she was crazy to buy a loft in an old factory in Brooklyn.

As always, she didn't listen. Hazel rarely listens to anyone but herself, but she's very charming about it.

"That's an interesting idea—I'll be sure to think about it," she'd say to anyone, usually a man, who tried to tell her what to do. That person would walk away satisfied they'd influenced her decision, but I knew better. It was Hazel's way of telling them to take a hike.

Nowadays Boerum Hill is clean, manicured, and filled with people who look very similar. If there are still artists here, I suspect they're doing quite well for themselves—just as Hazel did. She built a business from the ground up, negotiating with companies around the world, and helping artisans in developing countries—women, especially—get paid for their valuable handiwork. It wasn't easy, I know that much.

But Hazel is fierce, always willing to speak up for people, refusing to accept injustice.

My contribution to the world feels so insignificant compared to hers.

Standing outside the dented metal door of Hazel's building, I attempt to compose myself. I got muddled changing from the 6 train to the F train and ended up going two stops in the wrong direction. It knocked the small amount of confidence I'd gained about navigating New York City solo for the first time. But now it's my duty to be the strong one, even if I find the city nerve-wracking.

One more steadying breath and I ring Hazel's buzzer.

Instead of her usual quip crackling through the speaker—last time it was something along the lines of "Is that the troupe of male exotic dancers I ordered?"—the door just buzzes open.

I make my way up the creaking staircase that hasn't been painted or repaired in the entire fifty years Hazel's lived here. When I arrive on the landing, her front door is ajar.

"Hazel?" I call tentatively through the gap.

"Come in, Joy."

The voice sounds like Hazel, but lacks the vigor I'm accustomed to. Bracing myself, I nudge the door open.

At the sight of her, I do exactly what I promised her I wouldn't.

I burst into tears.

Sitting in her wicker peacock armchair, my friend looks like a shell of herself. Now I understand why she was wearing such flowing, layered outfits when I saw her in Beacon, and why she came to the breakfast table at my place fully dressed. Today, wearing simple slacks, a turtleneck, and no makeup, there's no sartorial curtain to hide behind.

And the reality is stark.

Limbs frail, skin sallow, once-robust cheeks reduced to bone, posture hunched. It's nothing like the woman who's always stood tall, facing the world with an impish glint in her eye. Cancer is especially cruel that way, creeping up on you silently, then accelerating to an unrelenting sprint with no warning. If anyone should be crying, it's her.

"I'm so sorry," I sniffle, dearly wishing I could force the tears back where they came from. "I know I promised I wouldn't make a big deal out of it."

How graceless to make this all about me.

Even Hazel's smile exudes effort. "Oh, Joy. You've always been too tenderhearted for your own good."

She eases up out of her chair and I rush to help her, but she waves me away.

"I can do it," she insists. "It just might take a little longer than it used to. There are good days and bad, and today's been more of the latter."

She beckons me over, and surprisingly puts up no resistance when I fold her into a hug in lieu of her usual air kisses. Brief as the embrace is, it's enough for me to register the boniness of her body, the looseness of her arms around me, as if they're barely even there.

What do I say to her? Asking how she's doing feels like a cruel emphasis that she's not doing well. So I say nothing, cherishing the rare embrace.

When she disengages, I hold up my bag of Tupperware. "I've brought you some food so you don't have to worry about cooking."

Her face lights up as she peeks into the bag.

"What an angel you are," she says. "Ordering takeout isn't as fun as it used to be. Now it's just a depressing reminder I can't stomach the spicy food I adore. That might be the worst part of all of this—the only thing I can tolerate is blandness."

I expected this. Hazel still hasn't said what kind of cancer she has, but from observing her barely touching her meals last week in Beacon, I knew her appetite would be diminished.

"I made all your favorites, but stayed light-handed with the spices and garlic."

Hazel peeks into the bag again. "Ohhh, do I spy moussaka in there?"

"And paella," I add, pleased that she is pleased.

I walk over to her open-plan kitchen where the skylight bathes the island counter in a cheerful burst of sun. A fleeting boost to my bruised spirits.

"I'll put these in the freezer for you," I say, unloading the containers onto the counter. I search my purse for a Sharpie to label them.

"It's just like the old days," Hazel says, sitting back down. "When you used to send me care packages every month, no matter where I was in the world. You must've spent a fortune on postage over the years."

I shrug. "You were worth it."

It was the one thing I put my foot down about with Thom, allowing me the money to send those care packages during Hazel's long stints living abroad. My tastes were otherwise very simple—I rarely asked for any money to spend on myself—so I suppose he deemed that one extravagance acceptable.

I loved putting those care packages together, filling them with the comforts of home that Hazel mightn't have had access to in the far-flung place she was in—her favorite candy and cookies, the lavender hand cream she adored, practicalities like new underwear, and always a copy of *The New York Times* and *The Village Voice* (Thom would begrudgingly pick up the latter while in the city for work). Often those packages would arrive at her destination a little worse for wear, but at least she got them. It was my way of reminding her that I was always there waiting for her, whenever she was ready to come home. That someone in the world was thinking of her.

Hazel commences a slow, painful walk across her loft to join me in the kitchen. "I'll make us some tea."

"No, no," I say quickly. How do I take care of her without robbing her of the little autonomy she has left? "I'm right next to the kettle so I'll put it on." I hold up one of the containers. "I also brought some sticky date pudding to have with it." Another favorite of hers.

"All right then," Hazel says, inching back to her chair. Just a year ago she was hiking up mountains in Thailand. It's surreal that this is happening.

"There should be enough to last you at least a week," I say. "And I'll bring you some more next week."

"Two visits in two weeks?" Hazel teases. "What an honor!"

"I'm happy to come down whenever you need me," I say, my tone firm so she knows I mean it. "Doctor's appointments, grocery shopping, anything—just say the word."

I clear my throat to dissuade the imminent lump.

"Thank you, my friend," Hazel says softly, leaning her head back.

I stay quiet, hoping she'll open up more about her situation. I'm desperate to hear the details—prognosis, treatment, everything—but those things aren't mine to know until she wants to share them.

"Actually," she says, lifting her head as if the thought has just arrived. "There is something you can help me with this afternoon."

"Of course, anything," I say, relieved to be useful.

There's a certain slyness in Hazel's smile. I know it well—it appears when she's about to do or say something she knows I'll disapprove of. I brace myself.

"The doctors have prescribed me some of that medicinal marijuana," Hazel says. "But the stuff from the dispensaries is nowhere near as potent and effective as what I get from my usual dealer."

I probably don't need to state the obvious that I've never done any drugs. Hazel, on the other hand, has tried most of them. I know she likes to smoke pot, but the fact that she has a "dealer" is slightly horrifying to me.

"I see." I'm afraid of how this fact involves me, but I did just promise to do anything she asked.

"He doesn't do home deliveries—for obvious reasons—and I was supposed to go out and meet him this afternoon, but my nausea and dizziness have been quite debilitating. I'm not sure I'd even make it down the stairs." I know she's not exaggerating, but that sly smile is still there, curling one side of her lips. "Would you be a doll and go and meet him for me?"

I stand frozen, processing her ask. Surely she's not requesting that

I participate in a drug deal. She knows I've never even smoked a cigarette, because my father disapproved of ingesting anything addictive. It wasn't until I was married that I even dared to try a glass of wine—and I certainly never told Daddy I drank alcohol, even occasionally.

"Um, well, I'm not sure whether I could do that," I stammer. "Isn't it illegal?"

Hazel folds her arms. "Technically, cannabis is legal in New York City now."

I did read that in the paper, but I'm quite sure it's only legal when you buy it from one of those dispensaries Hazel mentioned. And it's definitely illegal in most other states in this country.

Almost every ounce of my being wants to tell Hazel no. But it's that one ounce, the one telling me I can really do something to help my friend feel better, that wins out.

Before I can convince myself otherwise, I commit.

"Okay—where am I meeting him?"

# 12

Who would have thought that, at eighty-nine years old, I'd be involved in an illicit drug deal?

Apparently, it's a precipitous downhill slope from pinching a library book to this. Talk about sullying the family reputation; my father would be appalled. Thank goodness Elizabeth and Finn are all the way up in Beacon.

I'm sitting on a bench in a small park a few blocks from Hazel's place, wearing her vermilion-and-gold silk scarf patterned with magnificent horses (far too fancy for me) so the dealer can recognize me. He texted Hazel to say he'd be here at three o'clock, but it's seven after and he hasn't appeared.

I wonder what he looks like. Perhaps some tattoos and a beard like Rowan? Not to say that Rowan's past indiscretions were drug-related, but he's really my only reference to someone who's acted illegally, aside from what I've seen on TV.

I double-check the cash Hazel gave me is in my purse and scan the park for anyone who seems like they're here to sell me marijuana—and for anyone in a police uniform. No sign of either. On any other day, I'd be delighted to be able to watch the children frolic on the playground, reveling in their squeals of delight. Today I feel like a menace to society, buying drugs in the vicinity of such pure, precious souls.

Two women sit with empty strollers, chatting to each other, mostly in English but with the odd Spanish phrase peppered in. One tells the other that she can't wait to see her kids when she gets home because she's hardly seen them all week. The other shares a similar lament, saying that she never gets home in time to put hers to bed. When their two tiny charges come running from the playground, the women greet them with such presence and enthusiasm that I would've assumed they were the kids' mothers, not their nannies.

What a tough emotional conundrum, giving your best to other people's children just so you can support your own. I'm grateful Thom was able to comfortably support us so I got to tuck Elizabeth in every night.

"Hazel's friend?"

I almost jump out of my skin.

Self-consciously adjusting my scarf, I turn to the man speaking to me. He looks to be in his early twenties, fresh-faced, clean-shaven, and wearing a well-ironed button-down shirt, as if he's just come from his office job. Not what I pictured at all.

"Oh, hello," I whisper, pulse galloping. "Yes, that's me."

"Nice to meet you, ma'am," he says. "Sorry I'm a bit late—signal malfunction on the subway had us sitting at York Street forever."

Well, it's nice of him to acknowledge his tardiness.

"That's quite all right," I say. "I know the subway can be unreliable at times."

I look at him expectantly, unsure whether I'm supposed to initiate the deal or if he is. What's the etiquette in these situations? It feels a bit boorish to just give him the money. Do we need to make small talk first?

Finally, he sits next to me and pulls his leather satchel onto his lap, the buckle jingling as he opens it. He retrieves a paper bag with a Starbucks symbol on it and passes it to me.

Golly, it's quite heavy. How much marijuana did Hazel order?

"I put in a block of the mushroom chocolate Hazel likes, as a freebie," he says. "I know she hasn't been feeling well lately. Thought it might cheer her up."

I have no idea what mushroom chocolate is, but it's a gallant gesture.

"How generous of you, thank you." I scan our surroundings for witnesses; everyone is occupied with other things.

"Of course," he says affably. Now he's looking at me expectantly.

"Oh, goodness!" I quickly open my handbag and pull out the envelope with the money. "Here you go."

Are you supposed to tip drug dealers? He did go above and beyond with the chocolate. To avoid a potential faux pas, I take the last ten-dollar bill from my purse and push it into his palm. "A little something extra for you."

He pockets the bill discreetly without looking at it—someone has obviously taught him how to receive a tip graciously.

"Thank you, ma'am." He stands, slinging the satchel over his shoulder. "Please tell Hazel I hope she gets better soon."

My eyes prickle. "I'll do that, thank you."

It's not until I've watched him walk across the park and disappear down the street that reality sinks in.

I've just gotten away with a small crime.

I assumed I'd be racked with guilt. But instead, a heady rush spreads through my body, momentarily dissolving the sadness that I haven't been able to shake this past week.

What a surprising twist to occur in the twilight of my existence. After a lifetime of doing exactly what I'm told, following every rule that society has expected of me, I finally have a taste of what it's like to disregard them.

And let me tell you, I've never felt so thrilled in my life.

# 13

WISCONSIN, 1947

Selfishly, I wish this wasn't my last memory of my mother, her casket being lowered into the ground. But if I'm being picky, I wouldn't want any of the memories from the past couple of years to be the last one either—watching her gradually weaken, the light that once shone so brightly eventually dimming until I had to squint to see it.

I'd barely even seen her at all these past six months, not since she was moved from our home to a city hospital in Madison. My father allowed me to visit her every few weeks, but only for ten minutes at a time and always with him—and usually at least one nurse—hovering nearby.

I wasn't there for her last moments. I heard the phone ring in the middle of the night and woke up to find Mrs. Branxholm, the woman who lives next to us, making breakfast.

Later that afternoon, Daddy arrived home looking older than I recalled him being the day before.

"It's just the two of us now, Joy," he said somberly.

Then he disappeared into his study.

It might seem harsh on his part, but he had just lost his wife. And what else was there to say, except to confirm that the invisible clock that had been counting down had finally reached zero?

But I was grateful that Mrs. Branxholm was there. And that she didn't hesitate to engulf me in a hug, the smell of garlic and rosemary infused in the folds of her apron unexpectedly comforting.

Mrs. Branxholm and her husband are among the mourners now gathered beside Mama's grave site, hands clasped in front of them, heads bowed. I was surprised by how many people showed up—it seemed like every adult in our town had put aside their lives for the day to join us at the tiny cemetery, where only a few crisp leaves still clung to the skeletal trees surrounding us.

As I'd looked around the gathering in awe just before the service started, Mrs. Branxholm put her hand gently on my shoulder and whispered in my ear.

"You can see how much your mother was beloved," she said. "Such a good woman."

I smiled back proudly. What a nice thing to have people say about you when you're gone.

The small crowd murmurs a prayer as the casket disappears from view.

I summon as much poise and courage as I can, standing next to Daddy at the front. I want Mama to be proud of me in this moment; I don't want to break down and make it about me.

I step forward, throwing a rose into the rectangular chasm that will now and forever hold my mother. As I step back, I reach for Daddy's hand.

It remains stiff, like he hasn't felt my gesture at all. My body runs cold, as though an icy breeze has blown across the cemetery.

And then I feel a gentle touch on my other hand, someone pressing their palm into mine, enclosing it tightly with their fingers.

I turn, a mixture of surprise and gratitude returning warmth to my body.

Hazel grins at me, squeezing my hand tightly. Her unruly curls are coaxed into two neat braids.

I didn't know she was even here; she must have been standing at the back of the crowd and pushed through. I wasn't sure she'd attend, given my father's unvarnished disapproval of her.

But here she is, coming to my rescue, again. I smile through tears, buoyant with thanks.

And I squeeze her hand right back.

# 14

have to lift the cemetery gate to open it, the warped and rusted metal a precursor to the generally unloved state of the grounds.

We could have buried Thom in one of the larger, more well-maintained private cemeteries in the area, but they felt so clinical and impersonal, all the headstones almost identical. Elizabeth and I agreed that this smaller cemetery had much more character, and that Thom would enjoy this particular plot under a grand oak tree.

Unfortunately, funding for this cemetery's upkeep is scarce, and the weeds get out of control if you don't tend to them regularly. Those yellow flowers might look pretty, but they're a menace if left unbridled.

I set my basket down and unload everything I need: my gardening mat (my knees aren't as hardy as they used to be), pruning shears, gardening gloves, a cloth and a spray bottle to wipe down the headstone, and a bunch of orange roses, freshly picked from my garden.

I've come here almost every Thursday morning since Thom died. It feels like keeping up my end of the bargain.

Just as Mama advised me to, I married a man who was dependable—at least in the sense that he made sure Elizabeth and I lived a comfortable life. And just as Mama said I would, I grew to love him, though unfortunately it was never that burning, star-crossed love that I enjoyed reading so much about. More of a deep affection.

I also felt indebted to Thom, for offering me a life outside of my father's purview. Had I not met him all those years ago, I might've lived out all my days in that same house with my father, working as his receptionist in his medical practice. In a way I went from taking care of one man to taking care of another, but it meant that, eventually, I got to experience motherhood. And best of all, I got to be closer to Hazel in New York City.

So the least I can do is keep Thom's final resting place tidy. Even if not all my years with him were rosy.

The midmorning sun climbs higher in the sky, vanquishing the remaining shade. I wish I'd thought to bring a bottle of water and a sun hat. A lifetime spent outside in the garden has left its mark on my body—many marks, in fact—and though none of them have turned out to be cancerous, a few have showed potential and had to be removed. The thing about sun damage is that it's there lurking under the skin, but it takes decades to actually show up, and by that time it can be too late. And since my generation wasn't the best about sun protection—I only started using sunscreen in the nineties—I need to be extra vigilant.

I hastily roll down my shirtsleeves and flip up my collar to cover my neck.

It takes me another hour to finish tidying Thom's grave. When I'm done, I can't help looking guiltily at the ones nearby, all in various states of unruliness. Perhaps their loved ones have moved away from Beacon, or are also buried here, so there's no one left to tend to them. I know I can't take care of them all, otherwise I'd be here all day. So I do the ones that look the most unloved, hoping that a stranger might pay the same courtesy to Mama and Daddy's headstones back in Wisconsin. I haven't been there since Daddy's funeral more than fifty years ago, so who knows what state they're in. It pains me to think of those graves covered in grime and overcome by weeds.

At least they're side by side; there's comfort in knowing that. There's no room next to Thom in this cemetery, but that's okay, because I don't want to be buried. A cardboard casket and a cremation is just fine for me. No need to be a burden to anybody.

I suppose I should ask Hazel what her wishes are. But how do you even work that into a conversation? I think I'll put it off as long as I can—especially since I still haven't broken the news to Elizabeth about Hazel's condition. I still remember her wail when I had to call her to let her know Thom had just had a ruptured brain aneurysm in our front yard. I can't bear the thought of having to do it again.

Gosh, I'm feeling gloomy, in spite of this beautiful day. Even the bird singing in the tree above me stirs no joy in my heart.

If only I could have held onto that rush I felt yesterday in that Brooklyn park——to somehow bottle it to use in moments like these. It was the most alive I've felt in weeks.

And what had made it even more satisfying was Hazel's reaction when I presented her with the goods.

"I knew you had it in you, Joy," she said, her eyes sparkling in a way they hadn't when I'd left the loft earlier.

I've missed that mischievous glimmer in her irises, her trademark ever since I met her as a spirited eight-year-old girl. The fact that I found a way to resurrect it gives me a smidge of hope.

Who knew that breaking a rule could yield such positive results?

I'm a bit surprised at myself—that something that would have seemed unfathomable, unconscionable, just a week ago, came to me with ease. How I was able to shrug off the creep of guilt by focusing on the reason I was doing it: Hazel.

Perhaps that's true of many people who commit crimes, especially petty ones. We only hear about the misdemeanor itself, but we never hear why the person did it—if we did, we might all be more compassionate. In truth, I've been an accessory to theft many times in my life. I've turned a blind eye at the grocery store when seeing a young mother sneak jars of baby food into her bag, or a man slipping a box of chocolates into his jacket the day before Christmas. They needed those things more than the wealthy corporation they were stealing from; they're victims of a system that doesn't support them.

But I'm much more tolerant of the misdeeds of others than of my own. If I'm being honest, I've spent my entire adult life trying not to disappoint my parents, even though they've both been gone for decades. I still feel my father's reproachful eye in any authority figure—the electricity company when I forget to pay the bill, the doctor when she tells me my cholesterol is too high, and don't get me started on my fear of running afoul of the IRS. Any time I step a toe out of line, I invariably feel like I've disappointed and displeased him—or that I've become an imposition in the way my mother cautioned against. Perhaps because I had so little time with both of my parents when they were healthy and happy, I've held on even more tightly to those moments when they told me I was a good girl. Once Mama became sick and my father became more distant, their praise grew increasingly rare. And yet I still believed if I did everything right, I might get that feeling of validation back.

In retrospect, it's absurd that I'm almost ninety and still defining myself by my mother and father's influence. As children, we are canvases, eager to be painted by our parents' brush of life wisdom. We don't question the quality of the tools or the paint, or the skill of the artist. We accept the things they teach us as sacred words to guide us through life. But I've now accrued the equivalent of two of Mama's lifetimes. Who's to say she knew the right way to live? Wasn't she just passing on what her mother taught her?

Do we ever truly shed the lessons ingrained in us as kids or are they part of our beings forever? Is there still time for me to try out a different way of being in the world?

I think I'd like to find out.

## 15

It's rather thrilling to return to the scene of a crime—even if it's to give back the very thing you stole.

Loitering outside the library entrance, I slip the book I pilfered into the after-hours slot to avoid the sensor going off when I walk through. It's a sweltering day, the kind where the humidity is so unforgiving that everyone gives up on trying to look anything but disheveled. When I step through the sliding doors, the air-conditioning is a cold compress on my skin.

I still haven't read any of the books I legitimately checked out the other day, so I don't need to browse for more. But that's not why I've come. I'm here to do research—albeit for a topic I wish I didn't need to be knowledgeable about.

I claim a chair at one of the public computers. I prefer to have Finn with me in case I need help, but that lovely young librarian Max is working again today, so I'll ask him if I find myself in a technology pickle.

Using my pointer fingers, I carefully type my word into the search thingamajig. I was quite the nimble typist back when I was my father's receptionist. But typing wasn't something I needed as a homemaker (I've always preferred handwritten thank-you letters) and the skill unfortunately disappeared after sixty years of disuse. So it's pecking at the keys for me, I'm afraid.

After a few tries, I manage to type my question without error.

How do you support someone with cancer?

I'm embarrassed I have to resort to asking a computer this important question that someone my age should know. Yes, I've lost a lot of people, but by some quirk of fate—I can't decide whether it's cruel or merciful—all those deaths were relatively quick. My father was taken swiftly by a heart attack and Thom by a ruptured aneurysm. Though my mother's illness was prolonged, I wasn't privy to most of it aside from those short visits my father allowed, so I gained no knowledge from that except how painful it was to lose her. I've had several close friends die in car accidents, one to drowning, and another in a plane crash. This might seem like a lot, but when you average it out over the years I've lived, it's actually quite normal. One woman I knew from my aerobics class in the eighties died while drinking a cocktail at an outdoor café in Tuscany, which, of all the ways to go, must be one of the best.

Of course I've had friends and acquaintances succumb after long illnesses, but I've never been the one to have to care for them. Am I lucky in that respect? Hard to say. Perhaps that experience would've been useful now that I need to step up for Hazel.

I click on the first link, preparing myself for the grim advice awaiting me.

The info is quite vague and only really suggests books to read, so I note down their names and click on the next link. It's only a touch more informative.

*Be present.*

*Be a good listener.*

*Respect their wishes.*

*Be patient.*

Well, yes, those are all pretty obvious.

The third link has more helpful suggestions, like assisting with cleaning and cooking, and offering to run errands. I've already been doing those things, though I do need to be more diligent about grocery shopping. It doesn't mention conducting drug deals on their behalf.

I sit back in my chair, discouraged, knowing this computer isn't going to be able to answer my most pressing question.

*How do I make it so that I'm not going to lose my best friend forever?*

Instead, I steel myself and type a different question, one I'm not going to like the answer to.

**How long will an eighty-nine-year-old with stage four cancer survive?**

I close my eyes and click on the button. When I open them, I immediately regret it.

Hazel's definitely not going to make it to our ninetieth birthdays.

I blink rapidly at the ceiling. I can't emotionally unravel in the middle of the library; that would make everyone uncomfortable.

I print the most helpful information and dash to collect it before anyone else sees it. If a well-meaning stranger asks me anything about those pages, tears will come flooding.

I have to get better at containing them. I'll visit Hazel again next week, and I'm determined not to fall apart like I did last time. I need to be as stoic as possible so she doesn't slip into her usual role of protector. She's never liked being taken care of—not even when she has a cold.

"Don't fuss over me, Joy," she'd say. "I can look after myself."

But I often wonder if that's just for show. Hazel's parents weren't attentive—likely because they were so young when they had her—so she's had to take care of herself since she was a child. It's probably a difficult habit to shake.

I've promised myself to visit Hazel weekly until, well, the end. If I could, I'd visit her every day, but that would mean letting down all my piano students. The disappointed look on those little faces whenever I've occasionally canceled or rescheduled lessons over the years is just too hard to bear. And I also want to honor Hazel's need to hold on to her independence.

I'm usually good at compartmentalizing unpleasant emotions so I don't burden anyone with my worries. "Chin up and smile," were Mama's instructions. She was unflappable, even in the most turbulent of times. I've tried to live up to that standard, but sometimes life throws you a particularly nasty curveball.

*Chin up and smile.*

I repeat it to myself several times until my body starts to believe it. I can pull myself out of this puddle of self-pity.

After collecting the warm papers infused with that distinct printer smell, I saunter over to the holds stand—I can't resist checking if there's another book that takes my fancy. A few tempting titles, but none that will bring that buzz I'm seeking. I need something bigger, like the drug deal. Something truly, dare I say, terrible.

Glancing around the room, I wait for something to plant a seed. And then I find it.

The fire alarm panel on the wall next to me.

How easy would it be to just lift up the glass and pull that lever? Back when I was working for my father, I used to stare at the fire alarm on the wall, daydreaming about what it would feel like to pull it. To step outside the tightly drawn box of acceptable behavior my father had established for me. Over the years, that same compulsion would return occasionally—on the subway, in the art gallery, at Zumba class—but I resisted it.

What if I didn't, just this once?

I surreptitiously check for security cameras facing my direction; they're conveniently pointing elsewhere, as if egging me on. One last check to confirm no one is looking my way.

Then I lift the glass cover, pull the red lever, and scurry away.

Even though I know it's coming, the shrill alarm abruptly barreling through the library gives me a fright.

Then the commotion starts. Heads look up from books, their faces all with the same anxious, puzzled expressions.

Max—bless him—jumps into action immediately.

"Okay, everybody," he yells. I've never heard him speak in anything but hushed, library-appropriate tones. "That's the fire alarm, which means we all need to stop what we're doing and move calmly towards the exit."

Everyone follows the first instruction; most ignore the second, grabbing their personal items and rushing to the exit with little regard for one another.

I stand in the middle of it all, stunned by what I've just done.

Misinterpreting the reason for my disorientation, Max rushes to my side.

"Mrs. Bridport," he says. "We need to evacuate right now. Let me help you."

He takes my bag and chivalrously guides me outside.

The crowd of people are fanning themselves with whatever they can—books, notebooks, their hands—and I feel a flash of regret. How inconsiderate it was to set off the fire alarm on an oppressively humid afternoon. I suppose I'm going to have to get comfortable with the fact that rule breaking brings collateral damage.

The fire trucks arrive with great fanfare, the urgent blaring of their horns elevating the drama. Everyone is watching the building anxiously, studying its architecture for telltale wisps of smoke.

Ah, yes, that's right—I'm the only one who knows there's no real emergency. I should at least feign some concern.

I turn to the woman next to me, who I recognize from the post office. She's the most efficient of the clerks—I think her name is Marie-Jeanne.

"What a frightening thing to happen," I say, trying on the skin of a flagrant liar for the first time in my life. "I hope everyone's okay."

Marie-Jeanne dabs sweat from her temple with her sleeve cuff. "They hustled everyone out pretty quickly, thank god."

"That's a relief," I say, a touch too dramatically. I'll have to work on my acting skills if I'm to continue down this rebellious path. "Do they know what started it?"

Marie-Jeanne shakes her head. "Not yet, but it's been a while since this town had any action. It'll give us all something to talk about."

I feel a surge of pride at being the instigator of such excitement.

Marie-Jeanne's eyebrows flatten with concern. "It's Mrs. Bridport, right? Are you okay out here in the heat? I know it can be challenging for people your age." She takes my elbow. "Let's find you some shade and somewhere to sit down."

Though her intentions are kind, her assumption stings.

I ease my elbow out of her grip. "Oh, don't worry about me, dear." I keep my tone playful to mask my annoyance. "I'm hardier than I look."

"Oh," she says, a trace of hurt in her expression. "Okay."

Empathy pierces my bravado. Marie-Jeanne just thought she was doing a good deed and it was rude of me to dismiss her so quickly. I know that feeling of rejection.

"I appreciate you being so thoughtful," I say with a smile. "Thank you so much for looking out for me."

She brightens. "No problem at all, Mrs. Bridport."

I excuse myself and continue milling through the crowd, waiting for someone to connect me with the crime. But everyone just smiles and greets me politely, or, worse, ignores me completely.

Max is conferring with the firefighters. I edge closer, pretending to admire the colorful mural on the library's exterior so they can't tell I'm eavesdropping.

"Looks like someone pulled the fire alarm," the firefighter says.

Her curls are peeking out from under her helmet, buoyed by the humidity—she and her colleagues must be boiling in those heavy-duty outfits.

I ignore the spark of guilt and listen closer.

Max's shoulders relax. "So there's no sign of any fire?"

The firefighter shakes her head. "Not that we can find. All those books would go up in flames pretty darn quick."

I'm charmed by the horrified look on Max's face—having them all burn down really would be a tragedy. What a treasure he is. It's a shame he's been impacted by both of my library misdeeds.

He frowns. "But who do you think would've done that?"

"Bored teens, probably," the firefighter says. "They love to cause havoc."

"Makes sense," Max says. I don't think he's long out of his teens himself. "Should I report it or something?"

My chest seizes—I hadn't considered that consequence to my actions. Would they fingerprint the fire alarm? It was reckless of me not to think of using gloves when I activated it.

The firefighter gives Max a resigned shrug. "You could. But, frankly, I doubt it'll go anywhere, even though it's technically a felony in New York State. The police department is understaffed as it is."

A felony! Does that make me an actual felon, or does one need to be officially charged for that? The gravity of what I've just done has suddenly become much more tangible.

Another firefighter strides over to join them. "Looks like everything's clear," he says with a lovely Southern accent. "You can start letting everyone back in."

"Great," Max says, relieved. "Thanks so much."

As he shepherds everyone back inside, I feel triumphant for having gotten away with "causing havoc" without anyone noticing me.

And I can't wait to tell Hazel all about it.

# 16



Everything about this place is overstimulating. The sounds—unrelenting car horns, drilling, yelling. The smells—rotting garbage, soured milk baked onto the pavement, headache-inducing car exhaust. The energy—everyone and everything moving at a turbulent pace.

And that's just New York City itself. I can't imagine what's waiting behind the door of this burlesque club Hazel and I are about to walk into.

I'm still shell-shocked from my arrival yesterday after enduring an eighteen-hour bus ride from Wisconsin. If it were up to me, Hazel and I would live our entire lives together in our town, raising our families and growing old together. But the minute we graduated high school—or, at least, the very next day—she packed her bags and boarded a similar Greyhound bus bound for New York City, armed with no plan except that she was never, ever, living in Wisconsin again.

That was four years ago, and Hazel has been pleading with me to come out here ever since. A visit to the country's largest metropolis was very far down my wish list, but I finally acquiesced, unable to say no to my best friend's persistence. I missed her so much that I was willing to spend a few days enduring the chaos of the city.

Of course, Hazel failed to mention that those days would include a visit to a burlesque club. In retrospect, it's best she didn't—it would've been the excuse I needed not to come.

In the frigid air of this November night, she hooks her arm through mine and raises a coquettish eyebrow.

"Ready to have your eyes opened, Joy?" Her cigarette perches glamorously between two fingers, smoke in tendrils above her.

What have I agreed to?

Hazel's bright red curls glow in the streetlight—I still haven't gotten used to this fiery new color on her. She tosses the cigarette to the ground and stubs it with the toe of her high heel in an elegant yet decisive twist.

She pulls me to the roped-off door and winks at the large security guard standing stoically in front of it.

"Evening, Miss Scottsdale," he says with a grin, unhooking the rope and stepping aside, much to the annoyance of the other people waiting in line.

"Thanks, Harry," Hazel says, brushing his arm with her fingers as we pass. She bends—her heels make her more than a whole foot taller than me—to whisper in my ear. "Now I'm going to show you why city life is much more exciting."

She leads me down a narrow staircase where the cigarette smoke is less a graceful tendril and more a suffocating plume. I squeeze my stinging eyes shut, holding tightly to Hazel's hand. As we get to the base of the staircase, the muffled sound of a trombone playing a sultry baseline permeates another set of double doors.

Suddenly they swing open and a group of drunken revelers stumble through, laughing and yelling. Hazel splits their group down the middle, pulling me through into a room packed so tightly that, for a moment, all I can see are shoulders. The air is hot, dense, and sweaty, thick with cigar smoke and spilled alcohol. On stage, voluptuous dancers—clad in various iterations of fishnets, lace, ruffles, and sequins—shimmy and shake. I marvel at how they're so at ease in their skin, in every purposeful movement they execute, in the flirtatious eye contact they make with captive admirers.

I can't even see Hazel now, but her hand stays firmly attached to mine, leading me through the throng. I've never been this intimate with a stranger's body in my life—and it's not just one body, it's dozens.

Just when I'm on the verge of panic, Hazel yanks me free of the crowd into an open space in front of a bar.

"Let's get you a drink!" Hazel yells over the din of the live jazz band, where the sultry trombones are now competing with cheeky trumpets.

"I'll just have water, please!" I yell back, unable to hear my own voice.

I can't hear Hazel either, but her response is clear on her lips. "Nonsense."

She beckons the bartender closer, pulling playfully on his tie as she purrs the order in his ear.

Minutes later she hands me a dark concoction of liquor and holds her glass up to mine. "To wild adventures!" she roars.

I clink my glass meekly, yearning to be back home in my bedroom in Wisconsin, tucked under the covers reading a book. She doesn't catch that I'm only pretending to imbibe the liquid through my straw. This isn't the night to try my first sip of alcohol—who knows where I'll end up.

Hazel waves to someone at the corner of the bar and grabs my hand again. "Come on, I'll introduce you to some of the most interesting folks you'll ever meet."

As we make our way over to the other side, people keep stopping to greet Hazel, sliding their arms around her shoulders, kissing her cheeks in that continental way. How does she have this many friends? And why does she even need boring old me? I stand dutifully by her side as she introduces me to a whirlwind of names and faces that I instantly forget, nodding and smiling until it hurts.

I wait until she's caught up in a spirited debate with a slick, mustache-clad gent to excuse myself to go to the ladies' room, edging my way around the crowd to avoid the sensory overwhelm of walking through it again. I don't even need the bathroom; I just need a break.

I navigate the perimeter of the room in search of a calmer space. The first corner I find is occupied by a couple canoodling with abandon, their hands and tongues in places I didn't know were even allowed in public. I hurry past them, averting my eyes.

Eventually I find a nook at the back of the room, empty thanks to whatever song the band has just started playing magnetizing people to the dance floor. I press myself against the wall, clutching my drink to my chest like a candle I'm praying over.

Hazel is now dancing with a different man than the one she was debating. He spins her around, her hips shaking so smoothly, eyes shining with that verve that makes her irresistible, even if she isn't a conventional beauty by society's standards.

"Mind if I hide back here with you?" a male voice asks from beside me.

I look around for someone else, certain he couldn't be talking to me. And yet it's only the two of us here.

There's something about his demeanor that feels as out of place in this club as I am. His hair is combed neat and flat, shorter than the slicked styles of the other men in the room. His suit is more conservatively tailored; his tie is sensible and tightly knotted. And he's holding a beer instead of the requisite glass of gin or bourbon.

"Oh," I say, blushing furiously. "Yes, if you want to. Though I'm afraid you might find my friend more interesting."

I point at Hazel.

The man follows my finger, then turns back to me. "I'm not sure she's my type."

"Oh?"

I'm not sure how to respond to this. I don't have much experience talking to men my age who aren't patients of my father's making an appointment. And most of those I grew up with.

"Yeah," he says, adjusting his tie with a smile. "I'm more fond of quieter gals."

I definitely don't know how to respond to that.

"This is all very new to me," I stammer, gesturing at the uninhibited gaiety happening in front of us. "It's my first time in the city. I'm from a very small town in Wisconsin, so it's a tad overwhelming."

The young man smiles approvingly and I notice his hazel eyes, the color of the rock pools in the small brook that runs behind the house where Daddy and I live.

"I'm a small-town boy too," he says. "Not from as far away as you—I'm from the Hudson Valley. It's just up the river from here, though it feels worlds away from this mayhem."

I'm relieved to have found another fish out of water. "So you're just visiting too?"

"Yes," he says. "Catching up with some law school buddies to celebrate us all passing the bar."

"Congratulations," I say. "I've heard that's very difficult."

The man shrugs. "Not if you're diligent about studying and don't get distracted by things." He nods disapprovingly at the dance floor.

A spark of courage kindles. "So you're not much of a dancer, then?"

Wholesome is the best way to describe his smile.

"I don't mind a spin or two around the floor on the right occasion," he says. "The waltz is my favorite—not really the kind of thing you'd do in a place like this, is it?"

"I suppose not."

He reaches out a hand. "I'm Thom Bridport."

I take his fingers shyly, a furious flutter of butterflies in my stomach. "It's lovely to meet you. I'm Joy Derwent."

"Well, Joy," Thom says. "I look forward to perhaps having our first dance someday."

**17**

The crowd crisscrossing Grand Central's main hall doesn't disorient me like it used to. I navigate it with ease, pushing assuredly between people with a firm "Coming through!" instead of the timid "Um, excuse me, please" I've relied on previously.

I'm not feeling so invisible these days.

Ever since the fire alarm adventure, a new confidence has inhabited me. I don't even bat an eyelid today when a man in an ill-fitting suit tries to cut in front of me at the subway turnstile.

I stand my ground, elbows out so he can't pass. Though I'm much shorter than him, his pungent breath—sour, tinged with onions—still assaults my nostrils.

"It's very crowded down here, isn't it?" I say to him, swiping my MetroCard successfully on the first go.

He huffs impatiently, marching towards the arriving train without a word.

It's amazing how decades of diligently doing what you're told can be undone in only a few rebellious acts. Turns out, life is much more exciting when you're living in spite of the rules rather than in fear of them. Next time I might even try entering through the security gate instead of paying my fare, just to see if I can get away with it.

I choose a different train car to avoid the foul-breathed man, claiming a seat opposite a father and his young daughter, who looks to be about seven.

As the train gathers speed, the girl turns around in her seat, kneeling so she can look out the window at the blur of dark tunnel outside.

Her father tugs on her arm.

"I told you to sit still, Alice—you're disturbing the other passengers," he says gruffly, even though no one seems bothered by her.

Hearing his tone, it's as if I've instantly regressed to her age. I can feel the shame of her father's admonishment, the way it spreads through her body, erasing all self-confidence, igniting anxiety instead. I see how she now sits, stiff as a statue and staring straight ahead, keeping herself small, reminding herself that breaking any of Daddy's rules means disappointing him. And how, in her flawed seven-year-old logic, she likely assumes that disappointing him might lead to him loving her less.

I want to tell her not to lose that curiosity, that adventurous impulsiveness; to assure her that her life will be much more interesting if she holds tightly onto it, even if the authority figures in her life try to scold it out of her.

When her father isn't looking, I catch her eye and make a silly face, crossing my eyes and poking out my tongue. She smiles, her body briefly relaxing before resuming its rigid vigilance.

As the train rattles downtown, I can't decide whether it's her father I'm angry at for stifling her spirit, or whether it's mine.

I'm elated to see Hazel dressed with her usual sartorial flair—I'd been prepared for the depressing version of her that greeted me last time I visited. Though her voluminous maxi dress—emerald-green with a glittering gold geometric print—hides the diminishing body I know is underneath, I'm glad to be able to pretend she's still her usual robust self, if only for a day.

"Come on in!" she calls brightly. A vocal mirage I'll also happily accept.

She's peering into a mirrored compact, applying her scarlet lipstick when I enter.

"I've been eagerly awaiting your arrival," she says. "Let's have an outing today."

Happy as I am to see her more energetic, I also don't want her to overexert herself. What will I do if she becomes too weak while we're out? I think I could get her into a cab, but I'm not sure I'm strong enough to carry her up the three flights of stairs to her apartment.

"What did you have in mind?" You never know with Hazel.

She plucks a large sun hat from the stand by the door. "I feel like going for a jaunt outside. My soul is craving some sunshine after being cooped up in here all the time. I want to be surrounded by humans living their lives instead of focusing on the fact that mine is dwindling precipitously."

"Sounds lovely!" I say, tamping down my apprehension.

If it makes her feel better, I'm willing.

My fears materialize within two blocks. We're only at Court Street when Hazel stops—we'd been moving at a crawl as it is—and grasps my shoulder for support.

I sneak my hand into my bag, ready to pull out my phone to call for help. "Is everything okay?"

Hazel grimaces, palm to her stomach.

"Yes, everything's perfectly fine," she says, determined. "Let's keep going."

A block later she stops again, her grimace etched even deeper.

I want to whisk her home and have her lie down and rest, but I know she won't allow it.

So I make a show of flexing my knee slowly and wincing.

"My knee has been acting up this week after my Zumba class and it's really quite painful—would it be okay if we stopped and rested for a bit?" I point to the French-themed café we're standing outside. "Maybe we could have a cup of tea here?"

Hazel's so good at reading me that I'm sure she'll see through my ruse and reprimand me for it. But her face softens in gratitude.

"Of course we can," she says. "You shouldn't push yourself so hard in that Zumba class—we're not as limber as we used to be."

"I promise not to shimmy so vigorously next time."

Every smile I get out of Hazel now feels like a lottery win; anything to distract her from her pain.

"You find us a table and I'll order," I say. "I want a chance to peruse the cake display before I choose."

Hazel doesn't protest. "Just a peppermint tea for me, please."

I'm about to pressure her into getting something sweet, but stop myself; she's likely dealing with nausea on top of her pain.

"Coming right up!"

Inspired by the French theme, I opt for an almond croissant. While I'm waiting to pay, I look around to find where Hazel is seated. My heart sinks when I see her sitting in her chair staring straight ahead, the way you do when you're trying desperately not to vomit.

The old Hazel would have already made friends with the couple at the next table over.

I have to get out of this habit of comparing her to the way she used to be. Of mourning her while she's still here. It's clear that version of my friend isn't coming back.

I'd been saving my story about the fire alarm until a moment when she really needed a boost. I think that time has come. I wait until our drinks have arrived before embarking on my reveal.

I smile cunningly at her over my cappuccino. "Since we don't keep secrets from each other, I have a confession to make."

Hazel eyes me cautiously. "Please don't tell me you have cancer too."

Her somber response catches me off guard.

"What? No!" I'm flustered now. "At least, not that I know of."

Hazel's shoulders relax. "Good. What is it, then?"

"I've been trying to follow your example by not being such a Goody Two-shoes all the time."

Hazel pauses her cup midair. "Do tell."

"Well," I say, leaning forward and keeping my voice low, "I've recently committed what some might consider"—I glance sideways to make sure no one's listening—"a felony."

Hazel almost chokes on her peppermint tea. "Come again?"

I gleefully launch into my story—leaving out the part where I was researching her prognosis on the internet, of course. It's so strange to be the one telling the tale for once instead of listening to hers. Now I get why she loves it—it's addictive to have a captive audience hanging on to your every word.

I finish with the part about standing right next to Max and the firefighters as they discussed the potential culprit, never for a second suspecting it was me.

Then I sit back and wait for Hazel's reaction. She looks genuinely awestruck.

"I've never seen you so much as jaywalk, let alone cause public nuisance, Joy," she says. "I'm proud of you."

It's not just her approval that makes my heart bloom. It's the way she's reanimated into her former self, as if, for a moment, she's forgotten all about her pain.

I need to find a way to make that happen more often.

# 18

A little boy named Lincoln sits at my piano, staring at the keys.

This is how all our lessons together begin. I suspect it's because he's overcome with shyness about performing in front of someone, even his teacher. He barely says a word beyond "Hello," "Thank you," and "Okay" during our time, and that's fine by me. These lessons are for the kids to express themselves however they need to. It's not as if I'm training them to be concert pianists. It's for them to explore their musical inclinations, if they have any, or to just have thirty minutes where someone is focused entirely on them.

Oh, I don't mean to imply that their parents are neglecting them. More that they themselves hardly have a spare moment, between working to earn enough to support their family and taking care of several children at once. So if Lincoln wants to spend the whole time just sitting without playing, I'm more than okay with it. He'll still get his baked treat at the end of the lesson.

The thing is, I know he wants to play. He just needs some space.

So just as I do whenever this happens, I excuse myself to get a glass of water, leaving him alone at the piano.

Really, I just go around the corner where he can't see me, and I wait. After a few minutes, I'll usually hear a tentative note, and then another slightly more emphatic one, then a chord, and maybe even a melody. Works like a charm every time.

Patience is a magical salve. You just have to let people do things in their own time. But so often we're in a hurry, or we push, which makes people stubborn—and they do the opposite of what we want. I constantly wonder about the beautiful things that might have happened in the world if we'd all been a bit more patient.

I wait a few more seconds before reappearing next to the piano.

"What lovely music!" I say.

A mauve flush creeps across his face and he looks down shyly, peeking sideways enough that I catch the pride in his eyes.

I tend to sit on a chair next to the students, but I don't want Lincoln to feel pressured. "I'd love to hear some more if you wouldn't mind playing for me while I water the plants," I say. "I'm sure they'd enjoy it too."

Lincoln nods without making eye contact, then resumes playing. It's a pop song that's been in regular rotation on the radio lately.

Classical music is my thing, but teaching these kids means I keep up with the music that's popular. In the sixties and seventies it was the Beatles and the Rolling Stones. The eighties and nineties were a lot of Madonna, Michael Jackson, Elton John, and Prince, with the occasional Guns N' Roses. This year my students all want to play songs by a young woman named Taylor Swift.

It used to be that I'd have to listen to the requested songs on vinyl record or cassette and then work out the simplest version of chords—like I said, it's about the kids' enjoyment, their feelings of accomplishment, not their precision. But the internet has made things a whole lot easier. Finn showed me how I can just type a song name into that little window and it'll give me the chords already written down, along with the lyrics. I can even change the key the song's in to make sure it's mostly easy chords that are manageable for small fingers. I'll spend an afternoon at the library computers finding the chord charts for the requested songs online and printing them out. Finn also loads the songs onto my phone so I can listen and understand what I'm teaching. My, that Taylor Swift has had some bad romantic luck in her life, hasn't she?

I tilt the watering can into the base of the snake plant, watching the way Lincoln loses himself in the song he's playing. It reminds me of a small boy named Chuck I used to teach about thirty years ago.

Chuck was scrawnier than Lincoln and not quite as shy. I don't push the kids for details they don't voluntarily share, but from what I could tell, Chuck's home situation was especially unfortunate. His mother had left when he was very young and his dad was raising him alone, while struggling with his own addiction demons. Chuck's clothes were frequently stained, his shoes had holes in the toes, and his hair rarely looked washed. But in spite of it all, he was so sweet and polite, listening attentively to everything I told him. Regardless of the situation at home, Chuck would show up for his lesson on time, brimming with enthusiasm. I don't want the kids to feel like charity cases, but I so dearly want to be helpful to them, so I buy a few necessities—sneakers, T-shirts, books—and keep them in the hallway closet. I used to tell them they were old things that Elizabeth didn't need any more; now I say they were Finn's. Hand-me-downs feel like a lot less of a burden.

Occasionally I wonder what happened to students like Chuck. Many of them stop their lessons as they become teenagers and other things occupy their time and interest. Sometimes I've seen them out and about in town, but most of them moved away as soon as they were old enough, seeking their own paths in life away from their chaotic upbringings.

Lincoln and I finish our lesson with cupcakes and milk. He still doesn't say much, but the way his skinny legs swing from the chair tells me he's content. And when I ask him if he wants to take a book from the cupboard, he spends several minutes deliberating. When he holds the winner—one about the solar system—in front of him like it's a precious object, my heart pangs. These kids are so appreciative of every tiny thing.

It's hard not to compare them to Elizabeth, who got almost everything she ever asked for. And yet sometimes I sense that she feels her childhood was lacking some vital thing.

After Lincoln's mom comes to collect him, I sit down next to my landline. Hazel offered to break the news to Elizabeth herself, but I told her I would do it—no need to saddle Hazel with that. And I know Elizabeth calls her once in a while just to chat, so I can't risk putting it off much longer.

I'm relieved when my call goes to voicemail.

Isn't it a parent's instinct to protect their child from pain for as long as they can?

**19**

NEW YORK CITY, 1968

I sit alone in the fancy Upper East Side restaurant, anxiously watching the door. This isn't the kind of place Hazel or I would even choose to frequent—Hazel because she thinks the clientele are too stuffy and pretentious, me because I know how much I'll stand out as not being one of them.

But Thom insisted on booking a reservation for the two of us here. "It's where all of my colleagues' wives socialize," he said when I mentioned I was planning to meet Hazel for lunch in the city. "It's very hard to get a table, but I can pull a few strings."

I dared not decline. And I'm looking forward to hearing about Hazel's recent trip to Puerto Rico. Lately she's been abroad for months at a time, so it's been rare that we get to see each other in the flesh. Last year she spent six months in Turkey, which put our Sunday phone calls on hold—too logistically difficult—and I found myself checking the mailbox religiously for the sporadic postcards she sent. But from what I gather, this trip to Puerto Rico was no longer than a week. Not even long enough to send her a care package.

The waiter stops by to ask, for a fourth time, whether I'm ready to order a drink.

"Will your friend be joining us soon?" His tight smile betrays his impatience.

"Oh, yes," I say, with a certitude I don't feel. "She's minutes away."

He raises an eyebrow. We both know that, unless she telephoned the restaurant, I would have no way of knowing that. And thirty minutes late isn't unusual for Hazel.

I drain my water glass to give him something to do, relieved when someone at another table summons him with a taut gesture.

There's not a thing in this place that isn't tasteful and refined—the decor, the clientele, and even the soft jazz music. I dressed up as best I could—in the cocktail dress I usually save for weddings—but I suspect the level of refinement here is embodied rather than worn. In other words, out of reach for me no matter what I'm wearing.

I mentally run through the table manners my mother instilled in me, just in case my nerves rob me of them in the moment.

*Napkin placed discreetly on your lap, away from the knees. Elbows off the table. No eating or drinking, water excepted, until everyone is seated. Utensils from the outside in; fork, held delicately in the fingers—not tightly in the fist—tines pointed down. Small, gentle bites. Spoon soup outwards to avoid spills.*

I almost cry with happiness when Hazel makes her entrance minutes later, swanning between the tables in a satin pantsuit adorned with a gold Chinese dragon, smiling grandly at the ladies tittering into their napkins as she passes.

I'm so eager to greet her that I almost knock over my water glass.

"Hello, my friend!" Hazel kisses the air beside my cheeks. "Sorry I'm *un poco tarde.*"

"You're here now and that's all that matters," I say, taking my seat again.

There's no point ribbing her about her lateness. I've long accepted it as one of the prices of admission for our friendship. Lord knows she tolerates my shortcomings—I'm sure she'd love it if I were as gregarious and adventurous as she is. Imagine the fun we would have had.

Hazel leans back to take in our milieu, the wrinkle of criticism in her brow.

"What made you choose this place?" She returns her gaze to me. "It's not very . . . you. And I mean that in the very best way."

"Thom arranged for the reservation." My thumbs work nervously at my napkin seams. "Our treat, of course."

He had handed me a smooth stack of twenty-dollar bills before leaving this morning. It irks him when I tell him Hazel has treated me to lunch, as if it's an insult to his capacity as a breadwinner.

"Well then," Hazel says, shaking out her napkin and draping it on her lap. "That explains it."

She flashes a winning smile at the waiter, who quickly approaches.

"The mystery guest has finally made her entrance, I see," he says, with a little more sarcasm than I imagine is permitted for staff in this establishment.

"She has, indeed." Hazel poses, hand to chin. "And she'll have a dirty martini."

The waiter scribbles, then looks at me expectantly. "And for you, madame?"

"Oh, just—" I frantically consider which cocktail seems most refined, but realize I have no idea about the hierarchy of fancy beverages. "A gimlet for me, please."

Hazel seizes her water glass in the meantime.

"So, tell me, what's new in Beacon?"

I should be grateful she's showing interest in my life, but I rarely have anything of note to report. No office politics to comment on, no child to gush about (despite Thom's and my efforts to conceive one). While I enjoy my days, they're comparatively unremarkable to hers.

"Let's see . . . Well, my azaleas are in bloom." I plumb my memory for something more exciting. "Oh, and a stray dog somehow managed to break into the butcher's last week when it was closed."

Hazel's eyes light up; a win for me. "Brava to her. I hope she got away with a worthy prize for her efforts."

"I think she managed to escape with a string of sausages." I'd have loved to see that. "But tell me all about Puerto Rico. I imagine it was beautiful. Did you go snorkeling?"

Hazel's focus shifts to the table behind me and then returns. "Ah. No, I didn't."

"What about the food? You must tell me all the delicious things you ate."

"Oh, you know, the usual—tostones, mofongo, that sort of thing." She picks up the menu. "Speaking of food, I do have to admit that this all looks delicious."

I study my friend for a moment—something's off. I can't recall her returning from a trip without something salacious, or at least scintillating, to recount.

I wait until after our meals arrive, and when no such tales have materialized, I press her.

"Is everything all right, Hazel?"

Though Hazel's forthrightness stings at times, the upside is that I know she'll answer me honestly.

She focuses on cutting her steak. "What do you mean? Of course it is."

Anyone else would read her delivery as nothing but confidence; thirty years' worth of conversations with Hazel tell me otherwise.

"It's just that I've never known you to come back from a trip and not have a million things to tell me. Did something happen while you were there?"

"No." Hazel puts her knife down. "I was just there taking care of some business."

"What kind of business?" Not an especially invasive question; she knows I'm fascinated by her adventures in entrepreneurship.

A forced laugh. "What's gotten into you, Joy? You're acting like a hard-nosed reporter."

What is this thing that she's avoiding telling me? Hazel gets a kick out of shocking me with the details of her wild antics. If it weren't for her, I'd still be as naive as a spring lamb.

"Nothing's gotten into me." I suddenly feel braver, like the dynamics of our friendship have momentarily reversed. "It's just that I sense there's something you're not telling me about this business you were taking care of."

Hazel looks everywhere but at me, her shoulders hunched forward.

I try again. "You can tell me anything. We don't keep secrets from each other, remember?"

We made that promise when we were still teenagers, but I haven't had to invoke the reminder until today.

I watch as Hazel's body language firms, like a balloon injected with helium.

The contrition in her eyes throws me off-balance.

"When I went to Puerto Rico," she says, allowing each word to float between us, "I was . . . with child." A pause, letting the sentence settle. "And now, by my own choice, I am not."

My eyes blink involuntarily, my body instinctively trying to clear the haze of confusion.

Finally, as if wiping condensation from a mirror, the reality of what she's said clarifies. I've heard why women of our generation go to Puerto Rico. I never in a million years could've imagined Hazel having cause to do so.

Suddenly it feels like the volume has been turned up on our surroundings—the clatter of cutlery on plates louder, the raucous laughter more grating and unkind. When I glance down at my hands, they're clutching the table so tightly, my knuckles are white.

I need to say something.

"But you didn't even tell me you were pregnant," I whisper, barely masking the betrayal taking hold. "I didn't know you'd been seeing someone special."

"That's the thing," Hazel says evenly. "It wasn't someone special. And I've always said that I'm not cut out to be a mother, you know that."

"It's just—" The words catch in my throat. "I always figured you'd change your mind."

"I'm sorry, Joy," she says quietly. "I didn't tell you because I knew it would be painful for you to hear."

Hazel inches her hand across the table so that her fingertips lightly brush mine, perhaps hoping, like a pair of jumper cables, it might re-establish the connection between us.

My body makes the choice for me, yanking my hand away in one brisk movement.

It's as if she's reached across the table and squeezed my heart like a soggy dishcloth.

I don't know if it's devastating because she kept a secret from me. Or because she was given the very treasure I've been yearning for since I married Thom.

And she rejected it.

# 20

There's a bounce in my step as I make my way down Main Street. Elizabeth has agreed to meet me at my favorite café—undoubtedly the highlight of my week. She's mostly been too busy for coffee dates since her divorce.

On my way, I pause outside the secondhand shop owned by Hazel's purported nemesis, Seth. Their decades-long feud does feel a bit ridiculous, but perhaps he might be more willing to part with the vase when Hazel isn't the one doing the bidding. And since I'm ten minutes early to meet Elizabeth, it couldn't hurt to pop in and try my luck.

Seth is leaning against the counter clipping his nails, making no effort to corral the shards as they fly in all directions.

Suppressing a grimace of disgust, I smile at him pleasantly, wondering if today will be the day that he recognizes me.

Apparently not.

"Hello, ma'am," he says. "Anything in particular you're looking for today?"

Mirroring Hazel's nonchalance from the last time we were here, I sift through the salad bowl of costume jewelry.

"Oh, not really," I say. "I'm supposed to be meeting my daughter for coffee but I'm a tad early."

Seth's lip curls in annoyance, already writing me off as a potential customer, thus not worth his time.

His rudeness piques my courage. I point to the vase sitting next to him on the counter.

"That's a very unique vase," I say. "What kind of deal would you give me on that?"

It occurs to me that even if he does agree to sell it, I might not have the funds to cover it. I wonder if I could go on a payment plan.

Seth's posture inflates and he deigns to bestow me with his full attention. "I'm afraid that's the one thing in here that's not for sale."

"Oh?" An innocent tilt of my head. "I would've thought you'd want to sell everything in here to make room for new stuff."

Seth smirks. "You're right," he says. "But this vase is a bit of a trophy for me. It represents a victory over someone who denied me what was mine. And for the past fifty years, she's been trying to convince me to sell it to her."

"Fifty years? That's a long time to hold a grudge," I say sweetly. "Wouldn't you feel better if you unburdened yourself of it?"

An emphatic shake of the head. "Never. I'm not one of those weak people who soften in their old age."

I consider trying to appeal to his conscience by telling him Hazel is terminally ill. But she'd never forgive me if I did; it would be like conceding to her adversary.

"What a shame, then," I say, rummaging in my bag for my phone. "Oh, would you look at that—my daughter is a few minutes early too." And with that fib, I tug open the door. "Have a lovely day, sir!"

Seth grunts a farewell, then resumes his nail-clipping.

The café is unusually busy for a weekday. Amid the din, I hear snippets of a foreign language I don't recognize—word of our beautiful town must have reached international tourists. Or maybe it's those "digital nomads" I've read about in the paper. Apparently people can do their jobs from anywhere nowadays.

I regret having suggested to Elizabeth that we meet here. A busy café isn't the place to deliver devastating news to someone. Especially when it's her day off.

I'm just about to take my place in line when my phone dings.

**Hi Mom. So sorry but the hospital is understaffed and I need to cover someone's shift today, so we'll have to reschedule coffee :(**

I deflect my disappointment—I can't wallow when my daughter has canceled so she can tend to sick people. And I'm sure she could use the money from the extra shift.

When she originally told us she wanted to become a nurse, I was surprised—she'd been toying with the idea of law, like her father—but I'm so proud of her for choosing that path. It's such a noble one, even if she's exhausted all the time, and I know she loves it.

I quickly text her back.

**No problem, darling! But let's catch up soon.**

No response.

Well, since I'm here I may as well stay.

I join the line while keeping an eye on my favorite table. I like it because it's right by the door and I can see everyone come and go. Some people put their bag or jacket on a chair before they've even ordered, to signal they've claimed that table, but that's unfair to everyone else, in my opinion. I like to leave it up to chance—if I get my table, great, but if I don't, it's not meant to be.

Today, however, I really want it. I don't want to have to sit on a park bench again and consume my treats all on my lonesome.

As soon as I have my order, I move quickly—balancing my cappuccino on its saucer in one hand and a cake plate in the other—ready to claim my prize.

That's when I see another older woman approaching the table. In the past, I would've immediately conceded it to her, even though we're equal distance from it. But I hold my tongue, letting her make the first gesture.

We both pause awkwardly, the table positioned between us like a priceless object. Between two women of our generation—who were taught to be overly polite, to never cause a scene, to concede to others—this interaction would usually follow a familiar path. She would graciously offer the table, to which I would graciously refuse and offer it to her, and so on and so forth, until one of us finally gave in.

For a moment, I consider suggesting we share it. But then I see her adult daughter behind her on the phone, an absent-minded yet affectionate hand resting on her mother's shoulder. A stab of envy takes me by surprise.

The older woman smiles at me. "Please, you go ahead and take it."

I swallow the words that come to me at first, the ones society has ingrained in me.

"Thank you, that's very kind of you." I place my cake and coffee down, as if staking a flag in the land I've just claimed.

My adversary doesn't hide her surprise. We are two contemporaries and I haven't followed the rules.

"Oh," she says, hovering. "You're welcome."

I sit, beaming at her defiantly, and sip my cappuccino. She and her daughter take the hint and head to join the line to order.

Pleased with myself, I dig my fork into the cake. It's drier than usual; disappointing, even. My sleeve sticks to the table, tacky from the spill of something syrupy that wasn't cleaned up properly. My victory isn't as sweet as I hoped.

"Joy?"

Rowan is standing in front of me, his short T-shirt sleeves revealing even more tattoos than I'd seen previously. The colors are quite something.

Funny that I've run into him again, but that's small towns for you. Usually it's the people you don't want to see whom you encounter most often. In this case, however, it's a pleasant surprise.

"Oh, Rowan, hello there!" I point to the empty chair. "Would you like to join me?"

As soon as I say it, I'm embarrassed. Why on earth would he want to sit and have coffee with a little old lady?

But his eyes brighten. "I'd love to, thank you, Joy." He points to my plate. "You've got a weakness for the lemon cake too, I see."

I beckon him closer so I can keep my voice low. "Yes, though I wouldn't advise ordering it today. It's dismayingly dry."

"Noted." He winks. "Can I get you another coffee while I'm ordering?"

I'm tickled. "That's very thoughtful, but I can only manage so much caffeine in a day."

"Philippe is the same," Rowan says. "He tosses and turns all night if he has too much. Keeps Hettie and me awake too."

As he joins the queue, I notice some of the other patrons watching us curiously. I suppose Rowan and I do make quite an unexpected duo. But I don't mind that it's turning heads—it's nice to be noticed.

Rowan returns with his macchiato and shuffles his chair closer to me so he's not obstructing people coming in the door.

His coffee cup looks ludicrously small given his large physique. "Unfortunately, I can't stay too long," he says. "I'm going to a matinee at the Beacon Theater."

"How lovely!" I say. "Years ago I had a film club with three friends and we'd see a movie and then have coffee and cake here afterwards to discuss it." I wipe cappuccino froth from my lip. "And believe me, the discussion got heated at times."

Golly, those afternoons were fun, the four of us—Rosemary, Midge, Laurel, and me—sitting around debating the merits of the film. Without fail, our opinions were varied and strongly held. I liked the quirky foreign films best; the others leaned towards the more commercial, crowd-pleasing movies.

Rowan lifts his cup. "Years ago? You're not into movies anymore?"

I herd the cake crumbs with my fork. "Sadly, I'm the last remaining member," I say. "A film club for one is rather depressing, isn't it?"

I sure do miss those women. But as time whittled my social circle, I could at least still take comfort in the fact that my truest friend remained.

Rowan puts down his empty cup, having consumed his coffee in three sips.

"I don't know about that," he says with a smile. "I've been doing it for years. Philippe isn't much of a film buff—it takes a lot of cajoling for him to come with me."

"My husband, Thom, wasn't either."

"So perhaps," Rowan says, "we need to merge our film clubs for one." He looks at his watch. "If you don't have other plans, would you like to join me for the matinee?"

My initial instinct is to decline. I don't want to be invited somewhere out of pity.

But then I ask myself what Hazel would do. The answer is obvious.

"It would be my absolute pleasure."

# 21

When Rowan suggested I join him for the movie, I assumed we'd be seeing some kind of action blockbuster. I wouldn't have minded—I'd have seen anything if it meant spending a couple of hours in another person's company.

But yet again, I've tripped myself up with stereotypes.

Rowan had chosen a delightful Japanese film about a shy, solitary man whose job was to clean the public toilets around Tokyo. It was ever so charming and heartwarming, and I couldn't help shedding a tear at the man's isolation—the way the rest of the world seemed to overlook him, deeming his existence inconsequential.

After the movie, I'd suggested we walk home together so we could discuss the film. Rowan gladly obliged.

"What would your film club friends have thought of that one?" he asks as we turn off Main Street.

I notice he's keeping his strides short so he doesn't outpace me, and I don't even take offense. I'm quite sure my legs are about half the length of his, so it's less of a comment on my ability and more a question of physics.

"Well, Laurel was the most opinionated and would've complained about the subtitles," I say. "And Midge would've wanted more dialogue—she loved fast-paced political thrillers. But Rosemary would've enjoyed it."

My voice cracks on the last sentence.

"Losing friends is hard, isn't it?" Rowan says.

I turn to him, surprised. "Have you lost many friends?"

He's very young compared to me.

He shrugs. "I'm a gay man who came of age during the HIV/AIDS crisis in New York City, so I understand what it means to have survivor's guilt," he says. "That whole 'why them and not me' rumination that never seems to quite leave you."

"I know it well," I say quietly.

"Unfortunately, I missed a lot of their funerals and memorials."

"That's understandable," I say. "It's quite exhausting when you seem to be going to one every other week. Last year, I attended three in ten days."

Rowan shakes his head. "No, I would've definitely gone if I'd been able to, but I was, let's say, indisposed."

"Indisposed?"

Rowan turns to me with a wry smile. "You might've heard a rumor through the neighborhood grapevine that I've spent some time at Sing Sing."

My flaming cheeks give me away. "I don't believe anything until hearing it straight from the source."

He smiles. "And now you have."

I hang my head. "I'm sorry our neighborhood hasn't been as welcoming as it should've been."

Our community has long prided itself on looking out for one another. That shouldn't change because someone did something against the law long ago. In fact, Beacon runs several programs that help former inmates reintegrate into society. Our local bookstores even donate books to occupants at the nearby correctional facility. And every so often, I'm asked for directions by newly released people standing at the train station with their plastic bags of belongings, trying to figure out where to go to begin their new life of freedom. I'm disappointed in my neighborhood—me included—for being so sanctimonious about Rowan. Especially now I know how easy it is to overstep the line of legality.

"Thanks, but I'm used to it by now," Rowan says. "I was used to it before I even had a criminal record."

I look up at him, puzzled.

"My father spent time in prison when I was a kid—stealing cars and other shady business," he says. "Even though I'd never set a single foot wrong in the eyes of the law, everyone else decided I was guilty by association."

"I'm sorry, Rowan," I say. "That's a rough hand to be dealt as a child."

He smiles. "I'm tougher because of it. Though I still can't decide whether I ended up walking a criminal path because of my father's example, or because it's what people expected of me. You know, giving in to the inevitable."

"I see."

I'm dying to know more. But in moments like these, I find it best to say as little as possible, to give a person space to gather their thoughts before they articulate them. That's when they'll often tell you the very thing you've been wanting to ask.

"The worst part is," he continues, "they threw me in prison for something I got caught up in and didn't realize was illegal until I was in over my head."

"Oh?" The key is to show interest without interrupting.

Rowan shoves his hands in his pockets and hunches forward, as if regressing to the posture of his younger self, not the assured man I've been getting to know.

We walk in silence for a few steps and I hold my tongue, careful not to push.

"I got a job in college working for this luxury wine merchant who imported rare bottles from all over the world," he says. "I was his assistant, so I did a bit of everything, whatever he asked me to—bookkeeping, client liaison, research. It was all very secretive, which I figured was just the way things worked when you're dealing with that kind of exclusivity—it's wild how much rich people will pay for a single bottle of wine." He removes a hand from his pocket to scratch his beard. "I was so dazzled by it all, getting to be around all these fascinating people who seemed so cultured, worldly, and knowledgeable compared to what I was used to. I guess that made me less attuned to the fact that what we were doing wasn't exactly legal. Or maybe I subconsciously chose to turn a blind eye."

I nod. "Sometimes it's hard to see things for what they are when you're in the thick of them."

Rowan offers an appreciative glance. "The thing is, when we were busted and it came out what my boss had been up to—forgeries, embezzlement—I realized I'd unknowingly participated in most of it. The cops offered me a plea deal to rat on my boss, but I refused because I was so loyal and felt indebted to him for giving me the job in the first place. I figured the loyalty would go both ways, but I was just a stupid kid. Of course my boss and his fancy lawyers turned around and pinned it all on me. All I had was a useless court-appointed attorney, since I couldn't afford anything else, and when I tried to fight it, he just said that there was no point, especially since I come from a family with a known criminal history. So I went to prison for eight years."

Anger brews in my bosom. "But . . . that's terribly unfair."

Rowan shrugs again. "That's life, Joy. A lot of people in prison are there because they couldn't afford a good lawyer and took the fall for someone else. And then it sticks to you for the rest of your life, no matter how hard you try to prove yourself. Once the world sees you as a criminal, that's how they'll always see you."

"But that was thirty years ago," I insist. "People shouldn't be held accountable for things they did so long ago. And it's not as if you"—I lower my voice—"murdered somebody."

Rowan laughs. "Most folks don't share your generous perspective."

We walk a few yards in silence.

"So I've seen a teenage boy coming and going from your place," Rowan says. "Is that your grandson?"

"Yes, that's Finn." I can't help but beam. "He visits me a few times a week."

"You're lucky to have such a good relationship with him," Rowan says. "My grandmother was a horrible woman. My sister and I were scared of her most of the time—and for good reason."

"I'm sorry to hear that," I say. "It's true, I am very fortunate."

As we turn the corner, I see two figures outside Rita's house on the opposite side of the street from mine and Rowan's. If my eyesight were better and I'd realized earlier, I would've suggested we detour. But by the time the two figures come into focus, it's too late.

Rita and Celeste are deep in conversation while the former is hosing her lawn. Doesn't she know you shouldn't water your garden in the middle of a hot day? The water evaporates so quickly that it's an unnecessary waste. I'd tell her, but that would mean having to engage them in conversation.

When Rita spots Rowan and me walking up the hill, a cryptic smile spreads across her face. She not so subtly nudges Celeste, who turns around to look at us.

Rowan waves, then turns to me. "Do you want to go over and say hello?"

"Oh, no, that's okay," I say. "We're not the closest friends."

"Really?" Rowan says. "At Celeste's potluck she had nothing but wonderful things to say about you. I was surprised she invited me, actually, but she said you were the one who suggested it."

I'd forgotten about that. "Oh, yes, that was me—I hope everyone was kind to you."

Rowan glances pointedly at Rita. "Some more than others," he says. "I noticed quite a few people giving me a wide berth, but like I said, I'm used to it." He opens my garden gate for me. "Anyway, things are looking up now that I've found myself a film club buddy—I've enjoyed our afternoon together."

"Me too," I say. "Let's see another film soon!"

As I stand on my porch, watching him walk away, I glance across the street, where Rita is whispering to Celeste with a crafty expression that suggests unkindness.

If I wasn't worried about betraying Rowan's confidence, I'd march over and tell them what he just told me about his reason for spending time in prison. To demand he be given the chance to start afresh. It's unjust that he's instantly doubted because of his past actions, whereas I've been getting away with things because I've built up a lifetime of goodwill by always doing the right thing and following the rules.

It feels like fate that he and I are meeting somewhere in the middle.

Maybe it's time I spent some more of that goodwill I've accumulated.

# 22



Central Park is the rare place in New York City where my nerves remain unperturbed. I can still hear the faint din of car horns and sirens as we walk towards the Guggenheim museum, but the chirp of birds and natter of squirrels from the tree foliage are enough to neutralize it.

"Are you sure you can walk in those?" Hazel points to my kitten-heel pumps. "You've been hobbling since we left Grand Central."

I wanted to make an effort to look elegant for my trip to Manhattan. Well, it was Thom who suggested I make the effort. It was important that his wife look as polished as the spouses of his city colleagues.

But as the stiff leather rubs my skin raw, I'm longing for the comfort of my gardening shoes. The sky is lovely and blue today—perfect for an afternoon tending to my chrysanthemums.

"Have I?" I push my toes deeper into the shoes so the leather doesn't touch the flaming skin on my heels. "It must be these uneven sidewalks."

Hazel lets me off the hook. "I suppose it must be."

All the young women around me are teetering in those platform shoes everyone's been wearing lately, and I admire their daring, their confidence. Thom wouldn't approve of those; understated and chic is what he prefers. He wouldn't approve of Hazel's bright green clogs either, nor her loud-patterned kaftan. But he doesn't approve of much when it comes to Hazel.

Perhaps that should have been a warning sign.

We continue our stroll—or in my case, hobble—through the heart of the park, the first signs of autumn blushing the foliage.

It's not until Hazel yells at a stout man swerving his bike across our path that I realize I've heard nothing she's been telling me about her recent trip.

I glance at her, embarrassed. "I'm sorry, what did you say about Morocco?"

Hazel peers over her sunglasses. "Let's see, that depends on when you stopped listening, which I'd estimate was about ten minutes ago." She stops walking and puts her hand on my arm. "It's not like you to be an inattentive listener, Joy. What's going on?"

A contrite blush. "It's nothing, really. I'm sorry—I really want to hear about your trip. Keep going, please."

I try to keep walking, but Hazel keeps hold of my arm, guiding me to a nearby bench. I glance self-consciously at the young couple across from us, but they're caught up in their own private world for two. How I long for that feeling.

"Okay, spill it," Hazel says. "And don't even try to pretend it's nothing—we both know I can tell when you're lying, since it's such a rarity."

Hazel squeezes my hand, and I start to cry. This is not what I'd planned for my day trip to the city to see my friend.

It comes out as a whisper. "I think Thom is having an affair."

That Hazel isn't surprised should be another clue. Mercifully, she doesn't lord it over me; she squeezes my hand tighter, leaving silence for me to fill when I'm ready.

I focus on a frolicking squirrel to calm myself, its bushy tail swishing with curiosity. When I eventually summon the words, I say each one slowly, carefully, conscious of the gravity they hold.

"I'm not stupid," I say. "I've always known that he's had . . . dalliances on the side." An unfortunate affliction among many men of my generation—enjoying the moral halo of being in a long marriage while ignoring its very essence of commitment. And their wives, if they want to save face, have no choice but to turn a blind eye. "When he's working in his firm's Manhattan office, he often stays overnight, sometimes even weekends. And I've smelled perfume on him many times and found little notes in his jacket pockets. But I've always been able to overlook it until now, because I never knew who any of the women were."

Hazel can't help herself this time. "So he's succumbed to the age-old cliché of a man doing the deed with his secretary?"

I cringe at her vulgarity. Thankfully, the young couple are still oblivious to our presence.

"It's worse than that," I say ruefully. "I'm quite sure he's having an affair with the woman who lives across the back fence from us." Her name is bitter on my tongue, but I force myself to say it. "Celeste."

"And you're still trying to impress him?" Hazel scoffs. "Throw those torturous shoes in the garbage!" Then she softens, sliding her arm around me and pulling me in closer. "I'm sorry, Joy—I really am. How did you catch them?"

Anguish seeps through my veins as I recall the moment.

"Celeste and her husband, Ernie, host cocktail parties regularly, and we attend because it's the neighborly thing to do," I say through measured breaths. "At the last one, I noticed Celeste's cat was getting stressed with all the people inside the house, so I let it out into the yard—I've often seen it there in the past." Hazel nods, waiting for me to continue. "As I was about to close the door, I heard Thom's voice in the corner of the garden, so I walked to the side of the patio . . ." The shattering of my heart feels as fresh as it was in that moment. "And that's when I saw him with Celeste in the shadows, kissing."

The sound of her nervous giggle and the way her hand pressed into his chest are branded in my memory. Of all the women he could have pursued, he chose the one who lives closest to us. The one I've felt inferior to since long before this, for the ease with which she moves through the world, the way she always looks so effortlessly put together while exuding sophistication.

I assumed he would be merciful enough to have been more discreet.

Hazel tenses. "The bastard. Did you confront them?"

I look at her in horror.

"Of course I didn't," I say. "It was dark enough that they didn't see me, so I just quietly turned around and went back inside."

Hazel takes off her sunglasses. "Then please tell me that you said something once you got home."

I shake my head. "I haven't said anything."

"But you're going to leave him, right? That man has never deserved you."

I'm shocked she's suggesting this.

"I can't leave him," I say. "Elizabeth is only five years old—she needs her dad."

Hazel is unmoved. "Because he's such a sterling example of a good, honorable man? Or because he's such a present and attentive father figure?" Her sarcasm stings. "Joy, he's hardly ever home—you've said that many times—so what's the difference if you're not living with him? He can still see Elizabeth on weekends; if he's not off with that floozy across the fence, of course."

As my tears spill, Hazel squeezes me tighter.

"I'm sorry, that was insensitive of me," she says. "I know it's not as simple as that. You've built a life with him. I understand how it must seem impossible right now to walk away from that. But do you really want to spend the rest of your life with a man like him?"

I look up at her through my tears. "I haven't had a real job since my early twenties, and that was working for my dad," I sniff. "And I'm not a real piano teacher. What kind of job would I be able to get now as a forty-three-year-old woman with no professional experience? How would I support us?"

Hazel produces a handkerchief from the folds of her kaftan. She dabs a few of my tears, then hands it to me to take care of the rest.

"You can both come and live with me until you work things out," she says. "There would be more job opportunities for you in New York City, and I'm traveling all the time anyway, so you'll often have the place to yourselves."

"In Brooklyn?" I say. "That's a wonderful place for someone like you who enjoys the wilder side of life, but I want Elizabeth to grow up in a small town like we did. That was a great place to be a kid."

"It was a great place for *you* to be a kid," Hazel says. "I couldn't wait to get out. That's why I left as soon as I turned eighteen. How do you know Elizabeth isn't a city kid at heart? She's going to learn about the world sooner or later."

I know Hazel wants the best for me, but in this instance she just doesn't understand.

"It's best to keep the family intact for her sake," I say quietly.

Hazel sighs in resignation. "Even if you're unhappy?"

"Yes," I say. "If it comes to choosing between Elizabeth's happiness and security over mine, then I would choose hers in a heartbeat."

I don't want to say this to Hazel, but it's not just my daughter I'm thinking of—I've seen the way the world views unmarried and divorced women. A mother with two young kids and no husband moved to our block last year, and it pained me to see the way people treated her—like an odd sock no one knew what to do with. I tried my best to make her feel welcome, but she only stayed a few months. I think she moved to the city, probably in the hope of living somewhere more open-minded.

It makes more sense for me to be unhappy in a situation I know, than to be unhappy navigating one I don't.

We sit for a while, watching the tree boughs rise and fall with the breeze, as if inhaling and exhaling calm breaths.

"Well, at the very least, you should say something to Celeste," Hazel says. "Let her know that you're fully aware of the situation and to stay the hell away from your husband."

"I'll think about it," I say quietly.

But deep down both Hazel and I know that's never going to happen.

Instead, I'll put my chin up, pin on a smile, and pretend like everything's fine.

Just like I always do.

**23**

I'm a bundle of nerves as I pull the vegetarian lasagna out of the oven. Elizabeth and Finn will be here in a few minutes and I'm finally going to have to come clean about Hazel.

I've been telling myself that since Elizabeth is a nurse and sees terminally ill people all the time, it might be easier for her to accept. I have a feeling it's wishful thinking. You can't have a bond like she has with Hazel and not be devastated by the news that it will soon be severed.

I planned to do it before dinner—better to jump immediately from a high diving board than stand there and let the fear consume you— but I chickened out. Elizabeth worked a double shift today and I could see how tired she was. So then I decided to leave it until after dessert.

"Hey, Nanna," Finn says as we're clearing the empty lasagna plates. "Did you hear someone set off the fire alarm at the library the other day? They had to evacuate the entire place."

My pulse skitters. I search my grandson's face for signs he's testing me, that he knows something about my involvement. But all I see is his open, trusting smile.

"Did they now?" I say, shimmying slices of apple pie onto the plates with a spatula. "That must have created some excitement."

Elizabeth joins us in the kitchen with the empty lasagna dish.

"Those stupid kids probably didn't think about the taxpayers' money they wasted by having the fire department called."

Whoops, I hadn't even considered that. I'll have to make a donation to their Christmas fundraiser to make up for it.

Back at the dinner table, I wait until Elizabeth's dessert plate holds only crumbs before setting my fork down pointedly and clearing my throat.

"I'm afraid there's some quite upsetting news that I need to tell you both," I say, kneading the edges of the plate with my thumbs.

Elizabeth pauses dabbing her mouth with her napkin. "Mom, what is it? Are you sick?"

"No, I'm not." Thank goodness she's broached the topic, even if it's slightly off base. "But Hazel is." I allow a few seconds for the news to sink in. "She's been diagnosed with cancer."

"What?" Elizabeth straightens. "What kind of cancer?"

I'm embarrassed I don't know the specifics—a best friend should, right?

"She hasn't wanted to share the details, except that it's stage four."

"Stage *four*?" Elizabeth leans forward. "Mom, do you know what that even means? That it's metastatic—it's terminal." I watch the spread of red rising from her chest to her neck, as it always does when she's stressed.

"Yes, I did some research at the library last week about what the stages meant."

"Wait." Elizabeth shakes her head. "How long have you known about this?"

"A few weeks," I say contritely. "She told me after we all had dinner together."

The red now stains her face. "A few weeks? Why didn't you tell me? She might've only had that long to live!" She looks at me accusingly. "Is that why you've been going down to the city so often?"

Finn sits quietly beside her, studying his hands.

"I'm sorry, darling." A breath to modulate the tremble in my voice.

"I wanted to tell you sooner, but you always seemed so busy and exhausted and it didn't feel like the right time."

My daughter throws her hands up in exasperation. "There's never a right time! She probably thinks I don't care because I haven't called her."

Her chin wobbles, and for a moment it's like time has sprinted back decades and she's that sensitive five-year-old struggling to contain her big feelings. The one who would run into my lap for comfort.

Finn gently puts his hand on her back, rubbing in circles. At her son's touch, Elizabeth breaks into sobs.

"She doesn't think that, darling, I promise," I say, negotiating with my own tear ducts. "Hazel loves you so much."

As Elizabeth's shoulders shudder with sadness, Finn and I eye each other helplessly.

We both know there's no way through this moment, except to endure it.

**24**

It feels good to get my blood pumping.

When I woke up this morning, I didn't even have the chance to summon my daily gratitude. Last night's conversation with Elizabeth was lodged in my brain—in particular, the finality of it. I wasn't just trying to spare her the pain by not telling her sooner; I was trying to spare myself.

**You still aren't rid of me!**

Despite its reassurance that she's still alive, the dark humor of Hazel's morning text was hard to stomach. But I couldn't ask her to tone down something that's part of her very essence.

I reluctantly texted back with my own proof of life.

**Nor you me!**

I sank back onto my pillow in a funk, knowing I had to get out of the house before the cloud of depression consumed me again.

Zumba is my preference but there are no classes today, so I've had to settle for water aerobics. It's not my favorite physical activity, and not just because I feel self-conscious sliding into the pool in my swimsuit while surrounded by mostly youthful, fit, smooth-skinned people. (The only part of my body that could still be called smooth is the tip of my nose.) My aversion to water aerobics is mostly because I still can't quite shake the memory of when Lois Manning didn't make it out of the pool alive. One minute we were all waist-deep doing jumping jacks in not-quite unison and the next she was clutching her chest, a stunned look on her face. I'll never forget the image of her splayed on the side of the pool as our instructor administered CPR and everyone else looked on, horrified. It wasn't the most dignified way to leave the world—I didn't know her well, but I'm sure Lois would've liked to be wearing something less revealing when she took her final breath. She wasn't much younger than me, so it was a sobering reminder that we oldies need to consider those things whenever we do any kind of activity that gets the pulse racing. You never know which one's going to get you.

So as I tread water doing bicycle kicks alongside four other retirees in swim caps, I make sure to take it easy so my heart doesn't overwork. I have too many things going on in my life right now to be taking my final bow in this pool. Above all I need to stay alive for Hazel, but I, too, would prefer to be wearing something more flattering than my forest-green swimsuit with the generously ballooning fabric around my midsection when I do eventually go.

"Now, everyone float on your backs for flutter kicks," the instructor calls out to the group.

As I let my torso rise to the surface like a cork, I notice a familiar figure at the other end of the pool, standing on the starting blocks, about to dive in. Despite the water droplets clinging to my glasses—unfortunately, I need them to make sure I don't accidentally hit one of my classmates with my windmill arms—I'd recognize that bright pink neck-to-knees swimsuit and matching swim cap anywhere.

Rita.

She waves at me from across the pool, then executes a graceful dive. (It's a rare conversation with Rita when she doesn't slip in a mention of the fact that she was a champion diver in high school.) I pretend I haven't seen her—I'm just not in the mood to tolerate her today.

As soon as class is finished, I scoot into the locker rooms to gather my things so I can leave before running into Rita. I don't like getting undressed in there, anyway; I can feel the eyes of the younger women examining my body, fearing what's awaiting them in the future. It makes us all feel bad about ourselves. So I towel off as quickly as I can, and throw on my clothes over my bathing suit—I'll shower when I get home.

Of course my efforts were in vain. Just as I'm heading out the door, car keys ready in my palm, a flash of pink appears in front of me.

As I feared, Rita launches straight in.

"So, I saw you with our new neighbor the other day," she says glee-fully. "Never in my years would I have expected you to be fraternizing with a criminal, Joy."

I hug my bundled-up towel to my chest, indignant on Rowan's behalf.

"Rita, you need to stop spreading rumors about people without knowing the whole story," I say sharply. "Rowan is a lovely gentleman who's just trying to live a peaceful life in our neighborhood. He very kindly invited me to see a movie with him and it was a very pleasant afternoon."

She snorts. "He's already pulled the wool over your eyes, I see."

Rita is such a pot stirrer. The only reason I've stayed civil with her over the years is because I feel sorry for her—her only child died in a biking accident in his teens, and I suspect Rita's habit of sticking her nose in other people's business is a way to distract herself from her own pain.

"You should be spending more time with people your own age." Rita pats her palm to her chest and I dread what's coming. "I'm going to a crafting circle next week with some of the ladies from around town—the ones of our generation, not those young ones who are al-ways on their phones. You should come, Joy; there aren't many of us left. We should stick together."

In theory, she's right. Here I am complaining about having no friends left when, in truth, there are people my age who are actively seeking my company—they just happen to be the ones I consciously avoid. Crafting isn't my thing. Board games or even watercolor painting would be more enticing. But beggars can't be choosers—and once Hazel's gone, my social circle will be nonexistent.

"Thank you, Rita," I say, every word an effort. "I'd love to come along."

## 25

A harsh, gray midday light casts an unflattering lens on Hazel's neighborhood, spotlighting its blights—windows thick with grime, overstuffed trash cans regurgitating their contents onto the sidewalk, the faint smell of actual vomit plastered on the stained concrete.

A bleak setting befitting my downcast mood.

I'd be naive to think Hazel will be in better condition than when I last saw her. Terminal illness doesn't work that way. What can I talk to her about that isn't a depressing emphasis of all the things she can no longer do? Everything she loves—exploring unknown pockets of the city, sampling its different cuisines, bantering with strangers on the street—feels out of reach now.

I could ask her to tell me a story. Maybe the time when she got lost hiking alone in the rainforest of Belize, requiring a large search party. Or when she was charged by a rhino in Namibia. Or the months she spent as a life-drawing model in Sicily the year she turned seventy, standing naked on a podium for hours on end as strangers scrutinized every inch of her body in the name of art. Even recalling those memories myself eases my dread ever so slightly.

When I sneak into her building behind the UPS guy—glad to spare my friend the effort of buzzing me in—the strong scent of marijuana greets me in the stairwell. Not unusual for Brooklyn.

I knock tentatively on her door.

"It's open," her voice calls dreamily from inside.

The smell is even more intense when I open the door.

Hazel is reclined on the couch, a content smile on her face and a robust joint burning in her left hand.

"You're just in time," Hazel grins, waving the joint. "I'm enjoying the fruits of your labor—and I'd love for you to join me."

I loiter tentatively in the doorway. "Oh, Hazel, you know it's not my thing."

"I do know." Her grin now leans devious. "But won't you indulge me this once?"

"I'm not sure about that." I wheel my grocery caddy to the open-plan kitchen and start unloading things.

Hazel sucks on the joint, holding her breath for a few seconds before exhaling.

"And what if I told you," she says, each word punctuated by a dance of smoke, "that it was my dying wish?"

A puckish glint confirms she's joking, but I take the request seriously. If there's something I can do to cheer her up, I'm willing.

"I suppose I could try a bit." I pause my unpacking and cautiously join her on the couch.

She offers me the joint, but I don't take it.

"Can you show me how to do it?" I don't want to risk a coughing fit.

"With pleasure," Hazel says.

As I watch her demonstrate, it strikes me how at ease she is. It must really be helping with her pain.

"The trick," Hazel says, "is to relax and inhale slowly, but not too deeply. Let the smoke sail effortlessly into your lungs."

Gosh, what would Finn think of me right now? Perhaps he's already tried his first joint and would be pleased that I have too. That would make me a far more exciting grandma than one who does nothing but bake him treats and take him to the library.

I do as Hazel says, taking it between my pointer finger and thumb.

A cough still catches in my throat, but the overall experience is much more pleasant than I imagined.

I sit very still, auditing my senses for a noticeable change.

"What's supposed to happen?"

"You'll see," Hazel says, resting her head on the back of the couch. "Have one more hit."

I oblige, and this time my head starts to feel like there's a helium balloon attached to it. "Oh. This is quite nice."

I lean back next to her and marvel at the patterns in the exposed-brick wall.

"Remember the first time I tried to get you to smoke pot when we were sixteen?" she asks. "It's only taken me seventy-three years to finally convince you."

I smile involuntarily. "Well, it wasn't legal back then."

Even now, I still feel a bit naughty doing it. But what if I had defied my father and given in to Hazel back when we were sixteen? Perhaps my life would have turned out differently—at the very least, it would've been more interesting.

It might be the marijuana, but I somehow feel less inhibited.

I slowly shift my head sideways to look at Hazel. "Do you ever feel invisible?"

Hazel raises an eyebrow. "Two puffs and you're already gone!"

"I don't mean now," I say, though my limbs do feel pleasantly buoyant. "I mean, in life in general. It feels like once you get older—especially as a woman—the world has no place for you. Everyone overlooks you. Or if they do notice you, they pity you, assuming you aren't capable of anything."

Hazel removes some debris from her lip, considering my question.

"I can't say I've ever felt invisible," she says. "But that's because I made sure to take up space, even when no one was willing to give it to me."

"I've always admired the way you seize life." My words are coming out slower than I speak them. "You're so fearless and you really don't care about what anyone else thinks. It must be so freeing to live that way."

I rest my temple on Hazel's shoulder, trying not to notice how angular it's become.

She leans her head on mine. "Don't put me on a pedestal like that, Joy. There have been many times when I've been scared and second-guessed myself."

I shift my attention from the brick wall. "Really?"

"Of course," Hazel says. "You can't live a life like mine without making some spectacular mistakes. And there are a few things I would have done differently. Spontaneity isn't as whimsical as it first appears. Sometimes it's just stupidity."

I don't know how marijuana works, but I sure hope I remember this conversation.

"What would you have changed?"

Hazel reaches for the tarnished Zippo lighter on the end table; she flicks it several times to reignite the joint.

"I could have been gentler with certain people's hearts," she says, exhaling a controlled swirl of smoke. "I've wounded a lot of people over the years. Saying hurtful things when I could've held my tongue. Leaving without saying goodbye. When you're accountable to very few people, you develop a certain cruelness because you know you won't be around to face the consequences."

I know she can be brash and forthright but it's a harsh self-assessment.

"I don't believe you could ever be cruel, Hazel."

She frowns. "I'm not sure if Eric would have agreed with you."

Eric, her friend who made the vase—I always wondered if there was more to their story, but seeing her devastation when he died, I decided not to broach the topic. Some wounds are just too painful to be tended to.

But in my chemically altered state, I try. "What do you mean?"

Hazel sighs. "He and I were occasional lovers—just as I was with several of my male friends—but he ended up wanting more." She flicks the joint against the gilt ashtray. "One night I arrived at his apartment to find he'd created this entire romantic setting. Rose petals, champagne, dinner for two with his musician friend playing the violin—all those terrible clichés I loathe. And when he made his declaration, telling me he'd long been in love with me, I laughed." Regret creases her forehead. "Can you believe that? He'd made himself so vulnerable, and I just threw it in his face. In retrospect, I was caught off guard—I thought we had an understanding—and I didn't know how to handle this frank outpouring of affection. But I'll never forget the searing hurt in his eyes. We didn't speak for weeks afterwards. I kept telling myself that he just needed space, that there was plenty of time for us to repair our relationship. But then, a few months later, he was dead."

My heart aches for my friend, keeping this anguish to herself for so many years. And for poor Eric, who never had the chance to learn how important he was to Hazel, even if it wasn't in the romantic way he hoped.

"But his death wasn't your fault," I say without conviction. "I remember you saying that he'd always been reckless with drugs, just like many artists of that time."

It feels odd to be having this conversation while under the influence ourselves.

"Maybe," Hazel says glibly. "But the reason people often turn to drugs is because they're so sensitive and feel everything so keenly. They're desperate to dull that pain somehow. With Eric, it always felt as though his emotions were simmering just beneath his skin, so raw and electric. It made him wonderfully passionate, but also easy to wound. And I ended up just adding to his pain."

Suddenly I understand why she's spent so many years trying to get the vase back. I wish I'd been brave enough to talk to her about this when Eric died, but I'm not sure she would have opened up to me. The fact that she's sharing this information even now is surprising.

We sit in silence, the air rank with what we've been smoking.

It's such a rare occasion that Hazel lets her guard down that I feel like I need to make the most of this opportunity, in case it doesn't happen again. I work up the nerve to ask a question that's long pestered me.

"You know, I've always felt our friendship has been lopsided in a way," I say. "I'm so predictable and boring compared to you. What do you even get out of spending time with me? You must know so many more worldly and interesting people."

Hazel lifts her head to look me in the eye.

"A kite with a string that's not attached to anything might fly freely for a while, but it'll eventually get tangled up and destroyed," she says. "You keep me tethered and grounded, Joy. If I didn't have you to be accountable to, I'd have gone off the rails long ago. I certainly wouldn't have made it this far in life."

I've never looked at it that way.

"Your earnestness balanced out my cynicism," she continues. "And the fact that you so diligently sent me all those care packages over the years—finding a way to get them to me even when I was in the remotest of locations—meant so much to me, even if I didn't express that to you as well as I should have. They reminded me that I was cherished, that I was on someone's mind." Hazel pats my leg. "The truth is, I need you as much as you need me."

I settle back on the sofa, touched by her answer. But now it's left me with another question.

If we both need each other, what happens when only one of us is left?

# 26



've got red!" Elizabeth yells as she snatches a plastic pawn from the Sorry! board game box.

Neither Thom nor I would have argued; we always let our daughter choose her color first. What's interesting is that, unlike us—Thom favors blue, while I love the cheerful yellow—Elizabeth's color preference varies week to week. All part of the caprice of being sixteen, I suppose.

We're just happy that she inherited our passion, and that she's still willing to sit down and play with us. Thom and I are fierce board game rivals—we always have been. In the months after we were married and were cohabitating for the first time, it took us a while to find our rhythm. He was used to living alone, and I was accustomed to occupying myself in the evenings with a book, since my father usually retired to his study. Being social with someone after dinner was a new muscle both Thom and I needed to strengthen.

One evening, as we sat on the sofa next to each other making stilted small talk about something on the television, I took a chance.

"Would you like to play gin rummy?"

Thom turned to me, surprised. "You like card games?"

"Of course! I used to play with our neighbor in Wisconsin, Mrs.

Branxholm, when I was a young girl." His quizzical expression made me second-guess myself—were card or board games not a ladylike thing to partake in? Or perhaps he just thought they were immature? "Do you . . . not enjoy them?"

He broke into that wholesome smile I'd been growing so fond of.

"Actually, I love them," he said. "Used to play them with my mom, in fact."

Suddenly, it felt as if the stiffness of a new relationship had finally given way to comfort, the way a new shoe does after you've worn it long enough.

After that, we'd spend many of our evenings competing with each other over the toss of a card or the roll of a dice, bringing a spark to our marriage that we hadn't managed to find up until that point. We preferred backgammon, but when Elizabeth came along, we needed games for more than two players.

Fortunately, even as a teenager, she still deigns to play with us once in a while. Though even that's hard to schedule these days, since Thom's work keeps him overnight in the city more frequently.

We're about twenty minutes into our first game of Sorry!, with Thom in the lead and Elizabeth close behind, when he lands on the same square as her piece, sending it back to the start.

He grins gleefully as he excises her red pawn from the square.

"Don't worry, Dad," she says, elbowing him playfully. "You're gonna pay for that eventually." She does tend to hold grudges over these things.

He laughs, then leans over to kiss her cheek.

I'm about to pick up a card for my turn when the phone rings.

Elizabeth shoots out of her chair. "I'll get it!"

Thom and I exchange amused glances as she dashes into the kitchen. Ever since she started high school, Elizabeth has protected that phone as fiercely as a sentinel; if a boy happens to be calling, she likely doesn't want to risk either of us speaking to him first. While I would be perfectly polite to any potential suitors—I respect my daughter's independence and privacy—Thom would be a touch more taciturn, if only for his own entertainment.

After a muffled exchange with the caller, Elizabeth slumps back into the dining room.

"It's for you, Dad," she says, sliding back into her chair with an eye roll. "She said she's your assistant."

Thom swiftly stands. "I'll just be a minute or two."

Elizabeth sighs, her playfulness from moments earlier completely evaporated. Perhaps she was hoping someone in particular would be calling for her.

She motions at the cards in the middle of the board. "Well? Aren't you going to take your turn?"

How quickly the tides change with teenagers—she's gone from sunny to surly in a matter of minutes.

I smile calmly, used to weathering these shifts.

"I'll wait until your father gets back," I say. "He said he wouldn't be long."

She rolls her eyes again. "What does an assistant need at eight thirty on a Sunday night?"

"She's probably just preparing for the week ahead," I say, to persuade myself as much as Elizabeth. "It's very diligent of her."

Elizabeth's expression is unreadable. "Right. So diligent."

Thom reappears. "Sorry about that—some work stuff that needed taking care of." He takes his seat. "Is it time for you to exact your revenge on me, kiddo?"

As he reaches out to ruffle Elizabeth's hair, she dodges his hand, annoyed. "No. It's Mom's turn."

Thom retracts his hand, sheepishly. "Okay, then."

"Don't count me out," I say, rubbing my palms together for luck. "I feel a comeback is in the cards for me."

Soon enough the game is back in full swing and we can all pretend we're a happy family.

At least for tonight.

**27**

D oes Hazel like peppermint tea or Darjeeling?"

Finn is standing in the supermarket aisle holding up two boxes.

"Peppermint is better for her nausea," I say. "Let's get two boxes."

I've enlisted Finn to help me with getting all the groceries for my next trip to Hazel's. He suggested we order them online, but I still don't quite trust buying anything on the internet. And who knows when they would arrive? I wouldn't want Hazel to have to answer the door or, worse, lug everything upstairs if they only deliver them to her building's entrance. In any case, doing the shopping myself makes me feel more useful.

I steer the cart into the baking aisle, trying not to think about how much all this will cost. And then I freeze.

Celeste is at the other end of the aisle, perusing the flour.

Finn puts his hands on the cart. "Why are we stopped?"

Fortunately, his back is to Celeste.

"Oh," I say, scrambling for a diversion. "We need to get another pint of ice cream so Hazel can keep extra in her freezer. Would you be a dear and run and get one, please?"

Finn shrugs good-naturedly. "Sure. Chocolate, right?"

"Yes, please."

As soon as he jogs off, I back the cart out of the baking aisle and into the canned-goods section two aisles over, where someone has painstakingly built a pyramid of the cannellini beans on sale.

How many times have I had to avoid Celeste over the past forty-plus years? Too many. In a town of thirteen thousand inhabitants, you can't help regularly crossing paths with certain people.

Worst of all, no matter how much time has passed, I still feel a ripple of shame whenever I see her. Logically, I know I've done nothing wrong. But when you've been cheated on, it's hard not to blame yourself. Or at least question what you might have done differently. I'd been able to overlook Thom's other indiscretions because they never had a face, or even a name. But Celeste was right there, every day, through my back window. She became the painful symbol—and constant reminder—of the thing that, for years, I'd managed to stay numb to.

I don't know how long her relationship with Thom carried on after I saw them. But from that night onwards, there was a palpable tension whenever the three of us were in a room together—at a neighborhood cocktail party, at church. Thom and Celeste rarely interacted, and when they did, it was stilted and forced, as if they were hiding something.

What if I had confronted Thom about his affairs? Would things have turned out differently? Would he have admitted his infidelity and pledged to never let it happen again, rededicating himself to his family? Or would he have dared me to leave him if it bothered me so much? A braver woman would have taken the chance and found out. It wasn't just because I was afraid of being on my own and having to raise Elizabeth as a single mother that I kept silent. It was also the fear that if I demanded that Thom give up his mistresses and he refused, what would it say about me?

Hazel insists Thom's infidelity was all about his own issues, not mine. But how can I not take it personally? My husband, the man I devoted my life to, found my company to be wanting. Could I have been more attentive? Taken better care of myself? Spent less time in the garden and more with him? Should I have been more sexually adventurous? More confident in my body? Funnier? More intelligent? I know it's futile to ask myself these questions, and yet it's impossible not to. Each time I run into Celeste now—even though Thom is long gone—those questions resurface, scratching away at me like the tag on a piece of clothing. Persistent, uncomfortable, grating.

Suddenly the supermarket aisle feels like it's closing in on me. I need to get away from here—from Celeste, from this unforgiving lighting, and from the cloying pop song playing on the loudspeaker.

But I have to wait for Finn.

Since I can't flee this terrible feeling, I need to find a way to mute it, just as I did at the library the other day.

So with the slightest of nudges, I use my elbow to ease a can of beans out from the pyramid display.

Instantly, the formation crumbles, sending an avalanche of canned legumes tumbling over the floor, narrowly missing an attendant pricing pasta on the other side of the shelf.

Whoops, I should have checked for potential casualties first. Fortunately, he's unharmed—and the chaos that ensues is tremendously satisfying. One of the cans has, regrettably, burst open, creating an awful mess for someone to clean up. But like I said, mischief comes with collateral damage.

The man with the pricing gun hurries over to me.

"Are you okay, ma'am?"

I put my palms to my chest, feigning shock. "Oh gracious me, that gave me a fright! I hope it wasn't me who accidentally bumped it. I'm getting a little clumsy in my old age."

An undignified yet necessary lie.

He guides me away from the graveyard of dented cans.

"Not at all, ma'am. To be honest, I think that pyramid was against health and safety guidelines, anyway. It was an accident waiting to happen." He pauses, eyes wide, realizing what he's just said. "But please don't sue us—I don't want to lose my job for telling you that."

I wink at him. "It'll be our secret." Despite my recently questionable ethics, I'd never sue for something I instigated.

Finn appears beside me, ice cream in hand. "Nanna, what happened?"

"You've missed some excitement," I say. "That pyramid of beans toppled over out of nowhere."

"Seriously?"

For a second, I think I detect a flash of doubt in Finn's face. It reminds me I need to be careful about misbehaving around him.

Grocery store employees descend on the scene with brooms and mops, shooing curious customers away.

"We should get out of their way," I say to Finn.

I direct my cart towards the cash register farthest from where I last saw Celeste. Of course she'll want to stick her nose into the commotion.

It's not until we're out in the parking lot that I realize we forgot peanut butter, one of the few things I know Hazel can still stomach.

"Finn, darling," I say. "Would you mind running back inside to get two jars of peanut butter?" I fish twenty dollars out of my purse for him. "Creamy, no added salt or sugar, please."

"Sure thing," Finn says, stuffing the twenty in his pocket and loping back to the store. As I watch him walk, it hits me just how lanky his limbs are now. Soon enough he'll grow into them and into adulthood, and then he won't be interested in hanging out with me anymore.

Thankfully, he's not here to watch me looking around aimlessly as I try to remember where we parked the car. Oh, don't go thinking that it's anything to do with my old age that I can't remember—I've long had a tendency to forget where my car is parked. But any time your memory stutters when you're elderly, people try to pin it on a deteriorating mind or dementia. Really, I'm just bad with directions.

After a few moments scanning the parking lot, I see my Suzuki Swift glistening in the afternoon sun and push my shopping cart towards it. I'm about halfway there when I recognize another car: Celeste's Mini Cooper.

The sight of her vehicle—all cute and shiny, just like her—sends my shame rearing again, and I'm compelled by an inclination that, just one month ago, would've been horrifying to me.

Today, however, it feels perfectly natural.

On my way past Celeste's vehicle, I "accidentally" lose control of my shopping cart, sending it veering directly into the side of the car. It leaves a small, but satisfying, dent.

"Oh dear!" I exclaim, in case anybody happens to be watching.

When no one reacts—the only person who might is a young mother busy wrangling her three kids into their car seats—I retrieve my cart and continue on to my Suzuki.

I don't even leave a note.

**28**

'm lurking in the parking lot of the hospital in Newburgh, the town just across the Hudson River from Beacon, waiting for Elizabeth.

I wonder what it's like for her to work in the same hospital where her father died. It's hard enough for me just standing outside it, the proximity to a memory I try my best not to relive.

I text her that I'm here. Finn left his calculator at my place yesterday and I wanted to return it as soon as possible in case he needed it. I didn't dare bring it to him directly at school—I don't want to give his peers something else to bully him about. A visit from your grandmother during your lunch break is socially unacceptable, no matter how much you love her.

Elizabeth told me where she had parked and said she'd meet me there—perhaps it's also socially unacceptable for your mother to visit you at work. As I stand next to her little hatchback, I can't help peering through the windows at how messy it is—old takeout bags, crumpled clothing, and a half-open bag of sunflower seeds that have populated every possible crevice.

I'm not surprised. The last time I visited her apartment, the living room was in a similar state of disarray. Elizabeth has never been the tidiest person, perhaps because I always picked up after her. Not that I minded doing that—it felt like a way to take care of her and Thom, keeping their living spaces and clothes clean. It's not like I had much else to do. When my piano kids used to remark how neat and tidy my house was, I couldn't help imagining the states of their own domestic environments—visual chaos on top of the emotional chaos many of them lived with.

I'd be more than happy to spend an afternoon cleaning out Elizabeth's car, but I wouldn't dare suggest it. Once, when I offered to come by her apartment occasionally to do the laundry and tidy things up, she almost bit my head off. Perhaps she felt I was encroaching on her independence then too, but I just knew how busy she was at work and that she likely couldn't afford a cleaner to come.

I recognize my daughter's distinct gait from across the parking lot. It's the same as her father's—a little extra bounce in the toes that appears misleadingly cheerful. As she comes into focus, the forward slump of her shoulders and weary expression in her face tell a more accurate tale.

She lets me hug her; that's something.

"Thanks for bringing this," she says, accepting the calculator. "Finn's got a big test next week—calculus or something—and he'll need it for sure. I would've come by and picked it up after work tonight but I have something on until late."

"It's no problem at all," I say. "You're the busiest one of the two of us, so I'm happy to work around you. And it's a treat to get to see you, even briefly!"

She pulls her hair out of its messy low bun, holding the black band between her teeth while she reassembles the strands into a smoother iteration.

"Any updates on Hazel?" Her words are squashed by her clenched jaw.

"She was in good spirits when I visited her a few days ago," I say, omitting the reason why she was in good spirits. I will certainly not be telling my daughter about my recent foray into smoking pot, even if the conversation did allow a closeness and frankness that I don't often get with Hazel. "Though I suspect she's barely been eating."

Elizabeth nods. "That's usually how these things go. I called her after you told me the news and, of course, she acted like it was no big deal, in typical Hazel fashion." The hint of her smile is a balm.

"It wouldn't be her otherwise," I say.

Elizabeth refastens the band around her hair. "I have a Sunday off work in two weeks," she says. "Maybe we could all drive down to visit her? I want to make sure Finn and I get to see her at least one more time."

I fail to hide my surprise. "That's a wonderful idea—she'd love that."

"Great." Elizabeth glances at her watch. "I've got to get back inside for a staff meeting, but I'll call you tomorrow."

"Of course," I say. "And I'll phone Hazel to let her know this afternoon." Better to lock it in before Elizabeth changes her mind; she wouldn't disappoint Hazel.

I try to get Hazel on speakerphone while I'm waiting for the traffic lights to change. It's such a lovely day that I lower all the windows to enjoy the fresh air. When she picks up, I decide last minute to turn off at the intersection and take the long route home, so we have longer to chat.

Her monotone greeting dampens my upbeat mood. "Hello, Joy."

"What are you doing two Sundays from now?" I say, overcompensating with exuberance.

Hazel's voice lifts slightly. "Well, it sounds like you're about to tell me."

"Elizabeth and Finn and I are coming down to see you! And I'll be there again before that, of course."

Now there's an obvious cheer in her tone. "Lucky me," she says. "I've just had a rather arduous visit to the doctor and that news has certainly brightened my day."

If only I could help her hold onto that brightness somehow.

I scan the empty road ahead of me, searching for something interesting to entertain her—an animal, a funny billboard—and then I notice the speed limit sign.

I try to drive a few miles under the limit at all times, in case I need to stop suddenly. In fact, people told me I drove like a grandma long before I officially was one. But what would Hazel do?

I press my foot a touch harder onto the accelerator. Then a bit more. The engine surges in appreciation.

Thirty-five.

Forty.

Hazel's voice calls from my phone. "Joy? Are you still there?"

"Guess what I'm doing!" I yell over the noise of the wind through the windows. "I'm driving ten, no, fifteen miles over the speed limit!"

It elicits exactly the response I'd hoped. "Wooooooooo! Go, Joy!" Hazel yells. "Go faster!"

My limbs are giddy. I check my rearview mirror for the inevitable flash of blue and red lights.

Nothing.

Fortified by Hazel's boisterous cheers, I press down on the pedal until the speedometer nudges to fifty-five, intensifying my high.

It feels incredible—why have I waited my whole life to do it?

## 29

BEACON, 1993

My heart lifts as the loudspeaker announces the arrival of the train from Manhattan.

When Elizabeth had told me she was planning to spend her college spring break with Hazel in Brooklyn instead of coming home to Beacon, I strove to mask my disappointment. I've missed her so much since she's been away at nursing school, even if it's only a few hours from here. And I wish she'd at least stayed for lunch when she dropped her car at our place before taking the train to the city. But she's twenty years old now and free to do as she pleases. At least she agreed to spend the weekend with us before she returns to campus.

At first I don't realize it's her walking towards me on the platform. She's wearing a colorful dress I've never seen on her. In high school, she wore jeans and a sweatshirt almost every day and I'd assumed we were alike in choosing comfort over style. But this dress is bright and eye-catching.

In fact, it's something Hazel would wear.

And then there's Elizabeth's hair. Her natural light brunette tone, which we also share, has been replaced with a peroxide blond. All told, it feels like there's a completely different woman standing in front of me.

But she looks happy.

"Hi, Mom!" She does a little twirl to show off her outfit. "What do you think?"

I choose my words carefully. I've learned that, with daughters, what you might think is a harmless observation can often be interpreted as a criticism. "It's very . . . modern!"

"I know," Elizabeth says gleefully. "Hazel took me shopping and I decided to try something new." She pulls me into an excited hug, tranquilizing my bewilderment.

"I'm sure that was an adventure." I'm a touch envious that I didn't get to join that shopping expedition. "And your hair—it's so . . . striking!"

Elizabeth twirls a strand around her finger. "It is, right?" She rolls her eyes. "Dad's going to hate it, and Jack too, but I figured it's my hair and I can do what I want. They'll just have to learn to deal with it."

She's right about Thom. I can just imagine the expression on his face when he sees her—modest and refined is what he prefers. And Jack, Elizabeth's high school boyfriend, who's studying dentistry at the same college as her, strikes me as a more traditional kind of guy too. Thom and I like that about him—he's very calm and studious but still very charismatic. A great potential husband.

And yet I admire Elizabeth's attitude—that it's her choice, not theirs. I don't think there's a single time I've gotten dressed for a fancy outing without worrying about whether Thom will approve of what I've chosen. In fact, sometimes he even chooses himself, buying me dresses and jewelry that, in truth, don't feel like me, but I don't like to be ungrateful. I'm glad Elizabeth doesn't feel the same burden—one positive aspect of Hazel that's rubbed off on her.

"I'm sure Jack will love you regardless of your hair color," I say. "He obviously adores you, since he followed you to the same college just so you didn't have to do long-distance."

Elizabeth frowns. "I don't know. After talking about it with Hazel this week, I've been wondering if I should break up with him—he's so regimented. And predictable. He's never going to want to live in a big city or even abroad like I do." She digs through her purse until she locates her lip gloss. "And I want to know what it's like to feel a romantic spark that drives you wild."

Did Hazel really suggest that? I'm not sure she should be the one giving my daughter relationship advice. Though Hazel has had many partners, to my knowledge none of them have ever lasted more than a few months. She loathes being tied down.

I proceed cautiously, not wanting to obviously contradict whatever my friend has told her.

"It's only natural to wonder what else is out there." That much I have to admit, otherwise I'd be a hypocrite. "But predictable can be a good thing, especially if you want to start a family one day. A romantic spark doesn't always mean dependability or security for your family."

Elizabeth shrugs noncommittally. "Maybe."

I decide to leave it at that for now. Perhaps these doubts are just the natural impulsivity of being a young woman.

"What else did you do with Hazel?" I ask as we get into my car.

"God, so many cool things." I haven't seen her this lively since she was a kid and we took her to an animal petting zoo. "We saw this amazing show at MoMA by Philip-Lorca diCorcia, a photographer Hazel knows. And we ate some great dinners at these little hole-in-the-wall places you'd never find unless you're tapped in like she is." In other words, places I would never know about. "Oh, and yesterday we went to a protest."

My hands tense on the steering wheel.

"A protest?" Thom would definitely not approve of that. "What was it for?"

Elizabeth pulls down the sun visor to apply her lip gloss. "Abortion rights," she says, as if it were obvious.

This has been an especially topical issue since a big Supreme Court case last year, though I'll admit I didn't pay as close attention as I should have.

"I thought the Supreme Court ruling upheld the original decision from 1973?"

There's impatience in Elizabeth's sigh. "It did, but it gave more leeway for the states to regulate, which sucks."

"I see." I search for something to say that won't make me seem out of touch. "Well, I know that Hazel is very passionate about that cause."

My mind immediately goes to that lunch with Hazel on the Upper East Side all those years ago, when she revealed the reason for her trip to Puerto Rico. I'm ashamed to admit that I felt quite a lot of resentment towards her in the months afterwards, not because I disapproved of what she did—I've always believed that women have the right to make choices about their own bodies—but because she was able to get pregnant at all when I'd been struggling for so long. I was secretly glad that Hazel ended up spending most of that year in Chile so I had time to work through my negative feelings towards her. I'm sure she noticed that my care packages to her were much less frequent during that time.

Thankfully, Elizabeth came along not long after, and the resentment dissolved.

"It's probably best you don't mention the protest to your father," I say. "You know how he worries about your safety."

It's believable, even if it's not the real reason.

The hair and dress are already evidence enough of Hazel's influence on Elizabeth, an influence I know Thom won't approve of. But in truth, Thom isn't the only one.

Do I really want my daughter following such a wild example?

# 30

No matter how many times I punch the numbers into the calculator, its screen tells me the same thing: I don't have enough money to take my car to the mechanic. It's been sporadically making a clanking noise for the past few months that I've been ignoring, hoping it would work itself out on its own. But after my speeding escapade yesterday, the clanking sound has become constant and I'm too scared to drive it.

The money I've spent on train tickets and groceries for Hazel is partially why I'm more strapped than usual. I know she'd offer me money in a heartbeat if I mentioned it to her, but I don't want her to feel like a burden. The local music store also called me last week about a used electric piano that would be perfect for Sunny, and there's no way I could pass that up, even if it meant depleting my meager emergency fund.

But now I'm wishing I'd gotten Thom to teach me about managing our finances, instead of burying my head in the sand and letting him take care of everything. I've considered attending one of those free financial literacy classes at the library, but I'm too embarrassed to admit that I need one. How did Hazel manage all these things herself? What will I do if Elizabeth needs help with money and I have nothing to give her? I just pray that the leak in the roof above my bedroom doesn't get any worse. We get some pretty intense rainstorms in summer, and so far I've been able to get by catching the water in a bucket, but if the leak gets any bigger, I'm in trouble. And then there's the rotting floorboards on the porch—I hope they hold on a few more years before collapsing.

I might have to start selling my possessions, after all, instead of giving them away on the street. But is any of it even valuable? I already pawned all my jewelry—except my wedding ring—a few years ago, when my ancient refrigerator finally gave up the ghost.

A small seed of panic plants itself in my chest.

I abandon my calculations and step out onto the porch for some air. It's thick with the smell of freshly cut grass, which tends to aggravate my allergies. I'm about to take refuge back inside when a robin flies down to rest on the bird feeder, his little belly a lovely rusty red. It's as if he's come especially to cheer me up.

But then the sound of barking sends him quickly back into the sky.

I scan the neighborhood, annoyed, until I see who was responsible for the bark: little Hettie and Rowan are out for a walk. I wave in their direction, pondering whether our neighborly relationship is too new to ask for favors.

Rowan stops at the garden gate, lifting Hettie up so she can see me.

"Hello, Joy!" He wiggles her paw in a wave. "Out here enjoying the sunshine?"

I wave back to Hettie. "Actually, I'm out here trying to decide my best course of action. I'm in a bit of a pickle."

"A pickle, huh?"

"Yes, my car has been making a funny noise," I say, coming down the steps. "I'm not sure if it's safe to keep driving it." I glance nervously down at the path of mossy cobblestones. "I don't suppose you could take a look and see if you think I can? I've seen you tinkering away at your vehicle, so I suspect your knowledge is far better than mine."

"It'd be my pleasure." Rowan reaches to flick the gate clasp open. "I can take a look now if it's convenient?"

"That would be wonderful, thank you!"

Ten minutes later I'm in the driver's seat, Hettie on my lap, while Rowan inspects the engine. I turn on the ignition as instructed.

"Looks like your alternator bracket is broken," Rowan calls out from under the hood. "I should be able to fix that for you—I'll just need to get the part."

My heart sinks. "Will that be expensive?" I look down at Hettie, embarrassed. "I'm on quite a tight budget these days."

I'm surprised at myself, revealing that vulnerability. I've never mentioned my money troubles to anyone—not even Hazel and especially not Elizabeth. That would go against my parents' credo of not saddling others with your troubles.

Rowan appears next to the open car window. "I'm pretty sure I've got some extras lying around, so you won't have to pay anything at all."

I squeeze Hettie tight. "That's so kind of you, thank you. But at least let me pay you for the labor—I don't have too much but I'd like to pay something." Though it might be more insulting to pay him twenty dollars than not pay him at all.

"Unfortunately, I don't accept cash," he says solemnly. "My only accepted methods of payment are baked goods or homegrown vegetables."

What a treasure he is.

"Well, in that regard, I'm quite flush," I say with a grateful smile. "Would you like to come in for some coffee and cookies right now?"

Rowan reaches through the window and boops Hettie's nose. "We'd love to."

He walks around to shut the hood, then follows Hettie and me inside.

"I can't promise my coffee will be as good as at the café," I say, leading him to the kitchen. "But I'll do my best."

Rowan laughs. "You forget I endured years of prison coffee," he says. "I'm sure yours will outshine that by far."

I like how easily he speaks about his time behind bars with me, like I'm a trusted confidant.

After washing his hands, Rowan sits at the kitchen table.

"I just baked some snickerdoodles this morning," I say, opening the container of cookies and inhaling their still-warm scent.

"It's my lucky day, then." Rowan says.

I peruse the coffee cups on the shelf, contemplating which to give him. I like to be intentional about my choice for each individual, taking into account both their aesthetic tastes and their hand size. I've never given anyone Thom's khaki-green mug, I suppose out of sentimentality. But perhaps it's time things changed.

I extract it from its cohort of cups and place it next to my sunflower mug.

I put two cookies on a plate in front of him, then bend down to give Hettie a carrot.

"I don't have any dog treats, I'm afraid."

"No problem," Rowan says. "She loves her veggies."

He laughs as Hettie delicately accepts the carrot and then scurries under the table to eat it.

Rowan breaks his cookie in half. "How's your friend Hazel doing?"

I'm touched he's asking.

"It's hard to know," I say. "She's so independent and never really lets others take care of her, so I can't tell what she needs." I pour some milk in a small jug and put it next to the sugar bowl. "I want to be useful to her but she pretends she doesn't need anything, even though she's obviously in pain and not doing well. She doesn't want to discuss her prognosis at all. And from what I gather, she's refused all treatment."

Rowan nods his head. "It's a helpless feeling, when someone you love is suffering."

His expression tells me he knows the pain intimately.

"Was it like that with your mother?"

"Yes," he says, squinting up through the window at the cheerful blue sky, a contradiction to our melancholy conversation. "She spent so long having to look after herself—especially when my dad went to prison and she essentially became a single mom to my sister and me—that she couldn't let anyone else do it. I could never tell if she was hurting or upset, because she kept up such a stoic front all the time, even at the end when she was gravely ill."

"I'm afraid that's what the women of our generation were taught," I say. "We're told to keep our chins up and smile, no matter what we're feeling on the inside."

I stare at the deep lines etched into my palms like riverbeds.

"You know, at first with my mom, I was determined to help her in the way I thought was best," Rowan says. "But I finally realized that it wasn't for me to decide. It was up to her how she wanted to navigate her final months, and I needed to respect that, even if I thought she should do it differently. The only thing I could do was walk beside her through all of it. Hazel might be working through it in her own way."

"I suppose you're right," I say, heart heavy. "I just want her to know how much I care about her."

Rowan nods again. "I get that. My mother and I weren't ever very open with our emotions. I could tell she was embarrassed when I tried to express them. So I decided to write her a letter thanking her for everything she'd done for me and telling her how much I love her—and that I appreciate her for loving me in spite of all my missteps in life. That way she could read it in her own time when she was in the right headspace. And she could also read it over and over—so, in a way, I was with her even when I couldn't be."

"That's a good idea," I say, relieved to have a concrete plan of action. If I tried to tell Hazel all the things I love about her, she'd just brush me off for being sentimental.

"The most helpful thing someone ever said to me about having a dying loved one," Rowan continues, "is not to treat them like someone you're waiting to lose; treat them like the person they've always been to you. Otherwise it's just a tragic waste of the time they have left."

In theory, what he's saying makes sense.

It's much harder in practice.

**31**

Hazel insists on making our cups of peppermint tea when I arrive at her place the next day.

I acquiesce, sitting obediently as she labors over a task that should be a breeze—lifting the kettle to fill it with water, tearing open the teabag packaging. As I mentally catalogue the many ways she now appears to be a ghost of herself, one thing is most depressing. Ever since she moved to New York City at age eighteen, Hazel has had a mane of bright red hair. It's been such a long time since I saw her with her natural ash blond that I'd almost convinced myself she was a natural redhead. Even into our eighties, Hazel maintained her fiery locks without a strand of gray.

Today, however, there's a telltale swath of white hair striping the middle of her scalp. On anyone else, a little regrowth would be nothing to worry about—a question of no spare time or perhaps a tight budget. On Hazel, it's a sure sign she's not doing well. Even the time she was briefly held in a Russian jail for having the wrong visa, she kept her roots concealed by sweet-talking one of the guards into finagling her some hair dye.

I want to ask what the doctors are doing for her pain and whether she's able to keep down any of the food I made her. But Rowan's advice nags at me.

*Don't treat her like someone you're waiting to lose. Treat her like the friend she's always been.*

I sit on my hands, suppressing the urge to rush and help when Hazel brings me my cup, the golden liquid sloshing over the edge like the ocean invading a boat in a storm. I wait until her back is turned to mop up the drips with the clean handkerchief in my pocket.

What can I do to make her feel like things are normal when they clearly aren't?

I look around the eclectic decor of her loft for ideas. Hazel isn't a fan of board games (too tedious, in her opinion), and I wouldn't dare suggest reading books side by side. She thinks it's antisocial; I think reading a book beside someone you care about is one of the loveliest feelings. There's such intimacy in that shared silence.

I study the large artwork hanging on the wall, a chaos of paint splashes and splotches in contrasting colors. I've stared at this painting hundreds of times and still haven't been able to make sense of it, but I know Hazel adores it. And it gives me an idea.

"Would you like to go on a little excursion to the Brooklyn Museum? I saw a poster for the new exhibition on the subway."

I should've said it before Hazel laboriously lowered herself into the wicker armchair. It'll take double the effort for her to get out of it again, and I know she'll refuse my assistance.

"That's a fabulous idea," Hazel says, a fleeting sparkle in her eyes. "And we can stop by that sublime ice cream place on Vanderbilt afterwards."

The ice cream place is about a fifteen-minute walk from the museum—one we've done many times—but even the journey from the kitchen to the sofa has left Hazel exhausted. I'll just make up an excuse about my feet being tired and needing to take a taxi.

"I'd love that."

I sip nervously on my lukewarm tea. I'm glad my suggestion has cheered her up, but I'm worried it's going to end up being a bad idea. That it'll make her feel worse than she already does. But she's so enthused I can't take it back.

I wait until she gathers her bag and signature oversized sunglasses and dons a glamorous headscarf to mask her glaring regrowth.

It's not until she's buckling her sandals that I recognize something's wrong. She stays bent over like a horseshoe, hands resting on her knees. Her left hand reaches out blindly, searching for something to steady her.

"Hazel?"

I take her hand, my joints cracking as I squat beside her.

Hazel waves her hand. "I'm fine, I'm fine." She's trying to convince herself as much as me. "Just a pesky wave of nausea. I get them at the most inconvenient times."

"Maybe you just need to sit for a minute before we go out." Why did I suggest this stupid excursion? "I'll get you some water."

Hazel doesn't let go of my hand.

"Actually," she whispers. "Can you help me to the bathroom?"

"Of course." I drape her arm across my shoulders and put mine around her waist. As well as being almost a foot taller than me, she's also, historically, much sturdier. And yet I can support her weight with little effort. It's like she's been divided in half.

We reach the bathroom just in time for her to throw up. I position a rolled towel under her knees as she heaves over the toilet bowl. Then I gently rake my fingers through her red strands, restraining them for as long as she needs, softly rubbing her back with my other palm.

When the nausea relents, Hazel sits on the bathroom tiles and looks at me forlornly.

"I suppose it's not a good idea to go out, after all."

I run a facecloth under warm water and hand it to her.

"It's supposed to rain, anyway," I say. "And we've got ice cream in your freezer now."

This time she doesn't resist when I try to help her up. We inch slowly into her bedroom and ease her onto the bed so she can lie down. I'm about to leave her to rest when I hear her voice.

"Joy?"

I turn to face her.

She wearily pats the duvet. "Come lie with me."

Blinking back the sting of tears, I oblige, lying down beside her, the two of us staring up at the ceiling.

"We haven't done this since we were teenagers," I remark softly.

Hazel used to come over to my place after school sometimes, before my dad got home. We'd lie on my bed for hours, just chatting, until it was time for me to make his dinner.

"We should've done it more often," Hazel replies, in an uncharacteristic lament.

Sensing my opportunity, I take a chance, turning my head on the pillow to look at her. "Are you scared?"

Hazel keeps her gaze on the ceiling, but her forehead creases.

"I don't think so. But then I've never let much scare me, so I certainly won't let death be the first." She finally meets my eyes. "I would say I feel . . . inconvenienced."

"How so?"

"Well, I've enjoyed my life—I think I've lived a great one—and I wouldn't mind living more of it," she says, directing her focus back to the ceiling. "But to be told that my time is almost up, well, it gets in the way of my plans. And that is inconvenient."

We lie wordlessly for a while.

"Of course, I'm grateful that we've made it this far," Hazel eventually continues. "And I'm fortunate not to have many regrets."

I envy her for that.

"You've squeezed a lot out of your years," I say. "Much more than me."

"Perhaps that's true," she says, pensively. "But living life untethered to anyone or anything also has its drawbacks."

"In what way?"

Hazel laces her fingers together, resting them on her stomach.

She sighs. "When you spend your life avoiding commitment of any kind, you end up with just that—no one committed to you and very few who care about you deeply."

I sit up on my elbows. "I care about you."

She smiles wearily at me. "And I'm all the luckier for it," she says. "But there's no one else lining up at my door to visit me. You're the only lasting relationship I've ever had."

"Lots of people care about you," I insist. "Finn and Elizabeth adore you."

"And I adore them," Hazel says. "But it's not the same."

I lie back down. It's easier to ask a difficult question when you're both staring at the ceiling.

"Do you ever regret not having kids?"

For a moment, I think Hazel's lack of response means I've pushed it too far.

Then she turns her head to me, eyebrow effortfully raised. "So I'd have them to look after me now?" She laughs stiffly. "It's a terribly selfish reason to have children, to expect them to care for you in your old age as the price for having given them life." Her focus returns to the ceiling. "But to answer your question, no. You and I both know motherhood wasn't the right path for me. No child should have a mother who resents them for the things they've prevented them from doing in life."

My inclination is to protest, to tell her that she might have felt differently once she held that baby in her arms, that she still could have had an adventurous life as a mother. But in my bones, I know what she's saying is true for her.

Hazel continues her train of thought. "Our patriarchal society has convinced us that a nurturing instinct exists solely to be channeled into motherhood," she says. "But I disagree with that. I've known many women with that same inclination who have used it in other ways—to help build strong communities, to pursue social justice, to care for injured wildlife. And our society is better for it. So even if it means I'm facing my end alone, I know I made the right choice."

I think of all the women in developing countries that Hazel's investment helped build their own businesses making textiles and other fiber arts. It really did feel like the best use of her energy.

"Plus, I loved being an honorary aunt to Elizabeth."

I squeeze her hand. "Why don't you come up to Beacon and stay with me? I promise I won't be too overbearing or emotional. And you could see Elizabeth and Finn more often."

Hazel laughs, then winces, holding her abdomen. "That's very kind of you, my friend, but I want to spend the time I have left in the city I love so much, surrounded by its chaos and energy, even if I can't partake of it in the way I used to. You know small-town quietness has never been for me." She pauses, her voice growing soft. "It would feel like surrendering something that I'm not ready to let go of."

"I know." It was worth a try.

"And besides," Hazel continues, shifting her body to get more comfortable. "I'm not entirely fending for myself. I've gotten myself a death doula."

Now I'm sitting up straight. "What on earth is that?"

Hazel smirks. "Don't worry that tender heart of yours, it's not as ominous as it sounds. It's just someone who's helping me tie up loose ends and work through the odd existential question when I need it."

I tense, indignant. "I could help you with tying up things."

And why does she want to work through those questions with a complete stranger instead of me?

"No offense, Joy, but you didn't even know how to pay a heating bill until after Thom died and I had to teach you."

"I'm better at those things now than I used to be," I protest.

"But you've also got Elizabeth and Finn to think about," Hazel says. "And this woman lives in the West Village, so she's not far away. She's a little strange, but she's very good at her job—why anyone would choose her profession, I'll never know."

Hazel's words are slowing. She's exhausted.

"Well, please know that I'm also here for you whenever you need me," I insist.

"Thank you," Hazel says, eyes closed. She nudges me with her elbow. "I wouldn't mind if you came to visit more often."

"I promise I will."

I stay beside her until her breathing signals deep sleep, then sneak out into the kitchen for an audit of her cupboards and fridge, making a list of things she needs, regardless of how much they might stretch my budget. I'll find a way.

Then I grab a cloth and cleaning spray from under the sink, neatening things up. Surely she won't notice if I give the floor a quick sweep.

But in spite of my efforts, as I walk to the subway later that afternoon, I still feel impotent.

When my train glides out of Grand Central, the near-empty carriage is a stark contrast to the lively, full atmosphere from this morning's journey. Before the train left Manhattan, I looked around hopefully at the few people on the platform, in case Rowan and Hettie happened to be among them, but there was no sign of them.

I'm glad when the loudspeaker announces our arrival into Beacon, but as I look up at the silhouette of the town on the hilltop, I remember the loneliness awaiting me at home. Stepping glumly onto the platform, I begin my walk to the station parking lot, the squawking seagulls on the riverbank emphasizing the absence of human company. Now that I don't have to hold my tears in for Hazel's sake, I let them flow.

It's not until I pat them away with my handkerchief that I see a familiar figure standing at the other end of the platform.

Finn waves, strolling in my direction. "Hey, Nanna!"

My heart swells, my tears now of gratitude.

"What are you doing here?"

My grandson slides his arm around my shoulders, and I can smell the new cologne he's been experimenting with. "I know this is the train you usually take and I figured you might want some company on the way home." He takes my bag from me. "How's Hazel?"

I dab at the remainder of my tears. "Not great, I'm afraid."

Finn squeezes my shoulder and rests his head on mine—just like I used to do to him when he was small. "I'm sorry, Nanna."

I'm so infinitely grateful for this caring young man.

As we walk arm in arm to my car, it reminds me of all the times I've waited for people on that platform—Hazel, Elizabeth, Thom. When you live in the same place for most of your life, memories linger everywhere—every street corner, every restaurant, every train platform—to the point where everything reminds you of a time gone by.

And eventually it feels like you're spending more time with memories than with the present.

**32**

BEACON, 1998

The first thing I noticed about Percy was that he was dressed a little too formally for an afternoon spent weeding, digging, and picking up debris in the local park, which is what we were both there to do. His neatly pressed shirt was buttoned right to the collar, his breast pocket sported a carefully folded pocket square, the leather of his brown oxfords shone in the sun, and perched on his head was a tweed newsboy cap. And yet he embraced his tasks with gusto, the knees of his pleated trousers stained with matching circles of mud, his shirtsleeves darkened with sweat. He didn't even use gardening gloves like the rest of us.

The second thing I noticed was his charming Scottish accent—even if I didn't understand every word he said, at first.

He approached me shyly midway through our first volunteer shift, clutching his hat in his hands.

"Looks like we're the elders of the group, eh?" He gestured to the other volunteers busily tidying the flower bed next to us.

It's true—we were the only two with gray hair, and likely had at least two decades on everyone else. At sixty-three, I was still getting used to often being the oldest person in a room. That peculiar time in your life when suddenly everyone you interact with, be it your bank teller, your doctor, even your church reverend, is younger than you. It's oddly disorienting to realize you've crossed a threshold you hadn't realized you were approaching.

"You're right," I said.

"Perhaps we can teach them a thing or two?"

"Or they us?"

Percy grinned, his teeth endearingly haphazard. "I like your version better."

And so, as we knelt side by side sifting cigarette butts out of the playground sandbox, our friendship began.

Percy was a widower of five years and had moved to Beacon from Chicago a year prior to be closer to his grandchildren.

"How did you and your wife meet?" I asked.

It generally makes people more uncomfortable if you dance around the topic of their recently departed loved one, rather than helping them recall a pleasant memory.

I knew it was the right question from the way his dimples deepened.

"Myrtle was in Scotland working on a research project in botany at the University of Edinburgh in the early sixties," he said. "We met on a hike up the local peak, Arthur's Seat, and within a year, she'd convinced me to move back with her to Chicago, where she had a college teaching position waiting. I was a carpenter, so I could use my skills anywhere. And most importantly, I was besotted with her."

"A professor of botany! Goodness, she must have been clever."

"Aye, she was." Percy dipped his head. "Worked right up until she died, she loved it so much. And what about you, Joy? You seem rather clever yourself. What was your line of work before you became a sifter of sandboxes?"

"Oh," I said, embarrassed. "I never really had one except for working as the receptionist in my father's medical practice. After my husband and I got married, I stopped working—I suppose it was so common back then that I didn't really question it. And I was grateful to have the chance to be a mother, even if it had its challenges."

Percy's dimples deepen further. "From what I can tell, being a mother is one of the hardest jobs in the world, so you're already a champion, in my opinion," he said. "What would you have liked to do as a career, if you'd had the chance?"

I hadn't ever dared think about it seriously. It would've felt like dwelling on something I couldn't change, and thus something to regret. I'd always just tried to focus on the things I loved about the life I had.

But since Percy was asking, why not daydream, just a little?

"Let's see," I said. "Well, I do love gardening, of course, and baking—but I could still keep those as hobbies. And I enjoy giving piano lessons to kids but I wouldn't want to ever charge for them." For a moment I couldn't think of anything—as if there were a tight lid on my imagination, limiting its expansion. "I suppose I would've liked to do something that helped people. My daughter is a nurse, so perhaps I could have done that. Or maybe I would have become an elementary school teacher. Or a librarian."

Percy nodded approvingly. "All wonderful choices," he said. "The year after my wife died, even though I was retired, I got a part-time job as a library page—the person who shelves all the returned books and makes sure they're in the right order. It helped me feel less lonely and isolated, surrounded by all those books and people browsing."

"That sounds very fulfilling." I might have enjoyed that job myself. "You don't do it anymore?"

He shook his head. "There're so many young ones who need jobs these days, people who have families to support. I was just doing it for the fun of it, not because I needed the money, so I resigned to give them the opportunity. It's the perfect post for someone who's an introvert like me."

From then on, I looked forward to every third Saturday of the month, when I'd get to see Percy. As the summer wore on, we started spending time together outside our volunteer group. We'd meet down by the river near the train station, grab a coffee from the little kiosk—well, English breakfast tea for Percy—and meander along the bank together.

It was as if I'd found a kindred spirit. I loved his gentle nature, the way he spoke so softly that you often had to lean closer to hear what he had to say. And how, while he sometimes didn't say much, it was always worth hearing.

Soon enough, I began to notice how my mood would lift at the sight of him. He was always so comfortingly consistent. His cheeks a permanent pink, like he'd just walked in from the cold. Bushy eyebrows, and white whiskers growing from his ears. Little nicks and occasional bits of toilet paper stuck to his chin, as if he still hadn't gotten the hang of shaving, even in his seventh decade. And then there was his smell—a medley of soap, throat lozenges, and freshly cut wood.

If I'm honest, those six months of our budding friendship were among the happiest months I can recall. With Elizabeth and Jack now married and living together, Thom still working as many hours as he ever did at his law practice, and Hazel on an extended trip to India, my life felt more muted than ever.

Percy brought back the brightness.

It's difficult to explain why. All we really did was walk and talk about everyday things like trees or birds, or interesting stories we read in the paper, or our shared love of BBC Agatha Christie adaptations. And he would save up random facts to tell me, because he knew how much I enjoyed them.

"Did you know, Joy," he'd say, eyes twinkling, "that you can tell if it's about to rain by looking at the pine cones on a tree? If they're closed, you'll soon need your umbrella."

"Did you know, Joy, that almonds are in fact part of the peach family?"

"Did you know, Joy, that all mammals get goose bumps?"

Occasionally I would mention Thom, just as Percy would sometimes tell a story about Myrtle. But mostly it felt as though our worlds revolved only around each other during the few hours we spent together each week.

I never felt the butterflies I did with Thom; it was something different, more distinct. Whenever I'd come back from one of our outings, I found myself standing a little taller, more at ease with myself, like I could be exactly who I was without having to be vigilant about the emotions or preferences of others.

There's no other way to describe it, except that Percy felt like home.

One late-autumn Saturday after our volunteer session—the last one of the year before we paused for winter—we were seated on a park bench watching a gang of seagulls squabble over a discarded soft pretzel.

A peculiar melancholy lingered over us, akin to when you're reaching the final few pages of a book you love and never want to end.

Percy was very quiet—more so than usual.

"Do you ever miss Scotland?" I asked, mostly to break the silence.

A wistfulness clouded his eyes. "Every day," he said. "Even though this is my home now."

"Tell me what you love about it."

"Well, people say it's gloomy," he said, in his melodious lilt. "But to me it's magical. The way the green of the Highlands seems to glow against the gray clouds almost makes my heart burst. And I love the way the brisk, cool air just smells so earthy and verdant. When I was a child, I'd go out into the fields on a chilly day and sing as loud as I could, letting the air cleanse my lungs."

"How I would have loved to have seen that." The image of little Percy singing his heart out in a field was almost too enchanting to bear.

We sat a little longer with no words between us, until Percy finally turned to me.

"Joy, I have a confession to make," Percy said, his cheeks even rosier than usual.

"You do?"

"Yes," he said, removing his tweed cap bashfully. "I spend all week researching those random facts, just so I can tell them to you when I see you. I love the way they make you giggle."

My cheeks suddenly matched the color of his. "Well, thank you—I very much appreciate your efforts."

He nodded and looked down at the dandelion stems he'd been twisting together as we sat.

"It's more than just wanting to make you giggle," he said softly, eyes earnest. "You may have already guessed, but I've grown rather fond of you. And I think . . . we make quite a good pair."

Percy lifted the tangle of dandelion stems, which I now saw had been fashioned into a bracelet. Then he tenderly took my hand and slid it onto my wrist.

It took several beginnings of a sentence before I managed to form a complete one.

"Thank you, Percy," I whispered.

It wasn't just his frank openness that took me by surprise; it was the realization that I shared his sentiment.

We did make a good pair. In fact, in many ways, we made a better pair than Thom and I ever had. I wasn't sure when our friendship had shifted into the hint of something more, but now that Percy had spoken it into existence, it felt so obvious. I was embarrassed I hadn't realized it myself.

"I know it's very ungentlemanly of me to even suggest this," Percy said tentatively. "I never dreamed I would pursue a married woman. But I would regret it for the rest of my life if I didn't say something. And dare I say, you deserve a husband who cherishes you, one for whom you are the highlight of their day." A shy smile. "You've been the highlight of mine for quite a while."

The seagull squabble intensified, and I was glad of the momentary distraction, a chance to gather my thoughts.

Every part of me wanted to turn to Percy and tell him he too was the highlight of my day, that my heart bloomed for him in a way that it never had for Thom.

And yet, although I had every right to, I knew I wouldn't.

"I'm sorry, Percy," I said. "I've grown very fond of you too." A deep breath. "And that's why I don't think we can be friends anymore."

He sat for a moment, digesting my words, then he stood, donning his tweed cap, and nodded. "I understand."

That afternoon was the last time I ever heard from Percy.

Until ten years later, a few weeks after I'd stumbled across his obituary in the paper.

An envelope arrived in the mail from a local law firm, with a brisk letter informing me that the enclosed correspondence was from the estate of Percy Strahan.

When I shook the manila envelope, all that fell out was a notecard with two handwritten lines.

*Did you know, Joy, that giraffes communicate by humming to one another?*

*I never stopped humming to you, even if you couldn't be there to hear it.*

And that's when I learned what it truly felt like to have your heart broken.

**33**

My finger hovers over the doorbell as I consider going back home and spending an enjoyable afternoon gardening instead of attending this wretched crafting circle.

What Rita neglected to tell me when she first invited me was that this week's meeting was being held at Celeste's house. The very place I swore to myself I'd never set foot in again after Thom died.

What makes it worse is that I don't even know who these other women are besides Rita and Celeste, my two least favorite people in the entire town. Who'd have thought you'd still get the first-day-of-school jitters when you're almost ninety? Turns out, the fear of being the new person in an already-established group rears up no matter your age. We all assume that, once we're adults, we'll outgrow the catty politics of the schoolyard—cliques and social hierarchies that make all but a chosen few question their self-worth. The truth is, if anything, it worsens as we women grow older.

But I can't back out now. They've probably already seen me through the front window. Besides, I've discovered that the best way to distract myself from the pain of losing Hazel is to try new things—and not all of them can be against the law.

I force myself to push the doorbell. The chime is the generic descending major third interval, otherwise known as the "ding dong" sound most people associate with doorbells. At least my doorbell has more musical flair.

When the door opens, Celeste stares at me like I'm some kind of apparition.

"Joy," she stammers. "This is a surprise!"

Did I misunderstand the invitation?

"Rita invited me," I say nervously. "Did I get the time wrong?"

"Oh, not at all," Celeste says. "I just wasn't sure you'd make it."

It's a fair assessment, given my track record of attending events at Celeste's place.

"I brought chocolate mud cake," I say, offering her the plate. Beyond my mother's instruction to never arrive at someone's home empty-handed, bringing something also fills those awkward few moments when you first arrive.

"This looks delightful, thank you!"

Celeste ushers me into the living room, where Rita and three other women are seated. They all look vaguely familiar; perhaps I've seen them at the café. Or a recent funeral.

The air is thick with competing perfumes—a jumble of top notes that make my nose twitch. It would be too rude to request to open a window when I've been in the room for less than a minute.

"Hi, Rita." I wave meekly at the others. "Hello, everyone—thank you for letting me join your group."

The women are dressed in a similar style—elegant button-downs, delicate cashmere sweaters, and tailored trousers, all neutral tones and subtle stripes, with chunky gold jewelry and the odd diamond. Should I have dressed up a little more? Heavens, this is just a crafting afternoon. What do they wear to an evening event?

I fiddle timidly with my wedding ring—my only accessory—as Celeste introduces everyone.

"This is Bridget." She gestures to the tall woman with an immaculate ballerina bun, perched primly at the edge of the armchair.

"And Phyllis." The woman on the adjacent sofa twirls her fingers in a wave, her nails a glossy deep burgundy.

"And here's Maude." Celeste points to the remaining friend, who has distinguished herself from the pack with a silk scarf knotted chicly around her neck.

Maude smiles broadly, but the flick of her eyes appraising me from head to toe cancels out the warmth.

It's not just their clothing that's similar. It's the unnerving tightness across their cheeks and foreheads that seems counter to their aging necks and hands. They look glamorous, but in a way that's both mesmerizing and incongruous, like those old brownstones in New York City with modern additions on their exteriors. It feels disharmonious.

"It's a pleasure to meet you all." I say, pulling at the frayed cuff of my shirt.

When Celeste puts her hand on my back, I have to stop myself from flinching.

"Joy and I have been neighbors since I was in my twenties." She looks at me. "Can you believe it's been that long? So many memories."

Why is she acting like we're best friends when I've spent the majority of those years avoiding her?

"So many," I say with a tight smile.

To her credit, she didn't say the memories were good ones.

"These ladies, on the other hand," Celeste continues, "I've only had the pleasure of knowing for a year or so. They've all recently moved up with their husbands from the city."

"We needed a change of pace," Maude says. "This town is so quaint."

That doesn't sound like a compliment.

"We all met playing pickleball," Rita says. "And now we have a fierce rivalry."

This time it's Phyllis assessing my physique. "Do you play pickleball, Joy?"

"Oh no," I say. "I've never been good at racket sports. Though my husband, Thom, was quite the tennis player."

I sense Celeste stiffen next to me.

The other ladies tilt their heads and pout with pity, the way people do when your use of past tense implies the loss of a spouse. It's almost always followed by a clumsy pause, then a robotic uttering of "I'm sorry for your loss"—something we've all been taught to do by rote that rarely offers comfort. It just makes you feel more isolated.

I cut them off at the conversational pass by pretending to be captivated by the array of craft supplies laid out on the coffee table. "So, what are we making today?"

I hover at the end of the coffee table, since there doesn't appear to be space for me to sit anywhere.

"I'm working on my needlepoint," Bridget says, brandishing a round frame with a taut piece of fabric. The skeleton of brown stitches hints at some kind of animal—a horse, maybe, or a slender cow.

"Except she keeps having to undo the stitches because she refuses to admit she needs glasses," Phyllis teases.

Bridget lifts her chin haughtily. "I've made it to seventy without them, why should I bother now?"

"Well, I don't know," Maude chimes in. "Because vision deteriorates with age?"

I adjust my own glasses self-consciously.

"It took me a while to admit I needed them," I say. "But my life is much easier now that I've got them. I didn't realize how dusty my house had gotten because I couldn't see it!"

I meant it as a joke, but everyone is looking at me in horror.

"Don't you have a maid?" Bridget asks, needle lingering in the air.

"Oh, well, I've never really needed one since I've always been a homemaker. And I'm capable of cleaning the house myself."

"Apparently not," Maude mutters.

Celeste shoots her a look, then realizes why I haven't yet sat down. "Oh, god, Joy, let me get you a chair."

She disappears and returns with a dining chair, positioning it beside Bridget in the armchair.

I gingerly take a seat. "Thank you."

"The rest of us are going to try beadwork today," Rita says, removing the lid of a box to reveal a spectrum of beads.

"Oh, how fun!" I say, not very convincingly.

I'm about to reach for a strand of fishing line, when I notice the crescent-moons of dirt under my fingernails. I yanked a few stray weeds out of the garden on my way here and didn't realize my hands were dirty. I pull them back swiftly before anyone notices.

"I might just use the powder room first, if that's okay?" I prefer to call it a bathroom, but something makes me opt for the fancier moniker given my current company.

"Of course," Celeste says. "Down the hall, second door on the left!"

As I leave the room, the ladies start discussing another woman they know from pickleball, critiquing her skimpy outfits.

"So distasteful for her age," I hear Maude say as I close the bathroom door.

Once my nails are clean, I stare at myself in the mirror, questioning how long I have to stay with these women before it's acceptable to leave. I suppose I should give them a chance.

Reemerging into the hallway, I resolve to be more open-minded, reminding myself that I'm soon to be without a best friend. None of these women could ever replace Hazel, but it would be nice to have someone to have coffee with once in a while. I don't want to pester Rowan too much.

On my way back from the bathroom, I stop to examine the photo frame on the credenza in the hall—a wedding portrait of Celeste and her husband.

Poor Ernie. I've always wondered if he knew about Celeste and Thom. He was so kindhearted and devoted to his wife that perhaps he didn't suspect anything. Or maybe he just chose to suffer in silence, like I did. I wonder if she had multiple dalliances with other men, or whether she just singled out my husband.

Not long after I told Hazel about seeing Thom and Celeste together, she suggested I get revenge by seducing Ernie. I dismissed the thought immediately, of course—I'm no seductress. Was I going to make eyes at Ernie in my gardening gloves and rubber clogs and invite him for a secret rendezvous by the bags of fertilizer in my tool-shed? I don't think so. And regardless, trying to steal someone else's husband—revenge or not—is just not who I am.

Nor is emotional infidelity, even when it was very tempting.

When I return to the living room, I can hear Celeste rattling around in the kitchen. She reappears with a tray of coffee and hands me a little gold-rimmed cup on a saucer.

"I thought espresso would complement the taste of the chocolate cake," she says. "Ern and I got those cups in Milan during our fortieth-anniversary trip."

"How lovely," I say, pinching the small handle of the cup gingerly. "Thank you."

I'm a drip coffee or cappuccino kind of gal. Espresso sipping is an activity someone more sophisticated than me would do. Someone like Celeste.

I sneak a glance at her sitting at the opposite end of the sofa, one knee slung neatly over the other. Technically we're dressed similarly—trousers and a button-down shirt—but her outfit feels inexplicably breezier than mine. Perhaps it's the monochrome effect of her match-ing off-white linen, or the way her sleeves are rolled up just so, re-vealing delicate forearms that aren't a patchwork of sun damage. Or it could be her hair, a subtle buttery blond pulled back in a wispy bun. I keep my gray hair cropped short; it's more practical, and it requires regular visits to the hair salon, which gives me a guaranteed hour of conversation where I don't feel like I'm monopolizing someone's time.

I smooth my faded olive-green chinos, conscious of the discolored splotches from when I splashed bleach doing laundry years ago.

"I've never beaded before," I say. "What should I start with?"

Phyllis holds up her half-finished strand. "I like to start by selecting my color scheme." She wiggles her shoulders smugly. "I used to be an interior decorator, so I have an eye for palettes."

As far as I can tell, there's only one palette she prefers. Her strand of beads is a similar series of neutrals to her outfit. It seems a travesty to choose those when you have all these beautiful brightly colored beads at your fingertips.

A surge of creativity strikes me. "I might make one that reflects all the colors of my garden."

"Joy has always had the most beautiful garden," Celeste says, and the other women titter in approval.

It bothers me that she keeps making it sound like we're lifelong friends.

"I'll admit that's one of the advantages of living here, having a garden," Bridget says, pulling the needle through the fabric in one elegant swoop. "Though I suppose we did have Central Park right on our doorstep—not that I ever had the chance to enjoy it." She gives me the reason before I even have the chance to ask for it. "No time for strolls in the park when you're running board meetings."

I must look surprised because Phyllis chimes in for my benefit. "Bridget ran a multinational cosmetics brand."

Golly, these women have had impressive careers, just like Percy's wife did. Rita was a respected dermatologist and even Celeste had her own successful accounting firm until she retired. I know that running a household and raising a child is also a job in itself, but these women managed those responsibilities while also having fulfilling, robust careers. It's hard not to see my own contribution to the world as meager in comparison.

I glumly thread the fishing line through the first bead; my earlier optimism about turning over a new social leaf has faded.

Is it really worth trying to find new friends if they just make you feel bad about yourself?

**34**

The earthy, sour smell of the Hudson River seasons the breeze outside the Dia Beacon art museum.

I'd been pottering around in my garden yesterday when Rowan walked by and suggested we spend the next afternoon together wandering through its galleries.

"Are you sure you want to keep hanging out with an old woman?" I said, forcing a teasing tone to mask the emotional truth.

Rowan shrugged. "Age doesn't matter if you have interests in common, does it?"

He's now waiting for me at the museum entrance, gazing at the cloudless sky. The rhythmic rattle of the Metro-North train nearby reminds me of the fortuitous encounter that seeded our budding friendship.

Rowan gallantly pays for both of our tickets, even though I tell him it's free for residents of Beacon.

"That's okay," he says, handing over the cash to the clerk. "I like supporting the arts."

Now I feel selfish for not thinking to pay once in a while myself. This art museum is one of my very favorite places in Beacon, and I love to stroll around it once a month or so. Even when there aren't many people here, I never feel lonely; the art somehow keeps me company.

But what I love most is the building itself—an old box factory with gloriously large windows where sunlight streams in so joyously that it's hard not to feel a bit cheerful. I enjoy the scuffing sound of my shoes on the concrete floors in the otherwise reverent silence. And the best thing is that the window views change with the seasons—a flame of orange in October, a delicate blanket of ivory in January, and an exuberant swath of green in June. To me, that's artwork in itself, all at the genius hand of Mother Nature.

Rowan receives two metal pins from the clerk and hands me one before fixing the other to his shirt, the vibrant purple an aberration on the solid black fabric. I follow him into the first gallery, pretending to admire the sculptures I've seen dozens of times but really watching him closely, observing how he cocks his head for a different perspective, or bends closer to savor a specific detail.

When he lingers longer in front of one particular sculpture, which, to me, just looks like a large circle of sticks, I panic that he's going to ask me what I think of it. This museum favors abstract works and I'm embarrassed to admit that, while I admire them very much, I don't understand most. Hazel once told me you must gaze at an artwork for ten minutes to fully appreciate it, but even then I'm unsure what message I'm meant to glean from a heap of broken glass, a giant hunk of weathered steel, or in this case, a pile of sticks. I prefer the patterns the sunlight makes on the concrete walls.

Finally, Rowan speaks.

"I was never really into abstract sculpture when I was younger. I preferred classical works, like the paintings of the Dutch masters— and not just because they loved their dogs," he says with a wink. "But one of my favorite books I had access to at Sing Sing was about the artist Richard Serra. I was so fascinated with his work and how he made such a crude raw material so beautiful. I promised myself I'd see as many of them as I could when I got out."

Richard Serra is one artist I do know—there are many of his sculptures here. But I'm especially pleased for this conversation because it's right on the topic I was hoping to broach.

"Then I understand why you suggested coming here," I say. "Eight years must have felt like a long time when you were only just embarking on your adult life. Do you still keep in touch with anyone you were there with?"

Just because you're in prison doesn't mean you can't make friends.

"A few," Rowan says. "Like I said, it's a tough life out in the world once you've got a strike against your name. A lot of them ended up back in prison."

"Oh, that's a shame."

"It's hard to walk an honorable path because everyone's just waiting for you to trip up," Rowan says. "I tried for a long time, but then I figured, what's the point of doing that when most people already assume the worst of you?"

There's an unmistakably mischievous gleam in his eye.

Is he saying what I think he's saying? That he still isn't on the straight and narrow? I want to know more, but it's risky to ask without knowing for sure that's what he meant.

I dart my eyes around the gallery, checking who's in the vicinity. A lone gallery attendant—a wiry man with his hair in a bun—sits in the corner staring into the space.

I shuffle closer, conscious that loud words might echo.

"As it happens," I say, "I've recently been dabbling in some illegal activity myself."

Rowan coughs in surprise. "I'm sorry?"

"You might've heard about the fire alarm down at the library last week." I don't mask the glee in my voice. "The fire trucks came and everything."

"Someone did mention it to me at the grocery store, yes," Rowan says. "It was bored teenagers who set it off, right?"

"That's what everyone thinks." I straighten my five-foot frame, chest puffed. "But, really, it was me."

Rowan can't hide his grin. "I'm impressed."

"It's a felony, you know—pulling a fire alarm when there's no fire."

He looks thoroughly amused now.

"I didn't know, actually," he says. "What inspired you to do something like that?"

I don't want to dampen the conversation by bringing up my depression over Hazel, so I tell him another truth.

"I realized I'd been missing out on the fun all my life by always following the rules, and I wanted the chance to see what it felt like to break them."

"I see," Rowan says. "And how did it feel?"

I grin at him. "Amazing."

He puts his hands in his pockets and strides to the next gallery. "I agree."

Here we are, meeting again in that moral middle.

I hurry after him.

"Well, I've confided in you about my misdeeds," I say, emboldened. "So now it's only fair you tell me about yours—don't think I didn't catch that mischievous look you gave me back there."

Rowan looks up at the sunlight streaming in above the sculpture, deliberating. Then he looks back down at me. "Fair enough."

A flick of his eyes around the space confirms we're alone.

"As you probably know, piano tuning isn't the most well-paying profession." He rubs his lips together, choosing his words. "So Philippe and I run a little operation on the side."

"Oh? What kind of operation?" Playing innocent is the best strategy.

"Well, as I mentioned, Philippe is an antiques restorer in Manhattan," Rowan says. "But he also runs a side business—producing fakes and forgeries."

My first thought is how naughty Philippe is, but then I catch myself.

"I see." I try on my poker face. "And how does that work?"

Rowan's heavy boots make his footsteps especially percussive in the mostly empty space.

"Over the years, he's kept a long list of everything he's worked on and the addresses of where they're located," he says. "My job as a piano tuner also gives me the chance to see inside the homes of wealthy people with valuable antiques and art. Sometimes we switch the real items out for fakes and then sell the originals to another collector."

Now he's carefully studying me, waiting for me to flinch.

It really is a roguish thing these two are up to. But it doesn't make me think any less of Rowan; it makes me admire him. How thrilling it must be to take part in a real live art heist.

"How do you get into those fancy buildings and apartments?" I ask. "That must be quite the task."

"It's easier than you'd think," Rowan says. "As wealthy as these people are, they're often not the most generous, and their doormen and staff aren't treated that well. That's why these jobs take patience—we spend time winning those staff over, usually with a nice chunk of cash, in order to get our people inside the building."

They really do have everything worked out.

"Do you ever have any ethical issues with what you do?"

Rowan turns to me, eyebrow raised.

"Just a bit curious, is all," I clarify.

The eyebrow lowers. "It's a reasonable question."

And yet he doesn't answer it. He just studies the next sculpture—a concave form fashioned from dirt—for what feels like minutes.

"I guess you could say I see what I do as part of an ecosystem," Rowan finally says. "We all play our different parts. I'm just helping to ensure the appreciation of art."

"How so?"

"Well, a lot of people who own expensive artworks collect them for the prestige and the bragging rights, rather than because they truly cherish them. And often those objects sit on a shelf or in a vault somewhere, unappreciated. But there are others who can look at a painting and be moved to tears by the craftsmanship, the tireless effort and genius of the artist." He absentmindedly unrolls his shirtsleeve, then rolls it again more neatly. "Great art deserves to be in the hands of those who understand its inherent value beyond a dollar amount. And most people in the first category don't even realize when their objects have been switched for a forgery. They still get the enjoyment—or bragging rights—they've always had."

"But how do you know the person you're stealing it for will truly appreciate it in the way you're describing? They might just be telling you that so that they can get the bragging rights."

"Ah, but that's the thing," Rowan says. "If the piece is stolen, then you can't brag about it, can you? In fact, you can't tell anyone that you have it." He pauses to let his point settle. "Philippe and I mostly work for one main client. She's a collector of rare art and objects who buys a lot of the items she wants on the art market legitimately. But there are certain things she covets that people don't want to sell. And that's where we come in."

"So she doesn't sell them once she has them?"

"No. She enjoys them," Rowan says. "There's a temperature-controlled room in her townhouse in Chelsea where she keeps it all. She spends a few hours a day in there, just admiring everything—it's like a meditation for her. And she's quite an important benefactor for several art museums in New York City, so you could say her karma is more or less intact."

I'm not convinced it all balances out so neatly. "And what about your karma?"

Rowan laughs quietly. "I don't think I'm destined to achieve karmic balance in this lifetime," he says. "I might have to start from scratch in the next go-around. Though I do make sure to donate a portion of all our earnings to my sister's animal rescue shelter in New Mexico, so perhaps that will help tip the scales."

"How noble of your sister to do that," I say.

He nods. "She's the do-gooder of the family—she somehow managed to resist the pull of our family's criminal background," he says wryly. "Her shelter is where Hettie is from. Someone dumped her as a puppy in the middle of a field with no food or water. Poor thing, she was so frail and skinny and riddled with fleas and worms." He grins. "That's why I treat her like a princess."

Gosh, some people are monsters. If we're talking about karma, they'll be the ones who'll be exiting this life with a serious deficit.

We descend a flight of stairs to the room of Serra sculptures, the deep red of their oxidized steel harmonizing with the museum's exposed-brick walls. Rowan stands still, gazing at the enormous forms like he's greeting an old friend.

I glance at the DO NOT TOUCH THE ART sign by the door, its words begging me to disobey them. Then I follow Rowan inside an enormous sculpture that curves around like a coil, as if we're walking through a maze. With no gallery attendant in sight, I run my fingertips defiantly along the metal surface, relishing its cool, rough texture.

"That client of yours," I say to Rowan. "What happens to all the objects and art in that room once she dies?"

As if following my lead, he brushes his hand across the sculpture.

"Good question," he says. "Fortunately, her adult kids share her passion and will continue to enjoy those objects once she's gone, but they can also plead ignorance if it ever comes to light. I'm sure, eventually, someone in the bloodline will take issue with the ethics of it all." He smiles at me. "And when that does finally happen, there'll be a mighty scandal in the art world."

I stand in the middle of the sculpture, considering that prospect. What would it be like to leave behind such an explosive legacy?

**35**

Red rivulets flow down the sides of Hazel's bathroom sink as I rinse the hair dye from her head.

Even though I'll be seeing her with Elizabeth and Finn this coming Saturday, I decided to pop down for an extra visit. And since she doesn't have the energy for an outing—and refuses to be seen out in public in the wheelchair I suggested borrowing—I decided I'd create one for her in the comfort of her loft.

A spa day.

The manicure and pedicure were admittedly very basic, given that I've never done either before. The few times I've gotten a manicure for a special occasion, I've promptly ruined it while gardening. (I do have gloves, but there's something so pleasant and meditative about having my bare hands in the soil.) I just made sure to keep my nails neatly filed and my cuticles trimmed so I didn't embarrass Thom at one of his work gatherings.

So in preparation for today, I spent an hour at a library computer watching videos on how to give someone a manicure. Then I practiced painting my own nails at home, with lackluster results. I didn't manage much better with Hazel's nails, but I was determined to do everything I could to make my dear friend feel pampered.

Perhaps it was a touch ambitious to offer to color her hair too, but

I'd noticed the box of hair dye under her sink and knew how much it meant to her—I'd seen how she kept self-consciously covering the stripe of white down the middle of her scalp. I'll have to commit to giving her bathroom a thorough cleaning because that red dye has somehow managed to get everywhere. At least I had the forethought to wear dishwashing gloves.

Hazel squints as water dribbles in her eye. "Is everything okay, Joy?"

"Yes," I say, nervously. "Everything's looking great!"

Thank god one of the videos I watched advised me to put a thick layer of Vaseline along her hairline, otherwise her forehead would be red too.

I was quite proud of myself when I realized the detachable showerhead would stretch to the sink—one of those large farmhouse-style ones—so I could rinse her hair as if she were at the salon. Well, sort of. We had to improvise a little with a dining chair, an inflatable neck pillow, and lots of towels. I'm relieved when the rivulets turn pink and then eventually clear.

"Would you like a deep-conditioning treatment, madame?" I say with a flourish.

I stopped at a Duane Reade on my way here to buy some fancy-looking shampoo and conditioner, and also splurged on a hair mask. I'm not sure if you're supposed to add one after using dye, but in this case, the pampering is key, not the end result.

Hazel dabs her face with the corner of the towel. "Why not?"

I massage it into her scalp and feel her body relax, her smile sleepy and serene. I'm grateful to have found a way to care for her, even if it does nothing to ease her symptoms.

"I went to Dia a few days ago with my new neighbor I told you about, Rowan," I say, readying the showerhead to rinse out the hair mask. "I think you two would get along well—he appreciates abstract art too."

"The ex-felon?" Hazel's eyes open. "Of course we'd get along. Has Rita eased up on her rumormongering?"

I turn the water on slowly, wiggling my fingers under it to test the temperature.

"Not exactly." In fact, annoyingly, her instincts about Rowan turned out to be right. "But she did pressure me into joining her crafting group."

Hazel laughs. "And how's that going? I've never known you to be into that kind of thing."

"It's fine." *It's a reminder of how much I'm going to miss you*, I want to say. "It's a reminder that it's good to try new things, even at our age."


Hazel fell asleep not long after I finished blow-drying her hair, so I've decided to stroll around her neighborhood before taking the subway to Grand Central.

Walking down Atlantic Avenue, it's still hard to get used to its polished state these days—fancy houseware stores and fashion boutiques in buildings I recall being abandoned for years in the seventies. Live long enough and you'll eventually see every place you've ever been to gussied up and stripped of its imperfections—and often its character.

I can only imagine the bidding war that's going to happen over Hazel's loft. I hope it goes to someone who truly treasures it, perhaps a young artist who embodies Hazel's free-spirited approach to life. In reality, I'm sure it will be snapped up by one of those ruthless developers.

At least Atlantic Avenue's legacy of antique dealers is still intact, though there aren't as many as there used to be. I cup my eyes on the glass to peek in the window of one shop, recognizing a lamp identical to the one that sat on my father's desk. I used to marvel at the rich colors of its stained-glass shade and I can still picture my father's profile in its dim glow, massaging his temples while engrossed in a thick medical text.

My mind drifts to Rowan's revelation at the museum, imagining the kinds of objects that he and Philippe have switched over the years. It must be a true art, being able to create those believable replicas.

A seed of an idea starts to germinate.

Perhaps there is something else I can do for Hazel after all, in addition to the letter Rowan suggested writing her.

One last grand gesture to show my appreciation for our friendship.

**36**

Finn's mop of hair is unrulier than usual as he hunches over his laptop at my kitchen table. I'm tempted to tell him he needs a haircut, but that's not what grandmas are for. His mother should be on top of those things.

I slide some shortbread in front of him. "What's that you're working on today?"

Finn leans back in his chair, stretching his arms above his head.

"An assignment for my social studies class," he says. "About what makes someone a good leader. We've been talking about how some of the most charismatic leaders in history were also the most destructive."

I sit down across from him with my own piece of shortbread. "I thought being charismatic was a positive thing."

Finn relaxes his arms and checks his phone in that compulsive way young people do. "Not always."

"How so?" I love the things I learn from Finn, especially since I never got to go to college. They teach kids such fascinating things in school these days.

"Well, someone who has charisma generally has a kind of charm or magnetism that others are drawn to, right? And that helps that person influence large groups of people."

"Right."

"But they can also use it to do terrible things," Finn says. "Most dictators in history could be described as charismatic."

"I suppose that's true." My grasp of history isn't as detailed as it could be—even though I lived through a lot of it. "That Franco fellow sure had everyone in thrall for a long time. And he was very bad."

"But that's my point," Finn says. "I don't believe we're born good or bad. I think we have the capacity for both, and it just depends which side we choose to nurture."

His phone vibrates, and he grabs it eagerly, rolling his eyes at whatever the message says. He fires off a response, then starts scrolling through something else on his phone.

I suppose that's the end of our conversation; teenage boys have such short attention spans.

Watching Finn tapping away on his phone, I consider my fire alarm escapade. It wasn't that I'd never had the inclination to do that, to pull a forbidden lever. It's that I've chosen to resist that mischievous side for the sake of order and doing what's expected of me—being a "good" person in society's eyes, and in my father's, in particular.

In truth, my thoughts aren't always as angelic as people might assume. Yes, I ended my friendship with Percy so that it wouldn't lead to infidelity on my part. But it wasn't as noble as it sounds—it was self-preservation. Had I not told him immediately that we couldn't continue any kind of relationship, I would have had the chance to imagine the possibility of it. And then, perhaps, I wouldn't have made such a "noble" choice.

Finn's theory lingers on my mind later that evening, while I'm on my way to the pharmacy to collect my prescription for cholesterol medication. Especially because picking up the pills won't be the only thing I'm doing.

Prior to this, every questionable act I've engaged in has stemmed from a spontaneous impulse, or, in the case of the drugs, a favor for a friend. But the act I have in mind tonight is one I've been planning since I last saw Hazel. Let's call it a premeditated experiment.

Considering Finn's hypothesis, if you do something deemed "bad," but with "good" intentions, where does that place you on the spectrum?

The pharmacy door chimes as I walk in, but I don't see anyone at the counter.

Excellent.

Emboldened, I saunter into the makeup aisle. As I said, I'm not much of a nail polish person, but it would be very easy for one of those exuberantly hued bottles to accidentally "fall" into my open bag, wouldn't it?

In my peripheral vision, I see a tall woman browsing the lipstick a few feet away. She smiles and I reciprocate. I could wait until she's moved to another aisle, but what if I didn't? Am I brazen enough to do it while someone is standing right by me?

That coveted buzz cloaks my body like a cozy woolen shawl.

I run my finger along the bottles lined up neatly in their rack and pick the brightest color—a cheerful chartreuse. Easing it out of its shelf, I enclose it in my fist and then lower it to my bag, coughing when I drop it in to avoid any audible clinking against my spectacles case.

The woman turns to me again, this time with an alarmed look on her face. My pulse elevates until I see she's subtly shuffling away from me.

"Oh don't worry, dear," I say. "Just a tickle in my throat I've had for years—nothing contagious, I promise."

Her tight smile implies she's doubtful. To appease her, I walk in the opposite direction into the sun-protection aisle, patting my purse with satisfaction. That was too easy to fulfill the criteria of my experiment.

The sunscreen bottles would be harder to conceal, but you know what would really test my mettle? Stealing a bright blue sun visor by wearing it in plain sight.

I balance on tiptoes to pull it down from its hook. The vivacious color glows in the pharmacy's anemic fluorescent lighting.

Examining my reflection in the square mirror sullied with greasy fingerprints, I position the visor on my head. My white hair mushrooms out the top, and I'm pleased by how ludicrous I look. I don't even remove the price tag.

I approach the counter, pulse pounding in my ears.

Cedric, a stocky man with a listless ponytail, appears from behind the shelves.

"Mrs. Bridport! Are you here for your prescription?"

I wasn't expecting to be identified on sight. I've been coming to this pharmacy for years, but after it was sold to a large corporation recently, the staff don't often recognize me. Cedric is one of the few employees who survived the transition.

The visor digs uncomfortably into my temple.

"Hello, Cedric," I say, as casually as you can when your stomach is in your throat. "Yes, I had a phone call saying it's ready."

His eyes flick upwards, registering my visor, but he says nothing. If anything, he's hiding his amusement.

Well, yes, I do look ridiculous, but that's the point. I've never worn a visor in my life—I prefer a broad-brimmed straw hat while gardening. And come on, Cedric, it's eight o'clock at night and the sun is barely a whisper in the sky.

I reach up to adjust the visor, feeling the scratch of the tag dangling behind my ear. I look Cedric directly in the eye, daring him to hold me to account.

Instead he sifts through a basket filled with bags of medication until he finds the one with my name on it. "Here you are, Mrs. Bridport!"

I stand silently, testing whether he'll notice the glaringly obvious attempt at shoplifting happening right under his nose.

He looks at me expectantly. "Is there anything else I can help you with? Perhaps you'd like a carry bag?"

"No, thank you, Cedric," I say. "There's plenty of room in my purse." I accept the paper bag and stow it away.

"Then have a lovely evening," he says with a kind smile.

It occurs to me that Cedric might be held responsible when the eventual stocktaking reveals the loss of the visor. But then again, the heartless corporation that took over this pharmacy, canceling the jobs of many hardworking people who needed the income, likely won't even care about one lost hat.

"Thanks, Cedric," I say, nerves calming as I inch closer to achieving my goal. "You too."

I turn abruptly, almost colliding with the lady from the makeup aisle. Perhaps she'll note the discrepancy—I wasn't wearing gaudy headwear when I spoke to her earlier.

She barely looks up from her phone. So it's not just teenage boys.

It's not until I push through the glass door that I fear I mightn't have gotten away with it, after all.

A uniformed policeman is standing in front of me, about to enter the pharmacy. My pulse resumes its pounding.

The policeman holds the door open for me, studying me closely. The expression on his face is not the suspicion I expect. It's more like confusion.

"Oh," he says, like a child suddenly remembering their manners. "Good evening, ma'am."

"Good evening, officer," I say, walking through the door he's keeping open for me. "And thank you."

Though I'm inclined to hurry off into the night, I glance at his name tag, tempting fate.

"Charles," I say with a smile. "That was my father's name. Of course, he probably had more than a century on you."

Charles smiles, pointing to the barely visible flecks of gray in his sideburns. "I'm not as young as I look. I just turned forty a few months ago."

"Still a spring chicken, then," I say. "I hope it was a happy birthday."

"It was." Pride fills his face. "It coincided with the birth of my daughter."

"A lovely gift!" I say. "Congratulations to you."

"Thank you," Charles says, still studying me curiously. He gives a subtle shake of his head, as if wrenching himself from a daydream. "I'd better get inside and find that teething gel my wife asked for." He steps aside to let me pass.

"Good night, Charles," I say, tipping my visor. "And if the gel doesn't work, try dipping a washcloth in chamomile tea."

He nods cordially, then disappears inside.

Standing under the cone of the streetlight, I stop to reflect on what I've just done, waiting for the full-fledged guilt to send me running back inside to tearfully confess. But all I feel is a deep sense of satisfaction.

And that means I'm ready.

**37**

Rage isn't an emotion I'm well acquainted with, but on this particular morning, it boils furiously beneath my sternum. On the rare occasions I do have these bouts of anger, it's the same culprit.

The rabbits have been nibbling at my flower buds again.

As much as I loathe their presence, I'm not cruel enough to sentence the naughty bunnies to death via traps or poison. So I've tried all manner of other creative deterrents—netting, motion-sensor sprinklers, strategically placed garlic, cayenne pepper, marigold, and rosemary—and yet those crafty devils still munch away at my garden with abandon. Their timing today is an especially painful dagger to the heart: they've chomped off the buds of some roses, just as they were about to bloom.

I stand in the middle of my garden, looking for telltale signs of where the rabbits have made themselves at home. They must've tunneled a burrow somewhere in my garden and I'm determined to find it.

Then I remind myself that I have a more pressing task at hand.

The benefit of having a decades-old garden is that it produces far more than I could ever need, even when I preserve a lot of it for winter. So I like to put together baskets of excess vegetables to share with the neighbors. Today, I'm bringing one to Rowan, but it's not the good-hearted neighborly gesture it seems.

I have an ulterior motive.

I wander through the rows of vegetables, deciding which ones to bring. Beets, radishes, and carrots will add a nice mix of color to the basket, along with some kale, broccoli, and Swiss chard for volume.

Twenty minutes later, I arrive on Rowan's doorstep. I adjust my newly acquired visor, tucking a tuft of white hair beneath it. A reminder to myself of what I'm capable of.

Hettie is the first to greet me, sneaking out the door as soon as the gap is wide enough to accommodate her rotund torso.

I present the basket to Rowan before he even has the chance to greet me.

"Good morning!" I say, projecting my voice for the neighborhood's benefit. "I had an overflow of vegetables in my garden and thought you might enjoy some."

I've done this so often over the years that no one would find it out of the ordinary.

"Wow, thank you, Joy." He accepts the basket, brushing his fingertips across the ruffled kale leaves. "Would you like to come in and join me for some cupcakes?"

Exactly what I'd been angling for. This is simpler than I'd anticipated.

I pretend to consider his invitation. "Well, I did already have a cookie with my midmorning coffee," I say. "But my doctors have been telling me for decades to eat less sugar, and yet here I am, still standing."

"I should warn you the cupcakes are store-bought," Rowan says. "So they might pale in comparison to the ones you bake from scratch."

Who cares, as long as they get me inside.

"I'm sure they're delicious!"

Rowan opens the door wider. "Come on in, then."

I'm so curious to see inside his home. All sorts of images flash through my mind of what a criminal's abode might look like. Maybe this house is just a front for what he and Philippe are really doing. I don't want to jump to conclusions, but the shades are drawn in spite of it being a gloriously sunny day outside.

He leads me into what is a lovely—and impressively tidy—living room. A calm landscape painting sits above an elegant brocade sofa with old books arranged in stately rows on the shelves. And standing in the corner is a beautiful old piano.

I can't resist walking over to it and stroking its weathered wooden lid. "Such a beauty!"

Rowan stands proudly, hands in his pockets, an already-familiar habit of his.

"Isn't she? I found her at an estate sale for a great price—the daughter wanted it to go to someone who'd appreciate it, and when I mentioned I was a piano tuner, she was instantly convinced. Unfortunately, I have to keep the shades drawn so it doesn't overheat—I'm hoping it'll be less of an issue in winter."

I go to lift the keyboard lid. "May I?"

"Be my guest," he says. "I'm not much of a pianist, but I've been trying to teach myself."

I turn to him. "That's not how you became a piano tuner? Most tuners I know have been playing since they were kids."

He shakes his head. "I wish I'd had the chance to try it then." A pause. "I studied piano tuning as a trade while I was in Sing Sing, practicing the techniques on the old one they had in the rec room. At first it was just to pass the time, but then I found I really enjoyed it. And it gave me a way to earn money once I got out."

"I'd be happy to give you some lessons if you're ever interested." I say. "You'd be my first adult student!"

"I appreciate that," he says. "But things are pretty busy with work at the moment."

"With piano tuning?" A leading question.

"Ah, no." Rowan looks at me mischievously. "With the side business I mentioned."

I seize my opportunity.

"It's funny you bring that up, actually," I say, butterflies in my stomach. "I know you said that if I ever needed help with anything, I should sing out."

Rowan nods. "And I meant it. What did you have in mind?"

I blurt out what I've been practicing in my head since yesterday (and a few times in front of the mirror).

"I need you to help me steal a vase so I can give it to Hazel before she dies."

Rowan shakes his head quizzically, as if he's misheard me. "I'm sorry?"

At his feet, Hettie barks, as if shocked herself.

"Well, technically I'd need you and Philippe to create the replica so I could switch it with the real one. You wouldn't have to do the stealing or anything—that would be my job. In return I could offer you all the baked goods you can eat, in perpetuity, until I'm no longer around to make them."

Rowan's expression is difficult to decode. "I see."

"You can definitely trust me," I say. "Aside from making the vase, I'll keep you both out of it. I wouldn't want to put you at risk."

"I don't doubt that I can trust you, Joy," Rowan says slowly. "It's just that I question if you really want to do something like that. Premeditated theft is a lot more serious than pulling the fire alarm at a library. Are you sure about this?"

"Oh, you don't need to worry about me." I tap the brim of my visor. "In fact, I swiped this from the pharmacy in town just last night."

Rowan coughs, caught off guard. "Did you now?"

I nod confidently. "I even wore it in plain sight in front of a police officer and still got away with it." Should I have said "cop" to sound a little tougher?

He studies me for a moment.

"Why do you even want to do this, Joy?"

His frown is one of genuine concern.

"Because for our entire lives, Hazel has always been the one to take care of me in my lowest moments, even when she was on the other side of the world." My voice cracks, but I persevere. "I can't cure her cancer, but this vase is the one thing that's special to her that she's never been able to acquire. I want her to have it before she goes. It was made by a former lover who died too young, so it has sentimental value."

Rowan rocks on his heels, considering my appeal.

"What if we made you a replica and you could just give her that? That way you wouldn't be putting yourself at risk."

"No," I say firmly. "It has to be the real thing, otherwise it's meaningless." I look up at him tearfully. "Please, Rowan, I know you understand what it's like to be about to lose someone and feel powerless to help them. This is one thing I know will make Hazel happy."

It's emotional manipulation, but it's also true.

The silence is excruciating as he stands rubbing his beard, thinking. As much as I want to push him, I trust my instinct for patience.

Finally, he looks back down at me.

"I'll think about it—but no promises."

It's a start.

# 38



The absence of natural light feels intentionally brutal as I sit in this bleak hospital hallway with Elizabeth sobbing next to me. Four-year-old Finn sits quietly next to her, whispering to his toy dinosaur in a respectful tone that suggests he comprehends the gravity of the situation.

Thom is dead. He went out to fetch the newspaper from the front lawn and had a ruptured brain aneurysm before he even got to read the front-page headline. I was in the kitchen making our morning coffees, and it took me a beat to register the absence of the screen door slamming with his return. When I finally went outside to check, he was sprawled across the grass, barely conscious.

Three days on life support.

One final breath.

And now I'm a widow.

I suppose I'm lucky it hasn't happened earlier; I had him for longer than others do their spouses. I try not to think about what might have happened if I'd realized sooner about the screen door. Would a few extra minutes have made a difference?

When I first met Thom in that burlesque club all those years ago,

I never considered how things might end. In the beginning of a relationship, the end rarely occurs to you. Neither does the painful middle. And yet they're both just as important as the beginning.

I was just grateful to have been noticed that night in Manhattan. Thom invited me to lunch the next day and behaved in all the ways my mother had told me a gentleman should. I left New York feeling much less trepidation than when I'd arrived days earlier. And for whatever reason, Thom saw something appealing in me. He was persistent, writing me letters every month, arranging to be in New York whenever I was there visiting Hazel. A year after we met, with only a few chaste kisses having been exchanged between us, he surprised me by arriving on my father's doorstep to ask for my hand in marriage. At the time I wondered why he deemed me suitable to be his wife—not whether he was the man I wanted to marry. I wouldn't say I was in love with him, but he had come to represent hope for the future. A chance to define myself beyond my small life with my father. It helped that he was exactly the kind of man my father had in mind for me.

Now, in this hospital corridor in Newburgh, the shock of Thom's death crystallizes. What it means to be married to someone for more than fifty years—your identities intertwined like the roots of two willow trees, inextricably connected, one forever reliant on the other.

But what happens when the dominant one, the one that stood so tall and vigorously in the forest, is gone? Can the smaller, feebler one survive on its own?

The truth is, I married Thom before I even had the chance to form my own identity, so he became mine. I'm not even sure I know who I am when not defined by my husband's existence. He earned all our money and made all our decisions, right down to who we would vote for (though in the privacy of the voting booth, I made my own choice). For many years, I couldn't even have a bank account, and it was only Thom's name listed in the phone book.

He set the tone for our entire life.

It's embarrassing that I've gotten to seventy-seven years old without ever learning to pay a bill. I wouldn't know the first thing about our finances, where the deed to our house is, or our marriage license, our insurance policy. Thom took care of it all. I can't ask Elizabeth to help me with these things—as her mother, I'm supposed to take care of her. Plus she has a little boy who needs her.

Nausea sweeps over me as I begin to reckon with my new reality.

The double doors in the hospital corridor burst open, reigniting the memory of our traumatic arrival here three days ago, Thom strapped to a gurney, me hurrying helplessly after him, still in my dressing gown. The only thing I could think in that moment was how embarrassed he'd be that I was out in public in my pajamas. He refused to even fetch the paper without being fully dressed.

I see that same helpless look in the young woman jogging behind the gurney that's come through the doors. A nurse takes her by the shoulders and guides her to the waiting room. I want to wrap her in a hug and tell her everything's going to be okay. But I'd probably be lying.

And that's when I see a flame of red hair, the tone of it so recognizable that it instantly floods my body with relief. When I'd called Hazel at the number I had for her in Egypt—where she's been living for the past six months—someone took a message on her behalf. I only wanted her to know that Thom was in the hospital; I didn't expect her to drop everything and jump on a plane.

Yet, here she is.

As soon as Hazel spots the three of us sitting forlornly on the hard plastic seating, I see from her face that I don't have to convey the news of Thom's death. She strides over, gathering the three of us into one embrace.

"Someone forgot to give me your message, otherwise I would've been here sooner," she says. "I'm so sorry you're going through this."

The fact that she showed up at all—despite her intense dislike for my husband—is all I need.

"Thank you for coming all this way," I sniffle into her quilted coat. "You didn't have to do that. I know your life is so busy."

"Of course I did," Hazel says. "You'll always be my priority, Joy. Especially when your heart is in pieces."

Elizabeth's husband, Jack, arrives a few minutes later to take her and Finn home.

"I can stay to help make arrangements if you need me to, Mom," she says in a small voice.

"No, darling, that's okay. You take Finn home and get some rest, and I'll call you in the morning."

She nods, giving me a half hug with Finn on her hip. When he wraps his little arm around my neck, I almost break down.

"It's starting to snow outside," Hazel says, as we sit down again in that unforgiving lighting. "We're in for a heavy storm, apparently."

The first snow of winter, unseasonably early—I haven't even had the chance to wrap my most vulnerable plants in burlap. An unnecessary cruelty of fate, the loss of a husband and a garden in one blow.

"When do you need to be back in Egypt?"

Hazel squeezes my shoulder. "When I'm no longer needed here," she says. "I'll stay as long as you want me to."

I'd love it if she stayed forever. But that would be like caging a bird that's always flown free.

"Thank you," I say, my head on her shoulder.

And that's when I finally do break down.

"I don't know how I'm going to survive without him," I sob, drawing in a wobbly breath. "I don't even know how to pay the heating bill."

"Then it's a good thing that I've been paying my own bills all my life," Hazel says. "While we're at it, I can also teach you how to check the fuse box, change a tire, and fix a dripping faucet."

I hadn't even considered all the home maintenance that Thom took care of. Hazel would have had to teach herself those things. How did she even start a business back when women couldn't have their own bank accounts? It's so privileged of me to see these things as insurmountable tasks when she had no choice but to learn them.

Hazel rubs my arm tenderly. "This is going to feel hard for a very long time, Joy. It's only natural that it will. But I'm going to walk beside you every step of the way."

I'm infinitely grateful to her. But once again, I feel guilty for burdening her with my emotions when I've never seen her so much as shed a tear.

How many times can one person rescue you without you repaying the kindness?

**39**

When I spot Elizabeth's car coming down the street, I lean over my porch rail to check one last time for Rowan's presence in his front yard.

Despite my best efforts—spending hours tending to my front garden or sitting on the porch—I haven't seen him since he told me he'd think about my proposal. Is he avoiding me? Time is ticking; I need to know whether he's going to help me with getting the vase or if I'm going to just have to find a way to go it alone. Even if stealing it outright would be much riskier than switching it for a replica.

Either way, I'm committed to this last act for Hazel.

I assumed we'd all take the train down to her place together, but Elizabeth insisted on driving, so we weren't beholden to the Metro-North schedule. I didn't dare argue—but I'm surprised when she gets out of the driver's seat and holds the door open for me while Finn puts my grocery caddy in the trunk.

"Can you drive for a while, Mom?" she says in a tired monotone. "I worked a double shift yesterday, and I'm zonked."

"To Brooklyn?" I never drive farther than the few towns surrounding Beacon—and definitely not on a five-lane highway.

"Well, at least half the way, so I can take a nap in the back seat."

"But I've never really driven on the freeway," I say timidly. "Your father always did that."

"You'll be fine, Mom," she says, her exhaustion breeding impatience. "Just stay in the slow lane."

Finn leans over from the front seat. "I'll be your navigator, Nanna," he says with his wonderfully asymmetrical grin. "You'll be great."

I'm terrified. But a grandmother with limited highway-driving experience is probably safer on the road than someone who might fall asleep at the wheel. Elizabeth is actually being sensible.

"All right, then." I slide into the driver's seat and adjust it so my feet reach the pedals. "But we might get there a little later than we told Hazel."

"I'll text her to let her know," Elizabeth says. "She's never on time, anyway."

Within ten minutes, Elizabeth is asleep, head resting against the window. Every so often, I glance in the rearview mirror, marveling at how peaceful she looks. I'd always wished I'd been able to bottle those moments watching her sleep as a child, so peaceful and innocent, so untarnished by the world, the soft rise and fall of her little chest, the dreamy sighs. Even now, hardened by five decades of life, there are glimpses of that peace, that innocence. My chest swells with adoration.

Traffic thickens as we get farther south, and I force myself to focus on the road. I've been sticking to the slow lane as Elizabeth instructed, but the car in front of us is inching along. This must be what it's usually like to drive behind me.

Checking over my shoulder, I glide into the next lane to pass the car. But instead of returning to the slow lane, I keep pace with the car in front of me.

Finn turns to me, shocked.

"Nanna!"

Startled, I scan the road for some kind of hazard. I glance at him, confused.

"What is it?"

He points to the dashboard. "You're speeding. I've never seen you do that in my life—you usually go five miles below the limit."

I feign innocence. "Was I?"

I ease my foot off the accelerator, but the impressed look on his face delights me no end.

"What's going on?" Elizabeth mumbles, her face arranged in the confused frown of interrupted sleep.

"Nothing, darling!" Finn and I exchange a sneaky glance. "I thought I saw a deer on the side of the road, but it was just a funny-shaped shrub—I'm sorry if we woke you."

She rubs her face with her palms. "It's fine. I can take over from you at the next gas station, if you want."

"Oh no, that's okay," I chirp to her reflection in the rearview mirror. "I think I've got the hang of it now."

Resting his elbow on the door, Finn hides a smile with his hand.

"Great," Elizabeth says, relaxing her head back against the window.

I feel a surge of confidence—turns out I'm capable of many things I've always avoided. What a treat it is to be on a road trip with two of my favorite people, on our way to see the third.

We're stuck in traffic on the George Washington Bridge when Elizabeth sits upright, as if remembering something.

"Hey, Mom," she says, leaning between the two front seats. "I ran into Rita the other day at the farmers market. What's all this about you hanging out with a convicted felon?"

Finn glances at me curiously. I like that I'm defying my grandson's perceptions.

"Oh, you know how Rita exaggerates," I say breezily. "She's talking about our new neighbor, Rowan. He just looks a little intimidating because he's rather burly and has a lot of tattoos."

Elizabeth frowns. "But is he really a criminal?"

The driver behind us beats her horn impatiently at the stalled traffic.

"He's a lovely and kind man who unfortunately got mixed up in some unseemly business when he was very young," I say. "It's not right for him to still be judged on past mistakes. Don't we all deserve some grace?"

My daughter's pursed lips imply skepticism. "Well, yes, but you do know the recidivism rates in America, right?

Finn turns to her. "Recidivism?"

"When people reoffend after spending time in prison, honey," she says, brushing his hair out of his eyes affectionately. "It tends to happen a lot."

A sudden heat injects my cheeks. I thought I'd gotten good at lying, but turns out that it's much harder to do with the people you love most.

"But that's often because society makes it hard for them to live a normal life due to their criminal background," I say. "Rowan just wants a quiet small-town existence with his dog, Hettie. And we've started a film club together—you're welcome to join us one afternoon. He loves foreign films, just like you do, darling." No lies there.

As if by divine timing, we start moving again, and Elizabeth sits back to let me concentrate.

I'm off the hook—for now.

# 40

The tension with Elizabeth starts a few blocks from Hazel's place, just after I've parked the car.

I was basking in the feat of driving us all the way down without a hiccup and executing the parallel park in one attempt. But as we approach Hazel's building, Elizabeth pulls me aside.

"Mom, do you mind if I go in by myself first?"

"By yourself?" My high is already disappearing. "But we all came down to see Hazel together."

Elizabeth's sunglasses frame two perfect reflections of the brownstone behind me, so I can't read her expression.

"Yeah, I know we did," she says. "But I want to spend some time alone with Hazel. This could be my last chance." The crack in her voice tugs at me. "I just want an hour with her—maybe you and Finn could go get smoothies, or something?"

She's right. I can't deny her this when it could be the last time. But it doesn't stop me from feeling rejected, like their special bond is something I can't possibly understand.

Finn slings his arm around my shoulders. "Come on, Nanna—I'll even treat you," he says. "And then maybe we can visit that comic book shop that's around here."

"A smoothie does sound good," I acquiesce. The quality time with my grandson is a welcome concession.

"Great," Elizabeth says. She kisses Finn on the forehead and takes the grocery caddy from him. "I'll bring this up and put the cold stuff in the fridge."

I feel a pang of jealousy. Providing for Hazel is one of the few ways I've been able to make myself useful to my friend, and now I don't even have that.

After we part ways, I sink into rumination over why she needed to spend time with Hazel without me. It's not like I would've monopolized the conversation. When all of us are together, it's always the two of them who talk the most with each other.

As we're waiting for our smoothies, loud reggae music competing with the racket of multiple blenders, Finn rubs my back sweetly.

"Don't take it personally, Nanna," he says. "Mom just wanted to thank Hazel for all she's done for her, especially the last couple of years—you know, with lending her the money and stuff."

Money? I'd never heard anything about Hazel giving Elizabeth money.

As far as I know, Hazel thinks giving money as a gift is gauche. And how long has it been exchanging hands? Given the way Finn mentioned it so casually, he must assume I know about it.

I feel foolish, ignorant, but I don't want him to think he revealed something he shouldn't.

"Of course," I say, pinning on that practiced smile. "That makes complete sense."

When we eventually return to Hazel's building, I'm glad when the rickety stairs declare our approach. Who knows what my daughter and best friend might be talking about?

"We're here!" Finn announces, once again making an uncomfortable situation bearable.

It pains me that the onus is often on him to play mediator. Some might argue that his ability to read situations and social dynamics at such a young age is an asset. But I can't help wondering if he learned those as a survival mechanism, just as I did, anticipating other people's moods to keep the peace. The way he tenses when his mother does, how he anticipates things that might upset her, cutting them off at the pass. Even that story he told me about trying to cheer her up by dancing in the car to cheesy music, subjecting himself to his classmates' ridicule.

And I can only imagine what he bore witness to in the months leading up to his parents' separation. The dissolution of a marriage is perilous for all who have to navigate its rocky shore, but especially children. Though my parents didn't divorce, I was forced to grow up long before I was ready to, filling my mother's void as domestic caretaker of my father. I wouldn't want Finn to suffer a similar fate; he deserves to just be a teenager.

Elizabeth and Hazel sit facing each other on the couch.

Is that disappointment on my daughter's face? Finn and I stayed away more than an hour, on principle, and I'm just as entitled to spend time with Hazel.

Finn bounds over to Hazel, and I'm worried he'll crush her with his hug. But as soon as he reaches her, his body language softens and he embraces her as delicately as if she were a precious baby bird.

Hazel kisses his cheek in appreciation. "How lucky am I to have you all gathered down here."

"It's only fair, since you visited us," he says.

How long ago that feels. Like a parallel universe of blissful ignorance.

Finn points to their empty water glasses. "Want a refill?"

Elizabeth lifts hers. "Thanks, honey, that would be great— sparkling water for me."

Finn collects them, then turns to me. "Nanna? Want some water?"

I'm lingering awkwardly against the wall like I'm at a school dance without a partner.

"Yes, please, darling."

"What are you doing all the way over there, Joy?" Hazel chides from the couch. "Come over and join us!"

"I wouldn't want to intrude on your conversation," I say, instantly regretting the childish passive-aggressiveness floating between my words.

Elizabeth raises an eyebrow at me.

Sheepishly, I take my place in the armchair adjacent to the couch and smile brightly.

And for the rest of the afternoon, we all pretend that the emotions simmering beneath never existed.

I wait until we've dropped Finn off at his friend's place for a video game night before broaching the topic with Elizabeth. The whole ride home, I debated whether it was even worth it, bringing up something I knew could widen the distance between us even more. But if there's one thing I'm starting to realize, it's that avoiding things has gotten me nowhere in life.

As we sit parked outside my house, the lights flicker on in Rita's front window. She's notorious for reporting suspicious vehicles in our neighborhood, but she should know Elizabeth's car by now. And if she happens to be peering through the curtains, as I assume she is, she'll see me exit the vehicle soon enough.

But for now, I keep my seatbelt strapped across my front, cherishing the false sense of fortitude it gives me.

Elizabeth eyes me strangely, likely wondering why I haven't yet gotten out.

A deep breath.

"There's something I wanted to ask you about," I say, twisting my wedding ring around my finger. "Finn mentioned it while we were getting smoothies."

Her phone vibrates; she grabs it from the console and I notice that she's hiding the screen from me. Could it be a message from Hazel lamenting that they didn't get to spend more time just the two of them?

"Well?" Elizabeth says, as if I'm keeping her in suspense. "What is it?"

"He said—" I choose my words judiciously, as if finding the sturdiest stones to safely cross a rushing river. "That Hazel had loaned you some money."

That deep pink flush streaks up Elizabeth's neck, spilling onto her face. "So?"

"I was just wondering what it was for." One more stone. "And why you didn't feel as though you could ask me for it." And another.

"It's not a big deal," Elizabeth huffs. "I just needed some money to pay for some of Finn's extracurricular activities and it made sense to ask Hazel."

Indignation balloons in my chest. It's a tormenting impotence, not being the one my daughter goes to for help.

"But he's my grandson," I insist. "You should have asked me first."

Elizabeth presses her lips together. "I knew you were already on a tight budget and I didn't want to make it worse by asking you," she says. "You don't think I see those past-due bills on your noticeboard? Or how you live off canned beans and pasta to save money?"

"I would've made it work if you gave me the chance," I insist. "You know you can come to me about anything."

Elizabeth puts her phone down and turns her whole body to face me. "Can I, though?"

I grasp the seatbelt, pulling it close to my body. "What do you mean?"

"Let's be honest, Mom," she says. "You've never really been comfortable with big emotions. Whenever I came home from school upset about something, you'd just tell me to look on the bright side and focus on being grateful for what I had."

"I just wanted to help you think positively!"

Elizabeth shakes her head. "But you made me feel like I wasn't allowed to have any negative feelings—because, in your opinion, I had a much better life than those poor piano students you cared so much about." Her eyes flash. "Do you know what it's like to feel second-best to some random kids?"

"Oh, Elizabeth," I say. "You weren't second best. You were—are—the thing I care about most. I did everything I could to make sure you were happy."

Elizabeth sighs heavily. "Your idea of making me happy was baking cookies for me, or teaching me the proper way to write a thank-you note, or how to be a good hostess—always with a smile on my face, of course," she says, her sarcasm thick. "But I didn't need that. I needed you to listen, to let me discuss my feelings without being judged. Even during the divorce, all you've done is offer to clean my house or make us meals, but what I've really needed is to talk about things. I can tell Hazel anything and she won't judge or pressure me."

Now I'm confused. "But . . . I never pressured you about anything." On the contrary—I tried to be as patient as possible.

Elizabeth laughs, incredulous. "Really? What about Jack? Back when I told you I was thinking about breaking up with him so I could maybe travel abroad—or at least try dating other guys—you convinced me to stay with him because he was the 'dependable' choice." I can feel the vitriol in her air quotes. "It's like you pressured me into living the same small-town life that you chose. And look how that turned out. I should've known better than to take advice from someone who wasn't even happy in her own marriage."

My stomach drops. "I'm sorry?"

I was sure I'd done my best to shield Elizabeth from my unhappier times with Thom.

"Mom," she says. "It was obvious that Dad was cheating on you—all those overnight trips to the city for 'business,' and those random women calling the house pretending to be his assistants? I overheard him talking to them sometimes from his study; they obviously weren't his colleagues."

I stare at her, the familiar sting of shame creeping over me. Did she know about Celeste too?

My voice wobbles. "I wish you'd said something to me."

"Would you have done anything?" Elizabeth's resignation hurts more than her anger. "Every time he came home with flowers or gifts for us, probably because he felt guilty, you just accepted them and pretended like we were one big happy family."

"I did it to protect you," I whisper. "So you could still grow up with a dad."

"Even if it meant watching him control you? Telling you how to dress, dictating every aspect of our lives, all while cheating on you?" Elizabeth stares up at the car ceiling. "Truthfully, I loved him as my dad, but sometimes I felt like I hated him as your husband. I think it would've been better for me if you'd left him."

Suddenly the seatbelt across my chest feels like a shackle.

I know I should stay and hash this out with my daughter, to explain my side of things, why I made the choices I did. But if I do, I'll unravel in front of her, and I can't do that, not now.

So I unbuckle myself, push the car door open, and flee.

**41**

D*ear Hazel*
These two words have been staring back at me from an otherwise blank page for the past forty-five minutes. I've been trying Rowan's suggestion of writing Hazel a letter expressing everything she means to me, but how do you capture eighty-one years of friendship in one measly note?

Though I'm an avid reader, I wouldn't say I'm good with words. Or better put, I'm not very good at distilling everything I think and feel into a sentence. I express my love for people in other ways. Their favorite sweet treat fresh from the oven. A basket of vegetables from my garden, grown with care. A warm, firm hug. A rendition of their favorite song played on the piano. But putting it all in one letter?

It feels impossible.

This isn't like writing a thank-you note—I'm adept at those, thanks to my mother's early tutelage. All you need do is thank the person for the thing they gave you or did for you, tell them how it impacted your life positively or how you plan to use it, mention how thoughtful it was of them, and then wish them well.

But how do you thank someone for their entire existence without simultaneously feeling like you aren't doing it justice?

Admittedly, it's not just my inability to articulate myself that's making this letter hard. I'm distracted by my conversation with Elizabeth last night, embarrassed that I fled her car without seeing it through.

I'm also ashamed that so much of what she said rang true.

At first, I felt indignant at her accusations. The reason I made sure she never had to worry about things like cooking and cleaning when she was growing up was because those were things my mother was never able to do for me once she was ill. I longed to have the freedom that Hazel's parents gave her—never having to worry about taking care of a house-hold in between homework, not having to get up at five in the morning to make sure the cleaning was done before I left for school. Being able to hang around with the other kids after class in high school, instead of rushing home to make sure dinner was on the table for my father.

And all those life skills I taught Elizabeth—how to be a good host-ess, how to stay gracious and composed—were because those were the few life lessons Mama was able to impart to me before she died. So I treasured them. I'd have loved to have her advice on other things—like how to love your body more, how to navigate a marriage, or the intricacies of female friendship—but I had to make do with the few things she was able to offer.

Now I understand that I was just seeing Elizabeth as an extension of myself and what I needed as a child. I failed to see her as her own person with her own unique needs. The ways in which I demonstrated my love were out of step with the ways in which she wanted to re-ceive it. Parenting isn't about creating someone in your own image; it's about giving them the clay to shape themselves as they see fit, and celebrating whatever form they end up taking.

Worse, it's true that I pressured Elizabeth into staying with Jack. On paper he seemed to fit exactly the criteria my mother had given me for a husband—affable, stable, dependable—but then again, so did Thom at the beginning. I wanted Elizabeth to be taken care of, to not have to struggle with money, and yet that's where she ended up, anyway.

Perhaps she would have been better off following her heart instead. I never even consulted my heart. If I had, and was brave enough to blow up my entire existence, I might have spent ten blissful years with Percy before he died. Or if I hadn't settled for Thom so early on, perhaps I would've crossed paths with Percy before he ever met Myrtle—Hazel did try to convince me to join her on a trip to Scotland in the late fifties—and then who knows where life would've led? Though if that were the case, I wouldn't have Elizabeth or Finn, so I can't really resent my choice. The point is, I should have encouraged my daughter to make exactly that: her own choice. What a mess I've made of being a mother.

The chime of my front doorbell gives me a reprieve from my angst.

I'm cautious about answering the door if I'm not expecting anyone. Elizabeth has warned me about scams targeting the elderly, tricking them into buying something they don't need, selling their house out from under them, or swindling their entire life savings. I'm not very good at saying no, so it's best to pretend I'm not home.

I sneak to the corner of my window, back flat against the wall so I can peer through the gap between the curtain and the glass unseen.

To my delight, it's Rowan.

I hurry to answer the door, counting to four before opening it so I don't appear too eager.

Rowan is holding the basket I'd brought with the vegetables the other day. I'd purposefully tied a little label with my name on it so he'd think I wanted it back and would have to come see me.

I might be getting good at this.

He points to the doorbell.

"'Ode to Joy,'" he says, referring to the tune of the chime. "A nice touch."

"It was a Christmas present from Finn," I say, tickled that he noticed.

Rowan holds out the basket. "I wanted to return this in case you need it. The veggies were delicious, thank you—Hettie especially enjoyed the carrots."

As usual, he's very tidily put together, his hair combed neatly with gel. I appreciate that his shirts, always rolled up at the sleeves, are infallibly well ironed. I must ask him his technique for keeping wrinkles at bay. But right now, I'm hoping we might have more important things to discuss.

"I'm so glad to hear it," I say. "Would you like to come in?"

Rowan glances at his watch and squints, as if calculating time in his head. "I can't today, unfortunately—I'm catching an early afternoon train to the city and I need to walk Hettie before we do. She gets a little restless on board otherwise."

Disappointment sets in—for a moment there I'd hoped he was here to discuss my proposal. In retrospect, it was a lot to ask of him and Philippe, especially since they have nothing to gain from it.

"Can't let Hettie miss out on her walk!" I say with forced cheer. "Perhaps we can see another movie sometime soon."

Even if he isn't willing to help me out with the vase, I want to make sure our film club stays intact.

"I'd love that," Rowan says, swaying to avoid the flight path of a bumblebee near his head. He checks his watch again.

"Don't let me keep you," I say. "And please say hello to Philippe."

Rowan nods. "Will do."

And yet he lingers on the doorstep. Maybe there's hope, after all.

"There is one more thing," he says. The ensuing pause feels interminable. "I've discussed your proposition with Philippe . . . and we'd like to help you, given the circumstances with Hazel." A hint of vulnerability reaches his smile. "You've been a good friend to me, Joy. It means a lot that you've been so welcoming despite what others might think. Not many people have extended that kindness to me in my life. I'd love to help you do this for your friend."

I want to hug him, but that would seem a bit over the top for a neighbor returning a vegetable basket.

"Thank you, Rowan," I say.

I hope my eyes convey my true gratitude—and also mask my trepidation.

What have I gotten myself into?

## 42

'm surprised to get a call from Elizabeth. I thought I'd have to be the one to reach out after our last encounter.

But she doesn't mention any of it when I answer.

"Hi, Mom," she says in the same emotionless, efficient tone of my doctor's receptionist calling to confirm an appointment. "I've just been offered a night shift last minute and I'd really like to do it for the overtime. Would you mind if Finn slept at your place tonight?"

Disappointment duels with relief—even though I'd hoped she'd bring up our recent conversation, I'm not sure I'm ready for it.

"Of course, darling," I say. "I'd love to have him stay."

"Great, thanks so much." At least that sounds genuine. "I'll drop him by in about an hour."

It's not until a few minutes before Finn is due to arrive that I realize Rowan is also supposed to be dropping by to discuss our plan for the vase. I don't know Rowan's phone number to call and warn him not to come. And he didn't give me a specific time, so I don't even know when to expect him. I'll just have to improvise—I've gotten used to telling the occasional lie lately in order to protect myself. But can I look my grandson in the eye and do it?

There's still no sign of Rowan when I start cooking dinner.

"A five-letter word for 'gusto,'" Finn says from the kitchen table, where he's hunched over the crossword puzzle from yesterday's paper.

I pause my chopping of tomatoes—made more difficult by the old, blunt knife.

"Five letters . . . ardor?"

"Nope." Finn presses the pencil on a square. "Last letter is E."

The shrill ring of the landline telephone startles us both.

"That's so loud, Nanna," Finn says. "You should get a cordless phone so you can adjust the ringtone—or at least the volume." He looks at me cheekily. "They even make them with buttons instead of dials now."

I bustle across the room to answer it. "I like it loud so I can hear it no matter where I am in the house," I say defiantly. "And the dial makes it more satisfying." I like the whirring sound it makes after each number.

I hold the army-green receiver to my ear. "Hello, Bridport residence."

Maybe Rowan found my number in the phone book.

A slight pause before I hear a woman's voice. "Hello, is that Mrs. Bridport?"

Immediately my guard is up. Elizabeth has also warned me about telephone scams targeting the elderly. These "spam" calls have become increasingly frequent.

"This is she."

I toy with the phone cord, its decades-old plastic split open, revealing the rainbow of wires running beneath like muscles.

"Hello, ma'am," the woman says in that same emotionless voice Elizabeth used earlier. "I'm calling in regard to your unpaid highway tolls. I'm afraid if you don't pay the bills immediately, they'll be sent to debt collection."

My lips curl into a crafty smile.

"Nice try! But I've never driven on a highway in my life. Good night!"

I hang up the phone triumphantly. Then I remember that I did, in fact, drive on one recently. But that was Elizabeth's car and she has one of those tags that pays the tolls automatically.

When I turn around, Finn is staring at me in awe. "Nanna, I've never seen you hang up on anyone."

"Well, it was one of those scam callers, so they deserved it."

"Even then, you're usually so polite that it takes you at least ten minutes to end the call."

He's right.

"Maybe I'm not as nice as people think," I say insouciantly, then wrap my arms around his shoulders while I study the crossword. "What about verve?"

He pencils it in. "Yessss, Nanna, you icon."


Of course Rowan chose the exact moment I went to the bathroom after dinner to finally drop by. When he'd visited earlier this week to let me know he was on board with my plan, I'd given him the details of Seth's shop and the vase.

"I'll get it, Nanna!" Finn calls when the doorbell rings.

I panic, willing my bladder to empty faster and my imagination to conjure a reasonable explanation for Rowan's visit.

By the time I'm out of the bathroom, Finn and Rowan are together in the living room.

"Oh," I say as breezily as possible. "Hello, Rowan!"

Finn turns to me. "Don't worry, I didn't just let a stranger into your house—I knew who he was."

"You did?"

Finn shrugs. "Yeah, you told me and Mom about him the other day, remember? You said he was your new movie buddy." He grins at Rowan. "Pretty easy to match him to the description you gave me."

I glance sheepishly at Rowan. "I was just telling him how much I liked your tattoos!"

Rowan smiles good-naturedly, then points to the tool bag on the piano stool. "Is now still a good time for that piano tuning?"

Brilliant.

"Yes, of course! It completely slipped my mind that you were coming." Inspired by Rowan's ingenuity, I summon some of my own. "Finn, darling, would you go outside and check if all the sprinklers have turned off? The timer doesn't work sometimes and it creates a minor flood. I wouldn't want my cucumbers to drown!"

"Sure, Nanna." He lopes out of the dining room.

"Thank you," I call after him. "And keep your eye out for those pesky rabbits!"

"Nice work," Rowan says.

"I'm sorry—my daughter needed me to look after him last minute."

"Totally fine." He waits until we hear the back screen door closing, then continues. "Okay, so I've paid a visit to the secondhand shop and managed to take photos of the vase from different angles. Philippe is working on creating the replica now and says it should be ready next week—the original is raku-fired, so he wants to make sure he follows the same process so it looks as real as possible."

Wow, this is really happening. I mean, I know it's what I asked for, but hearing the logistics and practical details suddenly makes it feel much more real.

"That's wonderful—please thank him for his efforts."

"Sprinklers are off!" I hear Finn's voice before I see him.

Did he overhear our conversation? Is Finn giving us a warning of his presence? His facial expression bears no indication that he's just heard his grandmother discussing a potential art heist.

"Excellent, thank you, darling." I button my collar to hide the flush of red on my neck.

Rowan begins rummaging through his bag and takes out his tuning hammer and muting clips, lining them up neatly on the piano stool.

Finn walks over. "Hey, man," he says casually. "Do you mind if I watch? I've always wondered how you tune a piano."

Has he? What a nice surprise.

"Be my guest," Rowan says.

He begins disassembling the front panel of the piano. It's a pleasure to watch him work; the ease of his movements as he opens the piano lid and begins his tweaks shows the confidence of someone who knows their trade intimately. But it's even more of a pleasure to see my grandson so engaged in something.

As I watch Rowan patiently talking Finn through everything he's doing, I can't help but feel a little teary.

Even though I'm preparing to lose one friend, I'm grateful to be gaining another.

# 43

The soft, ethereal light from the large screen fills Rowan's face, his brow flinching with emotion as the music swells.

For the second official meeting of our film club, we've selected a French movie about two young women, one of whom is sent to an island in France to paint the other's portrait. I'm so swept up in the beauty of it all—the saturated colors, the rugged coastal landscape, the profound longing between the women—that I almost forget that we're also here for another purpose.

When he invited me to today's matinee, Rowan requested I bring my grocery caddy, telling me he'd meet me at the cinema rather than walking there together.

He arrived with a leather duffel bag slung over his shoulder.

"I just came from the gym," he said, paying for our tickets despite my protests.

"It's good that you're keeping yourself in shape," I replied. "You'll be grateful when you're my age."

When I'm at the movies alone, I like to sit closer to the screen—my eyes aren't what they used to be and I also love the feeling of being immersed in the film, like I'm in a waking dream. But Rowan guided us to the back row of the cinema, and I'm feeling a tad guilty that my grocery caddy is taking up the wheelchair space. I suppose it doesn't matter, since we're the only ones here.

As the two women onscreen have an emotional conversation on a windswept beach, Rowan slowly opens the duffel, revealing an object swathed in a thick cloth. As he unravels the layers of material, there's a glimmer of glazed ceramic.

Rowan flashes me a knowing smile, then wraps it back up, nodding his head at my caddy. I follow his wordless instruction and transfer it safely to my possession.

Then we both return to watching the movie.

I'm glad he didn't try to do the exchange at the end of the film because I was a puddle of tears. What a touching, bittersweet love story it was. I caught Rowan dabbing his eyes with a knuckle as well.

After we stop for ice cream cones—mint chocolate chip for Rowan, pistachio for me—we claim a spot on the bench overlooking the waterfall and the beautiful red brick industrial buildings flanking it. We've had quite a bit of rain the past few days so the water tumbles vigorously, sending a refreshing mist floating in our direction.

Eager to hear about the next stage of our heist, I confirm that no one is in earshot, then nudge my caddy.

"It looks like Philippe did an excellent job," I say, catching a drip of pale green ice cream as it plunges towards my yellow blouse.

"He certainly did," Rowan says, tossing the last of his cone in his mouth. "I think he's especially proud of his work." He crunches down with a grin.

"I hope I get to see him again soon so I can thank him."

Rowan retrieves a bottle of hand sanitizer from his duffel. "As a matter of fact, he'll be up here on Thursday." He squirts the gel onto his palm. "If that suits you, of course."

We've already agreed that it's better if Philippe helps me make the switch, rather than Rowan. It's a small town, after all, and Philippe will hopefully blend in as one of the many city slickers up on a day trip to scope out antiques. There's enough talk about Rowan already and I don't want to do anything to jeopardize his reputation further.

"I'm pretty sure I'm available," I say coyly, as if my days are regularly booked out.

"Excellent," Rowan says. "Philippe will be at the shop at four o'clock and will be browsing when you get there. He'll distract the owner while you make the switch, and then he'll go straight back to the city."

"You won't even get to see him?"

Rowan shakes his head. "It's better he doesn't come anywhere near our neighborhood that day. We don't want to create any more links between the two of us and him."

What a rookie I am.

"Right, of course." I glance down at my soggy cone; it's sprung a leak. "I think it's time I gave up on this."

We find a trash can, then start heading home. As we pass Seth's shop on the way, butterflies begin a ballet in my stomach. This is really happening.

It's not until I'm back in my kitchen, washing my sticky hands in the sink, that I start to have second thoughts.

I've been so caught up in the caprice of it all—the thrill of plotting with Rowan, the idea of one last grand gesture for Hazel—that I haven't really accepted the fact that this isn't just the petty shoplifting of a cheap visor. It's a fully premeditated crime—with accomplices who have a lot to lose too.

Am I really capable of doing this?

Later that afternoon, eight-year-old Freya arrives for her piano lesson. I'd been so focused on my conversation with Rowan that I forgot she was coming until the doorbell rang. Thank heavens I wasn't still out somewhere.

Freya has only been coming for a couple of months, but she's obviously gifted. Once in a while, I have one of those students who possesses talent far beyond mine, and I feel like a fraud being their teacher, knowing they deserve someone of a much higher caliber.

But she isn't her usual sunny self today; she's listless and unfocused, fumbling over chords that would normally flow effortlessly from her fingers. Perhaps she's just exhausted from her day at school—they work kids so hard these days.

She sits back from the piano keys, frustrated with herself.

I gently cup her tiny shoulder. "Did you have a busy day at school today, dear?"

She shrugs. "Not really."

Her ever-present smile is noticeably absent.

"Are you feeling okay?" I touch the back of my fingers to her forehead—kids pick up all sorts of bugs, but Freya doesn't appear to have a fever.

She shrugs again. "Just a bit hungry," she says. "Mom forgot to pack my lunch today."

"You didn't tell your teachers so they could get you something from the cafeteria?"

Freya shakes her head. "I didn't want my mom to get in trouble. I know she didn't do it on purpose—she's just really busy."

I believe Freya—her mother, June, is a lovely and kind woman, but I know she struggles with being a single mother sometimes. I can imagine Elizabeth making a similar oversight with Finn.

And at least I now know the reason for Freya's lack of energy. It's four in the afternoon and the poor thing probably hasn't eaten since breakfast.

"Why don't we pause our lesson for today and have a sandwich instead?"

Freya's smile finally reappears, her two newly acquired front teeth still stumps at the top of her mouth.

"Are you sure that's okay?" she whispers.

"Of course it is," I say, standing up. "I'm a little hungry myself."

I prepare her a chicken salad sandwich with some carrot sticks and peanut butter on the side.

Watching her devour it like she can't get the food into her mouth quickly enough, my chest pangs. I wish I could do more to help these kids beyond the thirty minutes I spend with them each week. I send her home with a bag of snacks, telling her to keep them in her back-pack in case her mom accidentally forgets her lunch again. From now on, I'll make sure to have a sandwich waiting for her each time she comes.

As I'm cleaning up her plate, I realize I should have actually checked the calendar before agreeing to next Thursday for the "switch." Four o'clock is the lesson time for my student Annie—Thursdays are the only days that her mother can arrange to drop her off after school, so we can't even reschedule it for another day.

For a moment, I'm riddled with guilt. But then I tell myself to toughen up.

If I'm really going to go through with an art heist, the last thing I should be worried about is canceling a free piano lesson.

**44**

I got so distracted trying to find a good hiding place for the vase that I missed my train.

It wasn't just that I wanted to make sure Finn and Elizabeth didn't see it. It's that I feel guilty each time I catch sight of it.

I settled on squirreling it away in my dirty clothes hamper. No one is going to be digging in there anytime soon.

When I called Hazel to let her know I'd be coming down a little later than originally planned, she told me to let myself in, since I now have a key.

"I think after eighty years of friendship, you've earned the right to my spare key," she'd said, bestowing it to me as if it were a sacred stone.

Really, it was so she wouldn't have to expend energy buzzing me in, but I played along for her sake.

"What a great honor, your highness," I said. "I shall guard it with my life."

Her loft is silent when I nudge the door open. I leave my grocery caddy, along with the lavender plant I brought, in the kitchen and tread softly on the creaky floorboards near her bedroom.

My heart stutters when I see her lying on her back, hands arranged neatly across her abdomen, evoking memories of the too many funerals I've been to.

Thankfully, I can see her chest subtly rising and falling, but it still makes me consider what's soon to come.

I don't even know if Hazel wants a funeral. I've made a note in my own will that there's not to be a viewing at mine. But then, who's going to be there aside from Finn and Elizabeth? Perhaps I should state that there's to be no funeral at all, rather than pressuring people to come fill seats out of pity.

I've attended many funerals of people I barely knew, just to bump up the numbers so their families felt like their person was loved and cherished—a small kindness I could offer them in their time of grief. One time, however, I was at the funeral of a woman I was sure I'd met before, trying to recall my best memories of her, like her beautiful singing voice and the tremendous pumpkin pie she made for the church bake sale. But as people began filing out of the pews at the end of the service, the woman I thought I'd been mourning walked straight past me and smiled.

To this day, I have no idea whose funeral I was attending.

I stand in the doorway, taking comfort in Hazel's steady breathing for a while longer. I know there's a good chance I won't be here with her for her final moments, but the possibility that I might have missed them because I took a later train today would have been too much to bear.

Watching her sleep gives me the rare opportunity to really grasp how much her body is deteriorating. Of course I've noted her increasing weight loss and frailty, but I try not to look anywhere but her eyes when I'm talking to her—no matter how subtle you think you're being, people can tell when you're focusing on things they'd prefer you didn't. Most women know what it's like to have a man glance at their breasts in conversation, thinking they won't notice.

Even now, it feels intrusive—seeing how her perpetually tanned skin has grown sallow and paper-thin, how her beautiful clothes appear several sizes too big. It's hard to reconcile that someone so strong and robust can shrink so rapidly.

And yet it's not the first time I've witnessed that kind of decline.

Before my mother fell ill—Elizabeth suspects it was leukemia, based on the symptoms I recalled—I used to marvel at how strong and full of vigor she was. How she could carry a sack of potatoes or two pails of water with ease. Or how, when we'd go for long walks through the fields surrounding our house, she'd challenge me to race her to the next fence post. Somehow we always ended up in a dead heat—in retrospect, a motherly kindness on her part.

But then a sack of potatoes became too much, as did even a half-filled pail, and Mama no longer wanted to race. Soon she could barely muster the energy to rise out of bed, her body covered in unexplained bruises, her skin pallid. Every night I'd try to dislodge that image of her from my brain, trying my hardest to conjure the memories of her at her most robust.

What unfortunate bookends to have in my life, watching two of my most cherished people wilt away.

I take refuge in the kitchen until Hazel wakes up. After unpacking the meals I've prepped, I tend to the lavender plant, happy that it survived the journey down. I know it's a fool's errand to bring a plant to someone who won't be around to care for it, but it's the only way I could think of to feel less helpless—and hopeless. At least I know how to keep plants alive.

Filling an empty jar with water, I dampen the soil around the plant's base, but not too much. Overwatering is a death sentence to lavender—it thrives in dry, challenging conditions, and too much attention can cause it to rot. Hardy and independent, just like my friend.

I carry it over to the windowsill, to the jumble of pots already there—succulent, snake, and rubber plants in varying states of health. Even before she got sick, Hazel wasn't an attentive gardener and it was excruciating to witness the demise of many plants over the years. I'd discreetly tend to them, wiping the dust off their leaves, spritzing them with water until Hazel caught me.

"Are you here to visit me or to garden?" she'd say, eyebrow raised. "My ailing plants aren't your responsibility."

That's Hazel—a lone wolf for life. And yet, in the past few weeks, I've seen hints of vulnerability in my friend I didn't know she was capable of. Maybe that's why it's easier for her to have the death doula care for her instead of me. Just as I can't imagine not having Hazel around as the strong, brave one in our friendship, I know that she can't fathom a reversal of our roles. But perhaps I need to be more assertive with her too—starting with rescuing her forlorn houseplants.

I perform whatever triage I can to revive them, but what they all really need is more soil and bigger pots. I'll bring those next week, even if it means splurging on a taxi from Grand Central. I'll forgo my café treats for the time being. And I can handle a few more weeks of beans and veggies for dinner—come to think of it, I should've bought some of those discounted cans I knocked over at the grocery store.

The windowsill garden is looking markedly better when I hear Hazel's shuffle on the floorboards, wisps of her red hair defying gravity thanks to the pillow static.

"Hello, my friend," she says, subduing a wince of pain.

I pull her into a hug.

She doesn't brush me off or quickly tap out of it. She just lets me hold her, resting her head on my shoulder. In spite of her diminishing strength, it's the firmest hug she's ever given me.

As a rule, I try to hold onto hugs until the other person releases them, happy to embrace them for as little or as long as they need it. Today, Hazel and I stand in the middle of her kitchen, holding each other for what feels like minutes. I close my eyes and savor it, sending every ounce of healing energy I can muster between our aging bodies, committing every sensory detail to memory so I can treasure it forever. When Hazel does eventually disengage, she doesn't make her usual joke to dilute the awkwardness of intimacy. She just smiles down at me.

"Thank you," she says.

I expect bravado in her eyes. All I see is gratitude.

"How about I make you some lunch?" I say. "I've brought chicken and leek soup."

I know she can't resist that, but more importantly, it's packed with protein and nutrients.

"It sounds delicious," Hazel says, easing onto a bentwood chair. "But unfortunately, I've had trouble swallowing anything but liquids lately."

"Then it's lucky I blended it," I say, pulling out the container I'd put in the freezer. "I thought you might like to sip it from a straw."

We've arrived at the point when harmless quotidian actions like repetitively lifting a spoon have become a challenge.

A tired smile. "Let's give it a try."

As Hazel watches me prepare the soup, it occurs to me that while I'm savoring what's left of our time together, she's savoring what's left of her life.

The thumping bass of a pop song from a passing car floats through the open window and she sways along to it.

I pause my prep and stroll over to the turntable in the corner of the living room.

"Shall we put some music on?"

It suddenly dawns on me that the interminable silence is part of what's been making my visits here feel so depressing. Until her diagnosis, it was rare to be in Hazel's loft without music floating from that turntable.

She straightens, as if being reminded of an old friend she'd forgotten.

"Why not? I'd grown tired of having to constantly get up and turn over the record," she says. "But since you're here, be my guest."

Her taste diverges completely from my great love of classical composers. She prefers experimental jazz and rhythm-heavy music from distant parts of the world. A few times in our younger days, she'd taken me to obscure concerts in intimate venues where the crowds writhed as one to an irresistible beat. I felt completely out of place, but I loved watching the music bring Hazel alive, as if it were a spirit capturing her body.

I lift the needle from the record that's already on the turntable, something by a person named Fela Kuti. Hazel brightens instantly, her fingers tapping lightly on the table.

As I watch the music briefly revive her into that vibrant woman I knew, I remind myself of all the things she's done for me over the years, the way she's nudged me to be bolder and braver.

Despite my earlier reservations about my plan with Rowan, my mind is made up.

Getting her that vase is the least I can do.

# 45

My limbs are heavy from sleep deprivation, my mouth dry from stress.

I spent the night going over the plan I'd made with Rowan and Philippe, rehearsing all the potential outcomes.

Backing out is not an option—I'm getting this vase for Hazel, no matter what it takes. But it would be imprudent if I didn't consider the fact that I might get caught. Mine won't be as noble as Jane Fonda's arrest for protesting against climate change, but at least I'll be remembered for something. Perhaps it will even make the local news. Regardless, I'll have left a mark on the world, even if it's not one I strove for.

Even though I'm going to do my best to make sure that scenario doesn't happen, I've made some preparations just in case.

I lie still a while longer, savoring the soft pillow and cozy quilt, anticipating the discomfort of those prison cots. I wonder if they'd let me bring my knitted blanket for extra warmth—I'm sure those cells get drafty. I'll pack it just in case, folding it into the little overnight bag of things I'm hoping they'll let me bring if I'm taken into custody: a photo of Elizabeth and Finn on his tenth birthday, my hot-water bottle, a book of crossword puzzles, a romance novel I haven't read, and my gardening gloves (on the off chance they have a veggie patch at my prison).

I unplug everything in my house and leave a note for Elizabeth detailing where to find all my important documents and the bills that'll need paying, along with my checkbook and a letter stating my permission for her to use it on my behalf.

I give my garden a good soaking so it'll survive a few extra days without being watered (I included garden maintenance in my note to Elizabeth), and stand on my front porch, wondering if it'll be the last time. I try to memorize every detail—the pleasant jumble of smells, the distinct silhouettes of the leaves, the medley of color—just in case I don't get to see it again. Then I commence my walk to the bus stop (I don't want anyone to have to fetch my car), silently saying farewell to the neighborhood that's held me in its embrace for the majority of my life.

As the bus rumbles down the street, I pause at the mailbox to complete my last task: sending my finished letter to Hazel. Who knew that planning for the worst-case scenario could make you so uninhibited? There's a freedom to express exactly what you think and feel when the window to do so is closing. It was cathartic to put it all down on paper, to express my love and admiration without Hazel brushing off my sentimentalities or me getting tongue-tied. And at the end of it all, I included a list of ninety of my favorite memories together.

Now that I know how much you can get away with as an unassuming elderly woman, I've decided to lean into that persona. But it's hard to know what qualifies as little-old-lady attire, since I dress the same way I did thirty years ago. It's a bit of a stereotype, if you ask me. Maybe it's not that older women dress a certain way, but that we're all of the same generation and we dress accordingly. Elizabeth's cohort—Generation X, I think they're called—will likely dress in jeans and T-shirts when they're my age.

Still, it's better if I dress differently than usual to avoid the risk of someone I do know recognizing me. And having a "persona" also helps me summon the necessary courage for what I'm about to do. A while ago at the hair salon, I read an article in one of the dilapidated magazines about a young singer named Beyoncé who loved performing but was also painfully shy. She created an alter ego—the name was something like Sarah Fierce, or perhaps it was Sasha—that she would embody to help her feel brave whenever she was on stage. Now I understand what she was talking about.

Today, as "Bad Joy," I've opted for a slightly more glamorous look. After Thom retired and we weren't attending as many dinners and cocktail parties, I gave most of my fancier dresses away. Besides the one I wear to funerals, the only other dress I've kept—on the off chance I'm ever invited somewhere elegant—is a navy tea-length dress. I've added a long burgundy cardigan and a small string of pearls for good measure. I wasn't willing to part with my orthopedic sneakers; my uncomfortable-shoe days are long gone.

As the final flourish, I don my newly acquired visor.

Sweat prickles beneath my cardigan as I exit the bus on Main Street.

I'm not much of a performer. Hazel was in all the theater productions at our high school, but I was too timid for the stage, preferring to help with costumes. But right now the spotlight is on me and I need to put on a show.

Fortunately, I had the foresight to prepare last night by watching a movie featuring my favorite actress, Dame Judi Dench. I close my eyes and imagine how she'd handle this situation. It's a bit risky to try out a British accent without having ever attempted one, so I'll just have to channel Dame Judi playing an American.

I hunch my shoulders forward to exaggerate the hump in my back (earned from decades of bending over my garden). Then I slow my normally brisk walking pace by half, counting one second between each step until it feels like I'm moving in slow motion.

A block from Seth's store, I inch past a parking inspector, clutching onto my grocery caddy as if I need it for support. She pauses her vehicle surveillance.

"Good morning, officer," I say, adopting a drawn-out, frail voice.

Honestly, this feels ridiculous and I'm ashamed of contributing to the inaccurate stereotypes of women my age.

But it appears to be working.

The inspector removes her hat and smiles. "Good morning, ma'am."

I glance surreptitiously at my watch; four more minutes until my agreed meeting time with Philippe. I don't want to be caught loitering suspiciously outside the store. What would Dame Judi do?

"You know, dear," I say to the parking inspector in my exaggerated old-lady voice. "You remind me of someone I used to know many years ago. Marjorie was her name—or was it Alice?" I pause, pretending to think about it. "Anyway, she was a lovely woman. She used to work at the plant nursery where I got all my gardening bibs and bobs."

The inspector smiles and nods, as if encouraging me to continue.

"I remember I'd go in on Tuesdays because that's when they'd get the new seedlings," I say, thinking on my feet. "Wait, it might have been Wednesdays. No, it was definitely Tuesdays. Oh dear, all the days blur into one when you're my age!"

The parking inspector laughs good-naturedly. Heavens, this woman is patient. I wasn't expecting to have to improvise this much.

"But one day I went in and she wasn't there," I continue. "And it turned out that . . ." Fumbling for something to keep the story going, I glimpse a poster in the travel agency window across the street. "She'd been on vacation in Africa and. . . ." Come on, Joy, think. "She'd been attacked by a lion!"

Okay, that might have been a bit much.

The inspector's eyes widen. "Oh no, that's terrible!"

I've improvised myself into a corner. Where do I go from here?

Fortunately, someone is trying to park in front of a fire hydrant nearby, giving the inspector more important things to do.

I peek into my grocery caddy, ensuring the replica vase is safely stowed among the tea towels I stuffed around it for protection, and continue on my glacial way.

My nerves thrum when I spot the familiar red awning of Seth's store. I really should've gone to the bathroom one last time before I left. But it's too late for that; my bladder will just have to hold on for dear life until the task is done.

Standing outside the window of haphazardly dressed mannequins, I close my eyes to compose myself.

I can do this for Hazel.

Rowan said Philippe would already be in the store when I got there, so all I need to do is wait until he is distracting Seth to make the switch. But when I walk inside the open door, there appears to be no one else present.

The vase, however, is definitely still sitting on the counter, waiting for me.

I'm debating going back outside and walking around the block, but then Seth emerges from behind the shelves, an odd-looking clock in his hands.

I freeze, wondering if it was a mistake to have dropped in here on my way to meet Elizabeth at the café the other day. Seth has never seen me twice in such close succession.

He glances at my visor, then my pearls, then my cardigan, with no flash of recognition in his eyes. For once I'm grateful to have been so unremarkable that I've never stuck in his memory.

"Hello, ma'am," he says. "Anything particular you're looking for today?"

Oh, only that one-of-a-kind vase right by your elbow.

"Just thought I'd come in for a browse," I say, closing the door behind me. "It's a bit of a walk down memory lane for me in these sorts of stores. Highlights from every decade I've lived!"

Seth's laugh lacks sincerity and I'm kicking myself for not having prepared for a scenario where I have to make small talk with him. The longer I interact with him, the more chance there is of him remembering me—and that would be a problem, should he ever be required to give a police report.

"I sure did love that movie," I say, pointing to an old *Singin' in the Rain* poster on the wall behind him.

When he turns, I quickly scan the space for security cameras. As far as I can tell, there are none, just as Rowan promised. Hazel did say Seth was a cheapskate—perhaps he wasn't willing to spend the extra money.

"I'll give you a special price," he says of the poster. "Twenty bucks and it's yours."

"That's very kind of you, thank you," I say, unsure if it's actually a good deal, especially given the coffee-cup stain on the corner of it. "I'll keep that in mind."

He frowns—must've assumed I was a sure sale. "Just remember my deals expire at the end of the day."

"Duly noted."

I take comfort in the fact that he's already turned down my legitimate offer to buy the vase. He can't argue that I didn't give him the chance to resolve this honorably. But as I see the calculator next to the pile of receipts on the counter, it occurs to me that perhaps Seth isn't the cheapskate we assumed. He's only about fifteen years younger than Hazel and me, and he's still running a business. Is that because he can't afford to retire? If so, it's surprising that he's always turned down Hazel's lucrative offers.

I push the thought away; it's too late for empathy. And he wasn't planning to sell the vase, anyway, so it's not like I'm depriving him of income.

There's a rattling behind me—Philippe's on the other side of the door, jiggling the handle.

Seth hurries out from behind the counter.

"You just need to shove it a little," he calls to Philippe through the glass. "The wood must be swollen from the humidity."

Philippe nudges his shoulder against it until the door finally gives, sending him stumbling forward into the shop.

He dusts himself off sheepishly. Not the subtlest entrance, I must say.

Seth clasps his hands in apology. "I'm so sorry about that, sir— every spring I sand it down to stop it from sticking, and every year it still swells."

Philippe plucks a handkerchief from his blazer pocket and mops his brow.

"It's fine—I like to make an entrance," he says in his charming accent, which I now know is Egyptian via France. He nods at me politely. "Good afternoon, madame."

"Good afternoon," I say, hand tightening on my caddy.

What happens now?

Seth steps aside to let Philippe into the store. "Anything particular you're looking for today, sir?"

I wonder how many times a day he says that.

Philippe folds his handkerchief and returns it to his pocket.

"There is, actually. I'm opening up a restaurant in Brooklyn and we want to do something a little different and make all our dishes and silverware vintage." He smiles at me. "Adds character."

Clever. All of Seth's dinnerware is tucked away in an alcove at the back of the store.

"It's your lucky day," Seth says. "I've got piles of stuff out the back and some more downstairs in the basement. Come and I'll show you."

"Wonderful," Philippe says, following Seth, but not before giving me a wink. "Have a nice day, madame."

I tip my visor at him. "You too, young man."

He raises an amused eyebrow at my fake old-lady voice, then disappears into the shelves.

I wait until their voices are too muffled to discern, and then get to work before anyone else walks in.

From the top of the grocery caddy, I extract my second-favorite pair of gardening gloves—the ones I didn't pack in my prison go bag—since there's no way I'm risking any fingerprints.

As I slide them on, it strikes me that if Seth really treasures this vase so much, he should store it safely in his home. Does he really keep it here on the off chance that Hazel will wander in once or twice a year? His pettiness truly knows no bounds—and now it's his Achilles' heel.

Adrenaline courses through my body like a drug. As I set about making the switch, I briefly pause to admire the vases side by side and marvel at Philippe's handiwork. I'd take a picture to show him later, but I've watched enough TV crime shows to know better than to leave a digital evidence trail.

Just as I've slid the real vase into the bed of towels in my caddy, the door jiggles, almost giving me a heart attack. I'm not exaggerating—for a moment I thought I was going the way of Lois Manning at the swimming pool during water aerobics. What an exit that would've been.

It jiggles again, this time more violently. Panicking, I shuck off my gloves and cover the top of the vase with a gingham tea towel, then turn to the door. A woman in a UPS uniform is trying to open it.

"You have to push it with your shoulder!" I say to her through the glass.

Turns out it's quite difficult to project your voice while also trying to sound frail.

"Excuse me, ma'am!" Seth calls sternly from behind me.

I'm done for.

Was he watching me the whole time, waiting until I finished before confronting me?

I spin around to see Seth standing in front of me, hands on his hips.

I remove my visor in contrition, ready to accept his accusation. I just hope Philippe doesn't try to intervene on my behalf; he needs to keep himself out of this.

Seth looks at me impatiently, pointing to my grocery caddy.

"Excuse me," he says again. "I need to get past to open the door."

"Ah," I say, almost wetting myself with relief. "Yes, of course."

He carelessly moves the caddy aside, as if there wasn't a precious vase inside.

As I watch him yank open the door for the UPS lady—berating her for being a day late on what was supposed to be next-day delivery—I realize that I've pulled it off.

"It's getting a bit crowded in here!" I remark for their benefit. "It's probably time I skedaddled." Not a word I've ever used in my life, but it feels apropos.

Seth points to the poster on the wall. "I'll extend the deal to noon tomorrow."

"So generous of you," I trill on my way out the door. "I'll be in touch!"

I commence my tortoise-paced escape back down Main Street.

This must be what people feel like driving away in a getaway car, wind in their hair, the taste of freedom on their lips.

And now it's time to deliver the vase to its rightful owner.

<h1 style="text-align:center">46</h1>

My triumph is short-lived.

As I turn onto my street more than an hour later, there's a police car up ahead. My heart catapults into my throat.

I was sure I'd gotten away with it. Did the UPS lady see me make the switch and mention something to Seth?

Even with my glasses on, my long-distance vision is limited, so it's not until I'm almost there that I realize the police car isn't outside my place; it's outside Rowan's.

Oh no.

Was there someone in that empty movie theater after all who overheard our plan?

I abandon my slow walk and scurry to his house, my grocery caddy rattling behind me. I can't let him take the fall for the very thing I instigated, especially since it could incite an investigation into all the other things he and Philippe have been up to. If someone's going to take the fall and spend the rest of their life in prison, it's me.

I just hope the police will believe I'm clever enough to have come up with the whole thing alone. It's probably a stretch to say I created the vase. Perhaps I can just refuse to give up that information. Goodness, I'm going to have to channel a lot of Dame Judi.

I glance over at Rita's house to see if she's monitoring the situation through her curtains. She'll be dining out on this gossip for the next few years at least—little old Joy revealed to be a criminal.

My lungs are heaving when I finally reach Rowan's front lawn and see the back of the police officer in his doorway.

Like a lioness guarding her cub, I summon my courage.

"I think I'm the one you need to be speaking to, officer."

He turns in my direction, surprised. Behind him, Rowan looks confused, then wide-eyed, shaking his head subtly as if urging me not to do what I'm about to.

It's gallant of him, but I'm ready to face my reckoning.

"Oh," the officer says, removing his hat and tucking it under his arm. "Good afternoon, Mrs. Bridport."

So he already knows my identity. I may as well just offer him my wrists for handcuffing.

My courage dissolves, replaced by an all-consuming fear. Was all this really worth it? I told myself I was doing this for Hazel, but the truth is, I was also doing it for myself, seeking a thrill that could top them all. And now I won't even get to be with my friend in her final weeks.

"Good afternoon, officer." I should've discarded my caddy with the evidence, but my instincts to protect Rowan had propelled me directly over here. I straighten my shoulders and raise my head high. "Please have it noted for the record that I acted alone."

He tilts his head, as if he's misheard me.

Rowan cuts in before the officer has the chance to reply.

"Hello, Joy," he says evenly, his eyes trying to convey some kind of urgent message.

I shake my head defiantly in response; I'm not letting him talk me out of this.

Rowan perseveres. "Officer Launceston was just here to inquire about a complaint from one of our neighbors." Hettie barks in the background. "They weren't comfortable with the fact that I was receiving so many deliveries, even though that's what happens when you've just moved into a house. There were too many people coming and going, in their opinion."

Rita.

Of course she would call the police on Rowan for some small thing.

"I see." My hand loosens its grip on my caddy. "Well, officer, I am another of Rowan's neighbors, and I am willing to provide a signed statement saying that I have gotten to know him very well in the time since he moved here and he's helped me out with many things I couldn't manage by myself. I certainly haven't witnessed any kind of suspicious behavior."

I can't be suspicious of something I masterminded.

The officer bows his head, embarrassed. "To be candid, this is more of a routine call. We're obligated to look into every complaint, even if it seems unwarranted." He looks at me. "And I know you're a good judge of character, Mrs. Bridport."

I frown. How does he know that? "That's very kind of you to say, sir."

Now it's Rowan who clears his throat. "If that will be all, officer, I've got to get my things ready to catch a train to the city."

"Of course." The policeman puts his hat back on. "My apologies again for the inconvenience."

"Thank you," Rowan says, then looks at me pointedly. "I look forward to seeing you again soon, Joy."

He wiggles his eyebrows as he closes his door.

"I'd better be going too," I say, hastily maneuvering my caddy in the other direction. "Have a lovely day, officer!"

The policeman stands, hands in his pockets.

"You don't remember me, do you, Mrs. Bridport?"

I study his face for a moment, desperately trying to place it.

"Of course I do, Charles," I say, pleased my memory is intact. "We met briefly when I was on my way out of the pharmacy a couple of weeks ago. You were buying teething gel for your daughter."

"Well, yes, we did," he says. "And that chamomile tea tip worked wonders, thank you. But we also met quite a long time before that."

Perhaps my retention isn't as good as I thought. I search my brain but come up with nothing.

"I'm sorry," I say, reluctantly. "I can't recall when that was."

"That's understandable," he says affably. "It was about thirty years ago and you probably knew me by my nickname—Chuck." His eyes shine as he points to my house. "You were my piano teacher for a couple of years."

I finally place the smile and my heart swells.

"Chuck Launceston? Goodness! But you were a small boy when I last saw you."

A small boy with the kindest nature, despite his tempestuous life at home.

"That's right," he says. "My dad and I moved away from Beacon when I was ten, but I never forgot you." A tinge of sadness. "You were the one thing that brought me comfort during those years—I don't think I would've made it through without your kindness. I remember you used to give me clothes and shoes to replace my dirty, hole-ridden ones so I wouldn't get teased at school. And you'd never let me leave with an empty stomach."

"I remember you had a voracious appetite," I say. "And a wonderful musical talent. Do you still play?"

Charles nods. "Whenever I can—though it's tough with a newborn at home." He looks at me hopefully. "Maybe you could teach her when she's old enough. I can't wait to tell her all about the magical Mrs. Bridport who saved my life."

"Oh, I don't know about saving your life," I say, embarrassed. "But it would be my honor to teach her."

Charles's face stays serious. "Don't underestimate yourself, Mrs. Bridport. I'm positive I'm not the only kid whose world you changed with your kindness and encouragement. You should be proud of that."

My throat catches. Perhaps my existence has been a little more impactful than I realized.

"Thank you, Charles."

I hope he knows I'm thanking him for more than just the compliment.

<h1 style="text-align:center">47</h1>

Hazel sits regally in her wicker peacock chair, a blanket draped across her knees, her eyes squeezed shut.

"What are you up to, Joy?" she admonishes. "You do realize that buying someone a gift at the tail end of their life is a fruitless endeavor."

I smile to myself, arranging the vase on the coffee table in front of her, making sure the best angle points in her direction.

"I didn't buy it," I say mysteriously, then stand back, ready for my reveal. "Okay, you can open your eyes now!"

Hazel's eyelids spring upwards. I thought I knew the entire spectrum of her facial expressions by heart, and yet here is one I've never seen.

Shock.

She blinks several times, as if hallucinating, then stares at the vase.

"How . . ." She blinks again. "How did you get this? I thought you said you didn't buy it."

I clasp my hands behind my back, pleased as punch.

"I didn't," I say. "I stole it."

Hazel grips the arms of her chair. "You *stole* it? Joy, Seth is a very spiteful man, above all when it comes to this vase. He'll hound the police until they find the vase—and you."

Oh, how the tables have turned. It's entertaining to see Hazel's feathers ruffled.

"Except he doesn't know it's missing," I say smugly. "I switched it with a replica when he wasn't looking."

My friend throws her hands up, flabbergasted. "What? Joy, have you lost your mind?"

"My new neighbor, Rowan, helped me," I say. "Turns out he's not exactly an *ex*-criminal, after all. In addition to his piano tuning, he and his boyfriend Philippe have a side business forging art and antiques."

Hazel leans back, her face a progression of emotions. Confusion, astonishment, and, finally, gratitude.

"But why did you do it, Joy?" Her voice is soft with disbelief. "You could've easily been caught."

"I wasn't, though, was I?" I say contrarily. "Think of it as a thank-you present for everything you've done for me. For befriending me on that first day of school, for pushing me out of my comfort zone, for supporting me in my lowest moments, for always protecting me, and for teaching me how to pay a bill and check the fuse box."

Hazel studies my face. "I just can't believe you were able to pull this off. I mean, come on, Joy—you were wracked with guilt for years simply for telling Elizabeth that the Easter Bunny was real."

I shrug. The truth is, I haven't felt much remorse. "I suppose I've come to understand that the concept of good and bad isn't so cut-and-dried. And you were worth the risk."

"Thank you, my friend." She takes hold of the vase, gently turning it around to admire it. "But I do have one request."

I press my palms together. "Your wish is my command."

A smile quivers on Hazel's lips.

"When I'm gone, I'd like you to put my ashes in this and keep me on your mantelpiece. I want to be able to enjoy this vase in perpetuity."

I grin back at her. "It's a deal."

An osprey glides onto the rippling surface of the river, the blush of the departing sun injecting its dark feathers with a golden glow.

It has been a while since I've done this train journey home along the Hudson and felt peace. It's strange to feel that way, knowing Hazel's time is almost at its end. And yet it's as though the reason our souls intertwined in this lifetime has finally revealed itself.

I've always assumed I was meant to live vicariously through my friend, to be entertained by her adventures, her antics, her penchant for stirring things up. I thought that she was there to be my opposite, my complement, the yin to my yang. In reality, she was a mirror of what I was also capable of, in my own way.

All my life, I've defined my existence by its relevance to someone else's. I shaped myself in my parents' image, contorting to fit into the mold they presented of a "good" person. Then I met Thom—and again, I bent and twisted until I fit his mold of what it meant to be a "good" wife and mother. And throughout it all I saw myself as the same woman, the same self, living through all these decades. It's often said that, in a long marriage, you're really married to many different people, because your spouse changes and evolves over time. I accepted that with Thom, but I didn't offer the same grace to myself. The grace of nuance, of acknowledging that I contain multitudes, that I'm constantly shedding versions of myself. The grace of imagining that I could be someone, or something, new.

Putting others first doesn't always have to mean putting myself last. I can be kind to others while also being kind to myself. I can respect their wishes while asserting that they are not in harmony with my own. And I can acknowledge the rules set forth for me, and interpret them how I see fit, so long as I'm willing to accept the consequences.

Would I want Finn to know about the things I've been up to recently? No. But if he did somehow find out, I would simply explain that they are all part of who I am. And as his theory suggested, I've always had the capacity to be both "good" and "bad"—it's just that I've chosen to nurture only the former up until now.

Of course there are people who do terrible things with no reason or remorse, but what about the rest of us? It's simplistic to think that everything we do must fit neatly in the category of good or bad. And who gets to define those terms, anyway? As children we're given that clear binary by our parents, our teachers, even our government. But in many cases it's in the eye of the beholder. I suspect no one ever sees themselves as the villain—even if the world does.

In truth, we all inhabit the gray area in between. We all have our reasons, our justifications, and our best intentions, and yet often we stumble, we hurt one another, we make mistakes.

That doesn't make us good or bad.

It makes us human.

**48**

'm not sure brownies pair well with cocktails—Rita said she's serving them at our crafting circle this afternoon—so I've defrosted some mini quiches.

I put them on the ornate serving plate Celeste gave Thom and me for one of our anniversaries. I thought it was the pattern I loathed—a chintzy cluster of tropical fish—but now I realize that the gift-giver is why I detest it. Who gives an anniversary present to the wife of the man you've cheated with?

Rita's front door is open when I arrive, and I can hear distant laughter through the screen door. From the pairs of fancy sandals lined up on the shoe rack, I surmise that the other pickleball ladies have already arrived.

I ring the doorbell, then count to twenty before ringing it again.

When Rita still doesn't appear, I let myself in, add my sneakers to the rack, then pad down the hallway in my socked feet.

"Hello?" I call into the emptiness.

A peal of raucous laughter sails in from the back patio.

Rita, Celeste, and the other ladies—Bridget, Maude, and Phyllis—are seated around the glass table, champagne glasses in hand. A fancily arranged charcuterie board sits at the center. No sign of any crafting supplies.

I tap tentatively on the sliding screen door to get their attention.

Rita jumps, then laughs at herself. "Joy! You gave me a fright!"

"Sorry for letting myself in," I say. "I rang the doorbell a few times."

Maude turns to Rita in mock horror. "Rita, do you mean to say you left your front door unlocked after constantly warning us about the nefarious criminal you have living across the street?" The faint sway of her torso betrays her tipsiness.

I bristle, still resentful that Rita was likely the one who reported Rowan to the police for suspicious activity. Technically she now has two criminals living across the street, anyway.

I present the mini quiches to Rita. "I thought your cocktails might go nicely with these."

Next to Rita, Celeste looks at the plate, a quiver of recognition in her brow.

Bridget pours champagne into a glass. "Grab a drink, Joy—we're having mimosas." She adds a splash of orange juice and hands it to me. Her sickly rose perfume wafts from her blouse as she leans across the table.

"Thank you, Bridget." I slot into the remaining seat, cringing as the chair legs drag loudly across the patio.

Maude reaches for a quiche, gold bracelets jangling. "We were just drilling Rita for the latest town gossip."

"I bet you have some excellent gossip, Joy," Phyllis says, extracting a strand of hair from her mascara-clad eyelashes. "Haven't you lived here longer than any of us?"

I pinch the stem of my champagne glass, but I don't drink.

"Yes, I have lived here a long while," I say. "But I try not to spread rumors about my neighbors."

My pointed comment floats in the silence. For an instant I think the women are actually chastened by it.

But then Bridget sips her cocktail and shrugs. "Then we're lucky Rita doesn't have as many scruples as you."

Phyllis snort-laughs, then nudges Rita. "Go on then, tell us the latest."

I'm tempted to leave before the gossiping starts, but something keeps me planted.

Rita sips coyly on her mimosa.

"Well," she says, letting the pause linger to make sure we're all hooked. "You know Ramona, the plain woman who runs the green-grocer?"

Plain! Such a cruel way to describe a fellow woman. I've always found Ramona very pretty—made even more so by her kindness.

"Oh, yes," Phyllis says. "That woman needs to get her colors done. Everything she wears is so drab."

Maude sets her glass down impatiently. "What about her?"

Rita looks around slyly in one last dramatic flourish. "I have it on good authority that her husband has been stepping out on her for quite some time," she says. "He's got another woman in the city."

Bridget masks her glee with a feigned look of disapproval. "The dog."

"Do you think she knows?" Phyllis asks, helping herself to a mini quiche.

Rita tilts her head. "If she does, she isn't letting on. As far as I know they're still together."

Maude tuts sharply. "How could you willingly overlook something like that?"

The simmering anger in my chest becomes a rolling boil. I stare at Celeste, studying her face for a hint of acknowledgement at the irony of this situation.

But she's just sitting there, a stiff smile on her face.

"Perhaps she should have done more to keep her husband satis-fied," Bridget says, and the other women chortle.

Forty years of contained resentment finally bursts to the surface.

This time I'm grateful for the noise my chair makes when I stand abruptly. My own dramatic flourish.

"Is that what you think?" I say to Celeste. "That I didn't keep Thom satisfied?"

Her smile vanishes. "Um, I'm not sure what you're talking about, Joy."

The other women watch us intently, enthralled by this conversational twist.

I turn to them, Celeste stiffening in my periphery. "Why don't you ask Celeste about the night I saw her kissing my husband by her garden shed during one of her cocktail parties? And she still had the nerve to try to be my friend all of these years."

Bridget gasps, clearly delighted. "Celeste—you tramp!"

Phyllis snort-laughs again. "Now *this* is good gossip."

Celeste stares up at me, stunned. "Joy, I . . . I didn't realize . . . Let me explain."

"Don't bother," I say, wrenching open the screen door.

Celeste stands. "Joy, please."

I step through the door and slide it shut with a satisfying bang.

"You can keep that plate, Rita," I say through the mesh.

Then I stride back through the house with an unbridled grin on my face, collecting my shoes on the way out.

Gosh, that was cathartic. Why did I waste almost half a century keeping those emotions to myself? I should've said something to Celeste years ago.

I'm halfway across the street when I hear a screen door slam and Celeste's voice calling after me.

"Joy, wait!"

I turn to see her jogging across Rita's overwatered lawn.

Is Celeste a masochist? I've just exposed her in front of all her fancy friends—you'd think she'd never want to see me again. Out of sheer curiosity, I allow her to catch up to me.

Sweat beads her forehead; for once in her life, she looks disheveled.

I don't owe her any explanation, so I simply look at her expectantly, waiting for her to say her piece.

Celeste fingers her necklace nervously. "I want you to know that what you saw that night wasn't exactly . . . what you thought."

I cross my arms indignantly. "Oh? And what was it then?"

She looks around nervously—we both know Rita and the other women are probably huddled together at the window watching us.

"I'm not denying what you witnessed," she says awkwardly. "But it wasn't an affair." A grimace. "I'd gone outside during the party to make sure the garden lights were on, and Thom was already out there. We started chatting and then, all of a sudden, I felt his hands around my waist and he was trying to kiss me." Celeste looks at me, ashamed. "It took me by such surprise that I thought he was joking, and it wasn't until his lips were on mine that I thought to push him away. But I also didn't want to cause a scene in front of all our neighbors."

My pain feels as fresh as the night it happened, the wound deepening. Though I've replayed that scene countless times in my head, I'm suddenly viewing it through a different lens.

Could Celeste's giggle have been out of surprise, or even fear? Were her hands on Thom's chest there to resist, rather than encourage his passion? Was her distance afterwards because she feared he would try to make a move on her again?

What if the story I've been telling myself all these years has been terribly wrong?

Of course, she could be making it up. But it dawns on me that everything she's saying—coupled with Thom's history of indiscretions— well, for some reason, it rings true.

"I'm so sorry, Joy," Celeste says, the pain evident on her face. "I didn't want to tell you what happened at the time, because I didn't want to blow up your life when Elizabeth was so young. And on top of that, I felt guilty because I thought I'd inadvertently behaved in a way that gave Thom the wrong signals and made him think I was flirting with him."

I'm quite sure my face has turned a ghostly white. How could I have been so rude to Celeste all these years when she was, in fact, an unwitting victim of my own husband's shortcomings? If only I'd been brave enough to address it with her at the time, just as Hazel urged me to, things might have turned out very differently. I'd have at least saved myself a lifetime of resentment towards another woman—and maybe gained a friend.

What other things have I missed out on because I was so determined to keep up appearances, so desperate to avoid any kind of conflict?

"Celeste, it's me who should be apologizing," I say finally. "I knew about Thom's infidelity with other women, so I immediately assumed the worst of you. I'm so sorry you had to navigate that—and that you had to keep it a secret all this time."

Celeste shakes her head.

"It's not your fault, Joy," she says. "I'd have assumed the same in your position. I just regret that it ruined our budding friendship. I've always admired you so much—you're so kind and generous and everyone who meets you loves you." She nods at Rita's place. "I was so inspired to see you standing up to those women and their terrible gossip. If I'm honest, I don't enjoy spending time with them—I don't even like crafting—but I felt like I didn't have a choice because all my other friends are gone."

Now I truly feel like a cad.

"You shouldn't hold such a high opinion of me, Celeste," I say sheepishly. "I need to confess something."

"Oh?"

"Yes," I say, staring at my sneakers. "The other day when we were both at the grocery store, I dented your car in the parking lot with my shopping cart . . . on purpose." Heat rises in my cheeks. "I'm so ashamed of myself and I promise to find a way to pay for the damage."

Celeste laughs. "Truthfully, Joy? I hadn't even noticed. I've gotten into so many fender benders over the years that I've stopped bothering to get the dents fixed. One more won't matter."

"Are you sure?" I don't deserve this benevolence. "I certainly wouldn't want to take advantage of you in that way."

"Yes, it's really nothing to worry about." Celeste says smiling. "But I hope this means you might start coming to my potluck dinners again?"

I reach out and squeeze her hand, bathing in the glow of redemption. "That would be lovely, Celeste."

## 49

The coffee machine whirs through its motions and I'm buzzing with a new appreciation for life.

Not just that I'm still here, but that I've been gifted with time to make things right. Many people aren't that lucky; they leave this world with things unsaid, regrets untended to, and dreams unrealized. I can now see that I've never dreamed big enough to have to address the latter, and perhaps it's time I did.

Turns out it's never too late to start afresh, to truly begin living. I feel like a completely different person to who I was just a couple of months ago. Is it really possible to change when you're almost ninety years old? Or is it less about changing, and more about finally waking up to your true self? The way I see it, nothing but possibility lies ahead of me.

But first, I need to apologize to my daughter.

After my coffee and several rounds of sun salutations (aside from a niggle in my ankle, my body is still running smoothly), I hop in my car—also now running smoothly, thanks to Rowan.

Elizabeth and Finn used to live in a charming little cottage not far from me, but that got sold when the marriage dissolved, and they moved to an apartment on the outskirts of town. I offered for them to come and live with me—it'd be a dream having them around all the time—but Elizabeth immediately said no. Once children have flown the nest, they hold on tightly to their independence.

Finn works his part-time job at the farmers market on certain Sunday mornings, so I'm hoping to catch Elizabeth alone. Since our confrontation in her car after visiting Hazel, I haven't seen her, except for a curt wave when she picked up Finn after he spent the night at my place.

The building's cavernous hallway mutes my timid knock. Hazel said she's never felt invisible because she's made sure to take up space, even when people tried to refuse it. All this time I've been blaming society for making me invisible, when perhaps I'm the actual reason my presence has felt inconsequential. I've spent my life trying to make myself small and inoffensive, trying to attract as little attention as possible.

Not anymore.

I take a deep breath and rap louder.

Elizabeth opens the door, her hair messy and eyes bleary. Not unusual for someone who works irregular hours in a hospital, but it still tugs at my emotions. She looks life-weary.

She stiffens when she sees me.

"Mom?" she says suspiciously, looking around the hallway.

"Hello, darling," I say, holding a tea towel–swaddled container. "I made you an omelet—all healthy ingredients, just the way you like. I was even light-handed on the oil."

She frowns at my offering. "Thanks, but why are you here?"

I ignore the fear tapping on my shoulder, the voice telling me to do everything to avoid upsetting Elizabeth. Clearly that approach isn't as effective as I thought. A lifetime of avoiding conflict and confrontation with people I love has meant I often didn't get to deepen those relationships. Now I understand you need to endure the discomfort of difficult conversations in order to strengthen a bond.

Here goes nothing.

"I'm here to say what I should have said years ago. And to apologize to you."

Her frown softens and the door wavers slightly, as she debates whether to let me in. Eventually it swings open in my favor.

"Okay," she says uncertainly. "But you can't make any comments about the cleanliness of my apartment."

"Of course I won't."

When I walk inside, I see the reason for her preamble. Her living room is a mess—piles of papers, clothes draped over a drying rack, a vase of dead flowers with the sour tang of sullied water permeating the room.

She hastily moves a pile of unfolded laundry from the sofa so I can sit down. Since she doesn't appear interested in the omelet, I place it on the corner of the coffee table that isn't covered in papers.

I clasp my hands in my lap.

"I wanted to tell you that what you said the other night in the car was right," I say, making sure to look her in the eye. "Reflecting back, I did devote a lot of time and energy to my piano students, and I see now how that must have made you feel. I regret not telling you more often how much I love you and how you are the most important thing to me, and not giving you the chance to express all of your emotions— even the challenging ones." A breath. "And I'm sorry for assuming your needs as a child were the same as mine."

If it sounds rehearsed, it's because it is. I've been practicing the speech all morning so I don't mess it up.

Elizabeth glances away, blinking. When she says nothing, I continue.

"I'm also sorry you had to deal with what was going on between your father and other women. I'd hoped I'd been able to shield you from all that, but I suppose it was naive of me." Another slow breath. "In truth, I've been too naive my entire life—telling myself that I was merely seeing the best in people when, really, I was avoiding reckoning with them at their worst." My wedding ring feels constricting on my finger; suddenly I resent the sight of it. "I thought I was protecting you and giving you a stable home by staying with your father in spite of his infidelity. But the truth is, I should have at least addressed it with him. I don't know whether he would have changed his behavior, but he might have been more discreet. And I should have given myself the chance to consider whether it was a marriage I wanted to stay in. Regardless, I'm sorry we put you through that."

Elizabeth finally meets my gaze, eyes moist. "It's really him who should be apologizing," she mumbles. "And me. For judging you so harshly."

"You certainly don't have to apologize," I say. "Why would you ever think that?"

"Because Jack did the same thing to me," she says quietly.

My soul aches for her. "Oh, Elizabeth, I'm sorry. I never would have expected that from Jack."

That scoundrel; he really did fool me into thinking he was a decent man. I suppose Thom did the same, when I met him.

She shrugs helplessly. "Neither did I—I was kind of blindsided by the cheating."

"So was I, the first time I realized," I offer softly.

Elizabeth looks at the wall, embarrassed. "At first, I was going to let it slide and not say anything. But then I realized I'd be a hypocrite if I stayed with him, because I'd been judging you all my life for staying with Dad and tolerating his cheating. So I asked for a divorce immediately, to prove I could do things on my own and set a good example for Finn." She toes a carpet stain with her sock. "I didn't even give Jack the chance to apologize, or to try to work on our relationship. And it's turned out to be a lot harder than I thought it'd be. Now he's living with his mistress on the other side of the country—even though he always insisted he never wanted to leave Beacon." I understand her bitterness. "And he hasn't been paying the child support he was supposed to, but I've been too proud to take him to court, plus I didn't want Finn to know that his father wasn't supporting him. It's made things tough financially."

"And that's why you went to Hazel instead of me," I say, everything crystallizing.

She nods. "I meant what I said about not wanting to burden you, since you're already on a tight budget—I knew you'd loan me the money without question, but I was scared you'd deprive yourself of things to scrape it together."

It's true I would've willingly given up everything I could in order to help her.

"I'm sorry I pressured you into staying with Jack when you were younger," I say. "You were right that Hazel was a better role model for you. I'm grateful you had her as a successful, independent woman to look up to."

Elizabeth focuses hard on her cuticles. "It's not like I did a good job of following her example."

"Oh, Elizabeth," I say, wanting to go to her but also not wanting to scare her away. "You've done what you could in difficult circumstances. It must be so hard raising Finn by yourself, but you've done such a wonderful job—he's already such a caring and thoughtful young man."

She glances up at me hopefully. "That's because of you too, Mom. I don't know what I would've done without you to help take care of him. Even if I'm a little envious of the bond the two of you have."

Envious? I'm about to brush it off, to tell her she has nothing to be envious about, when I stop myself. Why not just tell her the truth?

"If I'm honest," I say. "I've always been a little envious of the bond you have with Hazel. She's much more fun and interesting than me—and much more accomplished. That's why I was so hurt that you'd asked her for money instead of me. It was one thing to have you admire her, but it was another to feel like she was performing the duties that belonged to me, as if she were the better mother."

"Oh god, Mom," Elizabeth says with a trace of amusement. "Can you imagine how I would've turned out if Hazel was actually my mother? I'd probably be living in a remote commune somewhere doing all kinds of drugs." Earnestness replaces her amusement. "Trust me, after having Finn, I understand how much kids need consistency and stability—and I do appreciate all you did to give that to me. You were steadfast and constant; you put me first. Hazel could never have done that."

"Thank you, darling." I sniffle. "And I admire you for leaving Jack, even if it meant having to navigate raising Finn alone. You're stronger than I was."

Elizabeth toes the carpet again, like she has more to say.

"Since we're being honest, I guess I should come clean about something else," she says.

Oh god. Am I not the only one who's recently been involved in illegal activity?

I brace myself, then nod encouragingly.

"When I called you the other day to ask if Finn could spend the night at your place," she says, "it wasn't so I could work the night shift." She looks up guiltily. "It was because I had a date."

"But that's wonderful," I say. "Why didn't you just tell me?"

"I don't know," Elizabeth says. "I guess because he's not really your idea of good husband material? He's an artist, and he barely makes any money." She pauses, and I see her face light up. "But he's considerate and funny, and he makes me feel so good about myself."

I think of Percy's rosy cheeks, the way his eyes lit up when he saw me. I knew that feeling for a brief six months. If only I'd been brave enough to embrace it.

"If he makes you happy, that's all that matters to me," I say, taking a tentative step towards her. "And I think we can both agree that my track record of picking husbands, for either of us, isn't the best. Even though I would have married your father all over again if I knew it would lead to you."

And there it is—an expression I haven't seen for decades. The same way she used to look at me when I was teaching her piano and she'd fumble a chord. I'd just smile and tell her that mistakes were how we learn and grow. It's only when you stop trying that you stop growing.

She looks at me like the little girl I once knew—tender, vulnerable, hopeful.

I take a chance, pulling her into a hug. Her body tenses, then relaxes into my embrace.

"Thank you, Mom." She buries her head in my shoulder, just like she used to after a bad dream, finally returning my hug in the way I've been yearning for.

Thank goodness I've lived long enough to receive it.

# 50

The rain patters against the glass as I tend to the rosemary on Hazel's windowsill. In the two months since I added the potted lavender, the gathering of plants has transformed from weak and listless to hardy and resplendent.

It helps that I've been here to care for them every day. After my reconciliation with Elizabeth, I decided there was no time to waste and temporarily moved into Hazel's Brooklyn apartment so I could be here for her until the end. I didn't take no for an answer when she insisted I needn't uproot my life for her. And when I arrived with my suitcases, the look of gratitude in her eyes, the way she crumpled in my arms, told me I'd made the right decision.

I just wish I'd realized sooner that beneath my dearest friend's tough, bawdy demeanor was a little girl who longed to be taken care of. And that the reason she assumed the role of lone wolf was because she was petrified of being vulnerable—fearing that, if she trusted someone to protect her, they might let her down.

I'm determined to show her that's not true.

Before I left Beacon, I arranged with the organist at church to fill in for me with my piano students so they didn't miss out. I'd have felt terrible if I'd had to pause those lessons, especially after hearing from Charles how much they meant to him. I offered to pay her for her time but, bless her, she was happy to do it as a volunteer.

And much to my surprise, Elizabeth offered to take care of my garden while I was away.

"It'll be good therapy," she said.

So here I am, a temporary resident of Brooklyn. And I'll continue to live here until the day that Hazel no longer does.

I spritz the orchid and delicately wipe the leaves of the rubber plant, tending to each one as lovingly as I do my friend. Then I make a steaming cup of ginger tea and carefully carry it into Hazel's bedroom, setting it gently on her nightstand. It's rare that she drinks it—she has trouble keeping anything down—but I know how much she loves the scent. It's small comforts like these, not the grand gestures, that are the most healing at this stage.

While arranging the cluster of medications on the nightstand, I spy a folded letter, its worn creases a clue it's been read many times. I silently thank Rowan for convincing me to write it, hard as it was. We've resumed our film club for two at the nearby art house cinema here in Brooklyn, whenever he's in town.

When I lie down on the bed next to Hazel, her eyes stay closed but her cheeks rise in a smile. Her hand fumbles across the bedspread until it finds mine. She pats it wearily.

"Hello, my friend."

I link my arm through hers, just like we used to as schoolgirls in the playground. We lie for several minutes in silence until Hazel speaks again.

"I've been thinking." Her voice has long been robbed of its vigor. "I've been lucky to have many passionate, romantic loves in my life." Her head tilts in my direction, eyes blinking open. "But you, Joy, have been the true love of my life. I'm so grateful for our friendship."

Dampness trickles down my temple onto the pillow.

"I love you too," I whisper.

Hazel's dry, pale lips part into the cheeky grin that's become as rare as a comet.

"I suppose I should let you know that I'm leaving this apartment to you."

"Me?" I prop myself up on my elbow. "What would I do with it? I'm eighty-nine years old."

Hazel shifts her head to look me in the eye.

"Exactly—you're still young." She smiles again. "I know you question why you get to be the one of us who lives longer, but that's precisely the way it's meant to be."

"What do you mean?"

"There's a reason your time hasn't come yet," she says. "You've still got things to do in this life. Of course, you can sell the apartment, or give it to Elizabeth or Finn, but I hope you'll use it to spend more time here in the city and experience a side of life you've always been afraid of. I bet there are plenty of kids in Brooklyn whose lives you could change with free piano lessons."

Would I dare do that? The thought is frightening—but also intriguing.

"It would be wonderful to be able to help more kids," I say softly. "Especially if it's in your honor."

"Glad to hear it," Hazel says. "Because I'm also leaving you some money to buy electric pianos for your students, instead of scrimping on your grocery money and living off canned beans to afford them. Call it the Hazel Scottsdale scholarship."

That suggestion feels much more doable. And I can't think of anything more meaningful than helping cement Hazel's legacy in the world.

"I'd love to be able to do that—thank you."

"Good," Hazel says. "I'm expecting you to honor our friendship by squeezing the hell out of every day you have left on this planet." She elbows me playfully. "I'll haunt you relentlessly if you don't."

I laugh. It's nice we're at the point where we can joke about her impending passing instead of tiptoeing around it.

"Well, I wouldn't mind if you 'visited' me once in a while," I say. "But please don't start moving things around, otherwise I'll think I'm losing my marbles."

Hazel looks at me slyly. "As long as you keep up your end of the bargain and live your remaining years with the same gusto I would have."

A tall order, but I'm willing. "I promise I'll try."

I lace my fingers through hers and lie still, listening to her steady breathing.

I'm no longer riddled with anxiety in these moments, panicking about whether they might be our last. I've learned to treasure them, to savor them, like the last bite of a delicious dessert. To think of each extra moment as a treat I'm grateful to have. Because, in the end, it's none of my business how many moments I have left with my best friend. What's important are the millions of small moments we've shared, ones that might've felt inconsequential at the time, but add up to a significant whole.

What greater achievement is there than a friendship that's lasted nearly a century, the fabric of it woven with the joys, sorrows, triumphs, and messiness of two lives forever intertwined? How lucky we both are, to have had that.

Who says your greatest love has to be a romantic one?

# EPILOGUE

Hazel's buzzer sounds and I pause my positioning of forks around the table.

"They're here!" I trill to her excitedly, hurrying over to buzz them in.

I'm still getting used to not getting a pithy retort from Hazel. But that's to be expected now that she's occupying the inside of that beautiful ceramic vase, currently holding court at the head of the dinner table.

Just as she requested, I've been spending a few days here and there in Brooklyn, dipping my toe into a life outside the one I've always known. And I must say, I quite like it.

Finn barrels through the door as soon as I open it, engulfing me in a hug that lifts my feet from the ground. He's about six feet now, and I still can't quite believe it.

"Be gentle with her, Finn, she's ninety!" Elizabeth chides, laughing.

She presents me with a bunch of flowers. "Fresh from your garden," she says proudly. "Which is doing very well, by the way—despite the rabbits' best efforts to devour it."

I'm glad she's taken up my (cruelty-free) crusade against those cotton-tailed menaces.

"Thank you, darling," I say, grateful when she reciprocates my hug with enthusiasm.

A tentative voice pipes up from behind Elizabeth.

"Hello, Joy."

I release my daughter and turn to the third guest.

"Hello, Celeste—it's a pleasure to see you."

And I mean it.

"Thank you for inviting me," Celeste says shyly and holds out a box of chocolates. "You're such a good cook that I didn't dare bring anything I made myself."

I accept the box and gesture her inside. "That's so kind, thank you."

She starts to shrug off her jacket, then pauses, shuffling closer. "I also brought you something else," she whispers.

After confirming Elizabeth and Finn are distracted by one of Hazel's artworks, Celeste pulls a book from her bag and discreetly hands it to me.

"I almost needed a cold shower after this one," she says, blushing.

"Noted." I quickly transfer the book to my grocery caddy by the door, ready to retrieve after everyone has left.

The buzzer sounds again a few minutes later—Rowan and Philippe are here. Unfortunately, Hettie had to stay at home because of Elizabeth's allergies, but I've been able to spend some quality time with her recently, dog-sitting while her dads went on vacation to Mexico.

"Just in time for appetizers!" I say as both men greet me with kisses and expensive-looking bottles of wine.

"Nothing but the best for Hazel," Philippe says as he delivers his bottle.

Once we're all seated around the cheese boards and crudités I prepared upon Elizabeth's suggestion, I raise my glass.

"It means so much to have you all here to celebrate my friend," I say. "While her parties were much wilder than this one will be, I know she'd be delighted to have you here." I take in the faces smiling back at me. "My wish for you all is that you get to experience a friendship as beautiful and fulfilling as ours was."

Beside me, Elizabeth puts her hand on mine and lifts her glass. "To Hazel."

Everyone reciprocates, toasting each other, and then the vase at the end of the table.

After dinner, when I'm in the kitchen dusting the sticky date pudding with powdered sugar, Rowan comes over with the dirty plates balanced up his arm.

He stacks them neatly next to the sink, pushing up his sleeves. "Would you like me to wash these now?"

"No, no, leave them," I say. "Sit down and enjoy yourself!"

He doesn't obey my instructions, instead moving closer to the fridge for a look at the photo of Hazel and me taken on my eightieth birthday.

"I wish you could have met her," I say. "The two of you would have gotten along so well."

"Well, actually," Rowan says, smoothing his beard. "I believe I did have that pleasure."

I almost drop the sieve of powdered sugar. "How?"

"I gave her a ride from the train station once in Beacon to what I now realize was your house. There's no mistaking that flaming red hair."

I clasp a hand to my heart. "Oh, that makes me so happy."

Rowan turns so his back is to the table, where Philippe has everyone enraptured with a story.

"You know," Rowan says, his voice lowered. "Philippe and I have been discussing it, and if you're ever interested in continuing your little foray into art theft, we'd gladly welcome you into our operation." He grins slyly. "No one ever suspects the sweet little old lady."

That heady rush surges through my limbs.

"I'm very flattered," I whisper back. "But I think I'm retired from all of that."

Rowan smiles. "Understood," he says. "It was worth a try."

He starts to walk back to the table.

"That said . . ." I say, raising my voice just enough to stop him. "Life is long, isn't it? You never know what the future might hold."

And then I wink at him.

The floorboards creak beneath my feet, the steam from my peppermint tea pirouetting into the chilly evening air coming through the window.

At almost midnight, it's one of the few times I've seen the street below without people. It's peaceful, soothing, like watching someone you love sleep.

My phone dings with a message from Elizabeth letting me know that she, Finn, and Celeste have made it back to Beacon. Rowan is staying at Philippe's place in Manhattan tonight, and I think of little Hettie waiting patiently for their arrival. I send a stream of hearts back to Elizabeth and return the phone to my pocket.

As I wrap my hands back around my mug, there isn't that familiar clink from my left hand against the ceramic. My finger feels oddly bare without the ring—having rarely taken it off in almost seventy years, I'd grown so used to its presence.

But it was time.

I appreciate the life I shared with Thom—the home we created, the family we built, the happy memories we shared among the ones that were less so—but I'm no longer willing to accept the things I turned a blind eye to during all those years.

It might seem pointless, given that it's all in the past and he's been gone for a long time. But I promised Hazel I would squeeze everything out of the life I have left. And that means discovering exactly who I am without shaping myself around my husband's existence—his preferences, his indiscretions, his memory. Who am I if I'm not defined by being someone's wife, someone's daughter?

I'm looking forward to finding out.

A lithe tabby cat tiptoes along the rail of the fire escape across the street, the moon glimmering in the window behind it.

I look down fondly at the lavender plant. I'll be taking it with me later this week when I return to Beacon, and I know exactly where I'll plant it—right at the bottom of the porch steps, next to the sage, so I can cherish Hazel's presence every morning.

I close my eyes, imagining myself sitting in my faithful rattan chair.

My entire garden is a scrapbook of memories. The rosebush that was the very first thing I planted when Thom and I moved in. The lemon tree I poured my energy into the first time I realized he'd been unfaithful, regaining my strength as it grew. The hydrangeas I planted when Finn was born, their cheerful presence always a comfort, just like he is. And it's there in that garden that I've felt most comfortable expressing my emotions, tilling the dirt to quell my anger, quietly letting my tears fall into the soil so they needn't bother anyone else.

I think back to my conversation with Rowan at the art gallery, when he described himself as being part of an ecosystem. All those plants play different roles. Some, like the lemon tree, are providers of fruit, while others are pollinators that attract the bees and butterflies. But then there are the plants whose contribution is less visible, harder to quantify. The companion plants that deter pests, or provide shade or support for other plants, or the ones that enrich the soil or cover the ground to help prevent erosion.

Perhaps it's true of us humans too. For some, their role in the world is visible, their impact on it measurable and unmistakable. People like Hazel who live out loud, making no secret of the fact that they're here to exist boldly. For the rest of us, however, our contributions might be quieter, less obvious to the naked eye.

And while it's easy to compare ourselves to those whose paths are more widely celebrated, we are equally important. Just like the worms who might envy the bees for the way the world cherishes their work, we must trust that our contributions matter. That without us, the ecosystem would be missing an essential piece. And perhaps we won't ever get to see the fruits of our labor, or the people we impact, or the lives we change. We just have to do our best, so we can sit back at the end of our life and say we tried our hardest, learned from our mistakes, and loved as hard as we could.

Small things really can add up to a remarkable life.

Every year, I've watched that garden bloom anew. And each time it's different. A plant might thrive one year and then be fallow the next. A shrub that's always produced flowers of a certain color might suddenly grow one of a different hue. And sometimes a plant that's struggled for years—one that's small and unassuming compared to the others—suddenly comes to vibrant life.

Everyone blooms in their own time, even if it takes eighty-nine years. Sometimes we need a few false starts before we come into our element, but it's never too late.

My eyes flutter open and a smile spreads across my face.

I am awake. I am alive.

And I'm not done living.

ACKNOWLEDGMENTS

I should begin with a disclaimer that, despite the antics in this book, I do not condone any kind of mischief towards libraries—they are among our most sacred spaces and should be revered and protected at all costs. A special shout out to my first branch, the Hobart Library on Murray Street in Tasmania (whose librarians were like gods to my five-year-old eyes) and to the Brooklyn Public Library, my current branch, which has made it their mission to make banned books accessible to readers across the United States.

Many people warned me that second books are often a challenge and I'll admit to thinking, *How hard can they be?* Turns out, they can be very hard! I'm infinitely grateful to the many people who have been devoted cheerleaders during the writing of this one.

A heartfelt thank you to my agent, Michelle Brower, as well as Allison Malecha, Elizabeth Pratt, Tori Clayton, and the whole team at Trellis Literary Management (Ollie included). And to Jemima Forrester, my UK agent, who also happens to be an excellent tour guide.

Thank you also to my tireless trio of editors, Sarah Cantin, Harriet Bourton, and Beverly Cousins for enthusiastically reading many iterations of "Book Two." And to Drue VanDuker for all her efforts behind the scenes.

To Katie Mouallek, Meredith Craig De Pietro, Jamie Finn, Eva

Munz, Trisha Ping, Natalia Sandoval, and Jesse Steinbach, thank you for your critiques, community, and friendship. What luck it is that our paths crossed when they did.

To Emma Brodie, Jessica George, Tracey Lien, and Tory Henwood Hoen, I'm so glad to be on this publishing journey with you, and I cherish your wisdom, your talent, and your delightful company.

To Annie Hartnett, Anna Johnston, and Natalie Sue, thank you for your generous blurbs and for the wonderful books you've put out into the world.

Thank you to Rosemary Ping for sharing your stories of growing up in rural Wisconsin, and to Christine Arroyo for your local insights into the town of Beacon.

To my mum, Jillian, and brother, Jeremy, thank you for always being so enthusiastic about my creative whims, wherever they might lead. And thank you to Kirsten, Hugo, Amélie, and Reuben for your cheerful encouragement.

To my great-aunt Hilda, thank you for your wry, warm presence, endless sense of curiosity and adventure, and excellent hugs. The shape of my life will always proudly bear your fingerprints.

I'm very fortunate to have several Hazels to my Joy, and Joys to my Hazel—and my only lament is that they're spread across the world, from Europe and the United States to Southeast Asia and Australia. Thank you all for your treasured friendship—may we continue our adventures together well into our eighties.

To all the readers who reached out or came up to me at events to tell me how much they loved *The Collected Regrets of Clover*, I appreciate you! And an enormous thank you to the libraries, bookstores, schools, churches, and book clubs who have championed it over the past few years and helped get it into the hands of so many people, in twenty-seven different languages to date.

And finally to you, the reader who has chosen to spend some of your valuable time and attention on this book—thank you. I hope it inspires you to cherish your friendships, seize life on your own terms, and perhaps dabble in a bit of mischief.

**Mikki Brammer** is an Australian journalist based in New York City by way of France and Spain. She is the author of *The Collected Regrets of Clover* and writes about design, architecture, and art for publications such as *Architectural Digest, Dwell,* and *Elle Decor.*

# THE COLLECTED REGRETS OF CLOVER
## MIKKI BRAMMER

*Discover Mikki Brammer's big-hearted story about figuring out what you want from life – and then finding the courage to go after it.*

Clover Brooks has forgotten how to live. It might be because she spends her time caring for people in their final days, working as a death doula in New York City. Or it might be because she has a regret of her own – one she can't bring herself to let go of. But then she meets Claudia: a feisty old woman who has one last wish . . .

As Clover begins a new adventure, will she remember how to live her own big, beautiful life?

'A beautiful, uplifting novel about unexpected friendship'
LUCY DIAMOND

'I fell in love with Clover, longed for her world to open up and cheered when she finally realised that comfort zones are designed to be stepped out of'
JILL MANSELL

'Charming, delightful and quietly powerful . . . this will warm your heart and change your life'  VERONICA HENRY

'Beautiful, poignant and the literary antidote to when life feels a little stationary'
JESSICA GEORGE

'This is one of those special books that will leave a handprint on your heart'
EMMA BRODIE

'Heartfelt and delightful . . . You will turn the last page with a fresh zest for life and absolutely no regrets'  ANNABEL MONAGHAN

On a station platform, with nothing to read,
and a four-hour train journey stretching ahead of him...

That's where the story began for Penguin founder Allen Lane.
With only 'shabby reprints of shoddy novels' on offer,
he resolved to make better books for readers everywhere.

By the time his train pulled into London, the idea was formed.
He would bring the best writing, in stylish and affordable
formats, to everyone. His books would be sold in bookstores,
stationers and tobacconists, for no more than the price
of a ten-pack of cigarettes.

And on every book would be a Penguin, a bird with a certain
'dignified flippancy', and a friendly invitation to anyone who
wished to spend their time reading.

In 1935, the first ten Penguin paperbacks were published.
Just a year later, three million Penguins had made their
way onto our shelves.

Reading was changed forever.

—

A lot has changed since 1935, including Penguin, but in the
most important ways we're still the same. We still believe that
books and reading are for everyone. And we still believe that
whether you're seeking an afternoon's escape, a vigorous debate
or a soothing bedtime story, all possibilities open with a book.

Whoever you are, whatever you're looking for,
you can find it with Penguin.